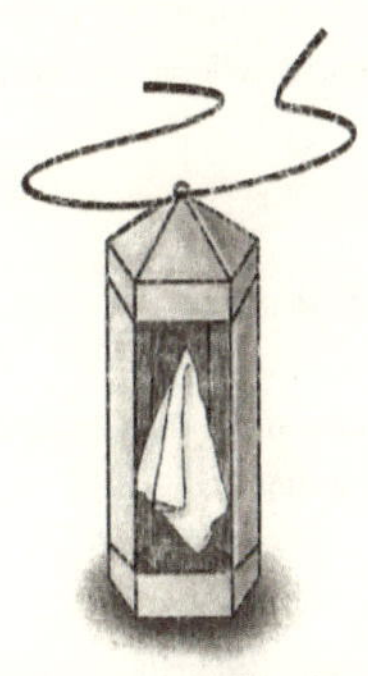

The Relic

Lloyd A. Meeker

WAYFARER
PRESS

Contact Information: wayfarerpress@gmail.com

Cover Art and Interior Design by Fablesmithy, © 2026 Fablesmithy

Wayfarer Press

Print ISBN: 978-1-939092-17-5

Digital ISBN: 978-1-939092-16-8

Published in the United States of America

To you
who sometimes reach
for a half-forgotten birthright –
a deep and knowing relationship
with all nature and its wisdom,
respectful and symbiotic,
full of wonder, beauty, and power.

May this book stir a memory.

Acknowledgements

Thanks and obeisance to storytellers throughout time
who have nourished our souls with stories of wonder,
of human relationship to nature and to each other,
calling us pause to think and feel more deeply.

Heartfelt thanks to all who helped create the book you hold!
Especially my beta readers, editors and support circle:
Amelia, Autumn, David, Doug, Sandy J., Sandy K., Sue, Joe, Clare;
my sisters Rose and Helen;

To Fablesmithy for this gorgeous cover art and book design;

And always, deepest affection and gratitude
to my very resilient husband, Bob.

Contents

Chapter One

Brother Magnus knew he was about to be punished. He felt a little sad, but perfectly calm at the prospect. It was appropriate. It was time to pay the cost of wanting to belong.

Father Xavier, Prior of the Monastery of San Fortunatus, had made things clear after dawn prayers yesterday. He'd ordered Magnus to return to his cell instead of taking up his regular early duties of feeding livestock and mucking out stalls. His instruction was to fast and pray in silence, reflecting upon his sins until summoned. The Prior's lizard smile told him exactly which sins were foremost in his mind, as his lips stretched back to his ears and tiny scales spread across his throat, a thin hard smile full of secrets.

Magnus didn't understand how it happened, but a man's face turned into a lizard's when he lied to protect himself. He'd first seen it a few years ago, when a married man who often hired Magnus to his bed for pleasure pretended not to know him when he said hello in the village square. Each time, the man's face had turned scaly and a sickly green, fading to the color of fresh cream along his throat.

Father Xavier was protecting himself.

Even with his current troubles, Magnus had been happier in his two years in the monastery than he'd ever been in his village. He loved the animals, and the hard work. The rites of the Mass; the incense and chants and prayers; and the unshakable order of things had created an overarching sense of shared purpose which held him in a nameless, sweet belonging.

To be held in that belonging, Magnus had been eager to turn his back on the snares of worldly life. But there proved to be other traps here, and he'd stepped in one last year only days after he'd taken his simple vows to enter the juniorate.

Just before Lent, the Prior had summoned Magnus to his apartment and ordered him to disrobe. He'd instantly understood that sex with Father Xavier would be necessary if he was to remain at San Fortunatus. It was out of place in a monastery, of course, but he chose to comply, thinking it a small price for the happiness he'd already found in his year as a novice.

Besides, he was no stranger to transactions in sex. He'd barely begun to shave when his own father had ordered him to find generous lovers to augment the family purse, since it was already clear Magnus preferred men. He'd been proud to help his family. For a time, it had earned him a place. When he turned twenty, he couldn't earn enough to satisfy his father, and was asked to make his way elsewhere. It hurt to not sit across from his father at the family table and count out the money he'd earned. Cold as those moments had been, they still bestowed a kind of belonging, and he'd treasured them. In that year between leaving home and entering the monastery, he'd felt lost and unbearably alone.

How could his ache to belong somewhere good bring so much trouble? Magnus sighed out a heavy breath. He should never have acquiesced to Father Xavier and then quietly moved on. He saw that now. As he always did, it seemed, when looking back. Too foolish in the moment, and oh-so wise in useless hindsight.

So now he sat in the Lord Abbot's antechamber and in his third hour of waiting. The bench he sat on had no cushion, but he didn't mind. He wasn't much used to sitting anywhere during a work day.

His stomach grumbled. Food was another matter. He'd never done well without food. He tried to distract himself from his complaining stomach as well as his looming fate, letting his gaze wander over the colorful hunting scenes on the walls.

In the one beside him, an antlered stag, already pierced by arrows, leapt at an impossible angle away from three brindle hounds as if he could fly. A hunter mounted on a horse readied his bow again, as another blew his horn in triumph. Too big for the central figures, a spirited tangle of vines, flowers, and songbirds surrounded the hunting figures, making a merry fence holding them all prisoner—victor and vanquished alike. All their best efforts won nothing.

He avoided giving more than a glance to the dark, heavily carved door he would soon pass through. On a table next to the door, a bronze bust frowned at him from under his cardinal's galero. The polished furniture smelled faintly of beeswax. Tall brass candlesticks glowed in the afternoon light streaming in through the single tall window.

Something tickled his left foot, and he looked down. A large winged ant, red-and-black-bodied, crawled across his instep. He held his foot perfectly still and watched, amused, overcome with a sense of hope and gentle encouragement for the little creature, caught up in its beauty. He couldn't tell where the ant was going, but he prayed it might get there without too much difficulty. Many dangers lay in wait for it, no doubt—especially indoors, where flying ants were not welcome.

Alates, the winged ants. It was the season for them, and they were everywhere. This one stumbled along the hemp rope of his sandal as if drunk, falling off only to climb back on, reversing direction. It flashed its wings now and then, catching the angled light like the stained-glass windows in their chapel.

It would shed its wings soon. On their way to vespers a few days ago, Brother Bernardo, the master gardener, had told him they flew only for mating—a brief few days. Such was their lot, he'd said with a finality that made Magnus shiver. To be able to fly only for such a short time seemed a harsh blessing. Perhaps it was better to never fly at all.

The carved door opened, and a stony-faced secretary peered at him. "Enter," he commanded, although his disapproving sniff said he'd really rather Brother Magnus stayed out, as if he still smelled of sheep and cattle manure—which he knew he didn't, as he'd bathed and even washed his robe only yesterday. He rose, swallowed against a dry tongue, and entered.

Chapter Two

The room was full of so much light it hurt his eyes. And so many books! Red, black, green, and brown, with gold lettering on their wide spines. Titles mostly in Latin and two that he could see in Spanish. He briefly lusted to fondle them all, hold them, and slowly read them one by one.

The air was warm and thick, smelling of leather and incense. Behind a dark wood table that gleamed in the blazing light of the long windows, a pale round man in yellow and green robes sat in an ornately carved chair, the back of which seemed to rise halfway to the ceiling. The Lord Abbot.

His great chair, almost a throne, made the man look small. Even though he appeared shorter than an average man, he easily had twice the girth. His white hair stuck out in coarse wisps from under his amaranth skullcap, and enormous eyebrows spread wild and thick, nearly meeting above the long hooked nose dividing the slack folds of his face. It was an unkind face.

Magnus scolded himself for judging the Lord Abbot by mere appearance, yet his appearance repelled him. He searched the face more closely, hoping to find some hint of other traits to disprove his shallow judgment—a spark of humor, traces of joy, even gentleness—and failed.

To the Lord Abbot's left, Father Xavier sat in a much less magnificent chair, looking pious and humble. His eyes were closed, and his pale soft hands were folded atop a small brown wooden box. As if lost in the ecstasy of prayer, he did not look up.

Brother Magnus stood behind the plain bench on his side of the table with his head bowed, braced in dread, feeling like a little boy waiting to be scolded.

"You may sit," the Lord Abbot wheezed. "Let's not waste time."

"Thank you, Father Abbot." Magnus wished his voice hadn't cracked, but he'd been sitting in silence all morning. He sat, folded his hands in his lap, and studied them. He should have cleaned his fingernails more thoroughly. He could do nothing about their roughness, but he should have made more effort to get the last bits of dirt out.

The Lord Abbot cleared his throat. "Father Xavier reports that you've made vain and wanton advances, advances of a carnal nature, toward him over many months; that he refrained from denouncing your behavior in hope that you would find your way back to the path of virtue, confess, and seek penance of your own volition. What have you to say to this?"

Magnus looked up. Across the table, Father Xavier's face had become a lizard's again. Scaly-smooth, cold and serene.

Magnus hated confrontation. It made him sick to his stomach. Contradicting Father Xavier would be taken as rebellion, and holy scripture taught that rebellion was dire as the sin of witchcraft. Claiming the truth—that it was actually Father Xavier who had repeatedly initiated those advances—would certainly be met with offended denial. And who would not take a Prior's word over his, a mere junior monk working in the barnyard with little more than a year since his simple vows?

Besides, it wouldn't be honest to claim innocence. He couldn't deny his own trespasses. Magnus had come to that conclusion yesterday as he'd fasted and prayed. He was, in fact, guilty. He had broken his vow of celibacy. Often. It didn't matter with whom, or why. He hadn't refused, and so he deserved censure.

But neither would he accept the Prior's lie, even if he couldn't deny it. He kept his gaze up so the Lord Abbot would see his knowledge of Father Xavier's deceit, if he chose. "Father Xavier knows the truth of this matter. Truth is sacred," he said quietly.

Father Xavier's eyes flew open. Eyebrows raised, he looked to the Abbot, who scowled across the table at Magnus.

"Surely you are not suggesting Father Xavier lies."

Magnus pulled in a deep breath. It was so tempting to shout, yes, that was exactly what he was doing, but he didn't have the courage. "Doctrine teaches us," he replied carefully, "that a Prior has proven himself insusceptible to worldly entanglements and to all untruth, for all such frailties have been purged from him through long and faithful devotion to the Divine Office. Father Xavier is our Prior. Ergo—"

"Yes, quite." The Abbot cleared his throat again, sharper this time. "The Monastery of San Fortunatus has no place for a junior monk who so shamelessly flaunts his youthful comeliness, tempting those who have taken their solemn vows."

The Abbot stretched out his hand toward Father Xavier, who surrendered the wooden box he'd been holding. "In his admirable compassion, our Prior has petitioned on your behalf, asking that you not be summarily expelled, but instead be given opportunity to redeem yourself through service."

So there was hope! Brother Magnus glanced again at his hands, heavily callused and marked with small scars. He would soon lose the nail on his left thumb, blackened when their ram butted him into a fencepost. What kind of hard task could they give him that was not already his to do? He fed the livestock morning and night, and labored all day in the fields. He mucked out the milking barn at night after his other chores were done. He loved his work, freely given in service to God, to his Brothers, to their home on this hallowed ground.

"Therefore," the Abbot continued, "you may render our order a service in penance, after which we may again be able to receive you into our sacred fold. We offer you a task. A difficult one. Accept it or be expelled immediately."

"What is the task?" asked Magnus, torn between hope and caution.

Father Xavier looked offended. "If that matters, we release you from your vows today and return you to the vicissitudes of the profane world."

At least there was hope. Magnus glanced up at the stained glass windows pouring many-colored glory into the room. He needed that glory desperately. At very least his days here had a comforting, reliable shape. He understood his few difficulties, and knew the great unpredictable world could not reach him. His chest tightened at the prospect of being thrown back, adrift, into the life which had so often overwhelmed him with its uncertainty. Far better to be punished and remain here, whatever the task. "I accept your gracious clemency, Father Abbot. Thank you."

"Very well." The Abbot set the box on the table between them. To Brother Magnus's alarm, the Abbot's face had now become a lizard's also, glittering brown, with orange scales covering his jowls. Magnus knew why Father Xavier had lied, but what would the Lord Abbot gain by lying to him?

"This holy relic is the Mantle of San Sarvras," the Father Abbot said gravely. "The only known remnant of the garment he wore in his

martyrdom. It received the tears of his agony and has healed many."
He lifted the lid.

Inside, on midnight velvet, lay a lantern-shaped reliquary of leaded glass, no bigger than Magnus's thumb. He peered closer. Encased within it lay a tiny scrap of brown cloth. He'd never seen this relic before, nor had he heard of it being brought to the altar during festivals or holy days. It was mysteriously beautiful in a rough way, as some things wrought by men long dead can be. Magnus stared at it, fascinated.

The Lord Abbot coughed, breaking the spell. "One of our order, Brother Calmas, a most gifted manuscript artist, has been detained by a self-styled general well beyond the southernmost reach of our diocese. In truth, this general is nothing more than a local strongman, but unfortunately, he controls our only year-round road to Santa Teresa and the sea. So we accommodate his posturing. It is fortunate that, despite his many failings, he remains steadfast in his faith. He has requested a sacred relic for his chapel as the price of Brother Calmas's release. We offer you the privilege—and challenge—of delivering the Mantle of San Sarvras to General Tun, then escorting Brother Calmas in his safe return to us."

He closed the lid, and leaned forward with a grunt, as if fighting against his own bulk to push the box to the center of the table. He sat back, breathing hard, his face flushed.

He could do this. Magnus leaned forward and drew the box to himself, cradling it in his hands. It was surprisingly warm. Of course—Father Xavier had been holding it, probably for a long time. No, that wasn't the likely reason. Father Xavier's hands had never felt warm to him before.

He'd heard of Santa Teresa but never of anyone traveling such a great distance. He swallowed down his dismay. "How long is this journey?"

Father Xavier shrugged. "On foot, three weeks. Perhaps four." He pursed his lips into a mean, thin smile. "You are fortunate to be young and strong."

Rather than wallowing in the uncertainties of the journey, Magnus concentrated on calculating the time. Four weeks, a few days between, then another four weeks to return with Brother Calmas. If everything went well, he could still be back well before harvest. They would need him for that.

He had no right to ask, but he asked anyway. "Who will care for the animals?"

"God has provided, as always," Father Xavier intoned, his palms together in prayerful gratitude. "Two healthy young novices have petitioned for entry to our order in just the last week." He shrugged again, smiling. "I have no doubt they will be well able to replace you in all your duties."

Magnus could feel his cheeks and ears heat. Father Xavier was mocking him now. Even the services rendered by his private parts would be assumed by others. He stared at the box on the table, burning in his humiliation.

"Until you return with Brother Calmas, of course," added the Lord Abbot. His giant eyebrows arched and flattened like furry white caterpillars trying to escape his forehead. "Then you may petition for reinstatement."

"Yes, of course," replied Father Xavier, his lizard face smug and smooth. "Should you return. Until then."

Father Xavier's suggestion that he might not be successful rang harsh. They knew something he didn't, and they weren't going to tell him. His heart raced, and he itched all over. He'd already said yes. "May I have a day or two to say farewell to the brothers and to my... to the animals?"

"Say your farewells quickly," said the Lord Abbot. "You leave to-morrow morning, immediately after first-hour prayers." He made a perfunctory gesture of blessing, no more than a wave of dismissal. "The shield of God, almighty in battle, go with you."

"Thank you, Lord Abbot, Father Xavier," he said, keeping his voice soft. He stood and picked up the relic's box, holding it close against his heart. Somehow, it soothed him. Then a sudden wave of hot certainty swept through, strengthening him. "I will deliver the Mantle and return with Brother Calmas."

Saying goodbye to the animals was proving to be as painful as Magnus had feared, especially now in the familiar, friendly reek of the brood sow's shed. He leaned over the rough wood rail and murmured to Nena as she lay on her side, grunting and snuffling. She was huge now, and her teats had begun to swell. He wouldn't be here to see her give birth. She was beautiful, he told her, over and over.

The door creaked open, and Brother Bernardo lumbered in to lean on the railing next to him. "I thought I might find you here." His rough gardener's hand landed on Brother Magnus's shoulder and squeezed. "I heard you're leaving in the morning."

"Yes. I'm saying goodbyes. Nena is last of my charges. I'm sad her little ones will come while I'm away."

"Ach. Perhaps just as well. Father Xavier is very fond of suckling pig. I still say you're too tender-hearted to be a good farmer. Too kind for your own good."

"Kindness costs nothing. It makes me feel good."

Bernardo shoved a bundle into Magnus's hand. "I brought you some apples. They're easy enough to carry."

"Thank you." Magnus laughed, feeling his face heat. "And who's being too tender-hearted now?"

"Not me. Give old Brother Bernardo a hug now," he said, his voice cracking as he wrapped Magnus in his arms, his calloused fingers rough and kind against his neck.

Bernardo let go and looked over his shoulder, as if to make sure they were alone. "You're not the first winsome lad our Prior has sent away, you know. Always before solemn vows, so there's less fuss. At least you can come back. That's different this time."

Magnus stiffened. "You know why, then?"

"Of course. Our Prior's appetites are no secret, even though no one dares say anything above a whisper. It's just your bad luck to be to his taste."

So everyone had known but him. He swallowed against the sudden thickness in his throat. His eyes stung. All this time, he'd thought he carried his ugly secret alone—a secret everyone else already knew but never mentioned. "I had no idea there were others, although I suppose I shouldn't be surprised. I just didn't think of it."

Brother Bernardo shook his head. "That's the price you paid for our silence. No one dared say. We never spoke to any of you. It's unjust, and I'm sorry for my cowardice." His shoulders sagged. "I'm truly sorry. It's not easy for a man to figure out where he belongs. After thirty years, this is where I belong, though perhaps only because of my silence and cowardice. I'm too old to start life over with nothing but my aching knees."

Of all the brothers, he'd considered Bernardo his closest friend. Magnus stared at Nena, reaching into his heart to forgive all his brothers who'd known he was being used and hadn't offered the tiniest kindness. He couldn't find any to give.

"I think it would have helped me bear my lot, though. And I would have known I'd eventually be sent away. I wouldn't have harbored false hope."

Bernardo squeezed his shoulder. "Harsh as it may sound, maybe you haven't found where you belong yet."

A flash of anger took him, and he wheeled on Bernardo. "That's for me to decide, not you, not the Prior! I've worked hard to belong here." Magnus scolded himself. Wrath was a sin. Maybe it was for the best he was going away for a while.

He didn't want to look at Bernardo, so Magnus stared again at Nena, letting the silence drag while he calmed. "Are you saying none of the others came back?"

"Not one. Just quietly gone. Made a life for themselves somewhere else, I suppose. Didn't miss them, really. Well, one, I did. Had the voice of an angel, did young Félix." Brother Bernardo poked Magnus in the chest. Hard. "You, I will miss. So come back if you can. If you choose. Take care of yourself while you're away, and come home safe. Animals and brothers alike will be glad to see you again."

If Magnus came back, Father Xavier would no longer be interested in his body, that much was clear. But he would be using someone else, someone more innocent than he. "I'll return. But I don't know if I could stay, knowing now what everyone else has known all along. I don't think I could stay silent about... the Prior."

Bernardo sighed and looked away. He swiped a leathery knuckle against his cheek. "That would be our loss," he said, his voice thick and sad. "But no less than we deserve."

The bell called them to dinner, but Magnus no longer wanted to break bread with his brothers. He would ignore their presence, and eat only for strength on the journey.

Chapter Three

The sun had barely broken the horizon when Brother Magnus paused on the footpath leading away from the barns. He wanted to weep, watching the animals being turned out into their pastures for the day. The dairy cows would still go to Sophia Meadow for another month before they rotated to another field. The sheep had just started grazing in Sebastian Meadow. His brothers were brown dots creeping across the field now, the clank of the lead animals' bells a distant music. He would miss this.

It was a sin, but he surrendered to envy. Only days ago, he'd been among them, pulling wide the gate or herding the animals through in the cool peace and long shadows of early morning. He'd belonged there with them. And now he didn't. Now he was just another of Father Xavier's discarded playthings.

He shook his head against such unseemly self-pity and turned again toward the abbey gate. The rucksack shifted on his shoulder, cumbersome and unpredictable. He wasn't yet used to accounting for it as he walked. He felt as though he needed more than two hands to manage his walking staff, his waterskin and his pack, which had a rolled blanket hanging below it.

Earlier in the kitchen, Brother Ignatius had handed Magnus a chunk of bread and a piece of dried meat, declaring that now he had everything he needed to start his journey. Charity of food and shelter along the way would sustain him, just as the honored tradition of hospitality to the Church had sustained countless monks traveling the same road before him. Magnus was careful not to show it, but he resented the lofty words. They rang thin and miserly. He was glad for the apples from Brother Bernardo.

He'd packed and repacked carefully: a book of prayer already shabby from use when it had been given to him; his alms bowl; a small knife and flint; a rough map drawn on a scrap of sheepskin that marked the road to San Pedro and then on to General Tun's stronghold; food. And nestled at the bottom, the wooden box containing the Mantle of San Sarvras, his sacred charge.

But was it truly sacred? He'd lain awake half the night wondering about that. The Abbot had obviously lied to him when he described the relic's provenance, so something about it was false. But by the time he rose for first-hour prayers, Magnus had decided it didn't matter to him. His task was real. His promise to perform the task was real. Every mile of the journey would be real, along with every hardship the miles might bring.

Therefore, he would treat the Mantle as real, too, as he carried it, honoring it with his deepest reverence. Otherwise, what was the point of making the long journey? It was a choice of his conscience, not someone else's.

He squinted at the late spring sky dotted with quick-sliding clouds. With luck and if the weather held, he would be at the fortress before midsummer. He didn't want to leave.

Brother Aloysius drew the bar from the abbey's foot gate and swung it open for him without a word, and without meeting his eyes. Yes, Brother Bernardo was right: everyone had known. Every one of his brothers had agreed to keep the Prior's secret, letting Magnus pay the price for his transgressions without the simplest kindness. The only way for him now was forward.

Magnus stepped out into the broad, unpredictable world without looking back. He strode through the town below the abbey and gained the open road before he'd broken a sweat.

As the sun lifted higher, he guessed by its position when his brothers would be observing the Hours, and sang the prayers as if he were with them. He was angry at them, and he missed being among them. The chapel would be cool, fragrant, and dim, with his spiritual family all around him, caught up in the undulating chants of worship. They were complicit in his plight. He stopped singing. His footsteps became the rhythm for his own prayer, steady and firm while the road shimmered before him in the midday heat.

Before it was time for the monastery's mid-afternoon prayers, the road came to a copse of cottonwood with a creek running through it. Magnus climbed down the ravine, drank, filled his waterskin, and sat in the shade for a while, listening to the languid, leathery chatter of the leaves.

As a boy, he'd imagined he could talk with trees like this. In a surge of nostalgia, he wanted to know what they were saying to each other, and take part in their conversation. He'd ask them what it was like to be forever in just one place, never having to wonder where they belonged. He laughed, chiding himself for such foolishness, but soft and low, a voice in his heart replied that perhaps by some miracle one day he could speak with them, and ask.

He ate sparingly, knowing the next village was more than a day away. He said good-bye to the trees and clambered up the slope to the road.

Just before sundown, he spread his bedroll on a small hill overlooking the road. He gathered dry leaves and sticks for a fire, but after many failed attempts to use his flint, he resigned himself to spending his first night without.

The darkness had its own beauty, he discovered. He sang his prayers to the stars and lay down, using his pack as a pillow. It occurred to him it might be sacrilege to sleep with his head on a holy relic, but he tumbled into a deep sleep before he could decide. A soft openness filled his dreams, moving in slow, heavy rivers through his limbs. More than once, he startled awake, only to feel the sweet pull of the dream rivers dragging him under again.

He woke before sunrise to pray. When the sun broke the horizon, his memorized prayers fell away to ash before the prayer of the earth rising to the sun. He wept at the way the sun lit every blade of grass like the flame of a candle set on a vast altar. It seemed to his heart as if he had never witnessed such a miracle, as if he had never walked out into the pastures of the monastery at dawn—which he had done every day for nearly two years—and seen this kind of light. This was an act of creation, the sun's immaculate benediction calling every green thing up into the fire of God's love, while he was its mortal witness.

Was it the Mantle of San Sarvras that made him so tender to the world's beauty? He drew the box out of his pack and reverently kissed the lid in thanks. It was a presumptuous gesture, but it also felt appropriate, even though he couldn't imagine how San Sarvras's tears of martyrdom could make his heart ache and sing like this, ache and sing for the beauty of trees and meadows blazing in morning sunlight.

He put the box back in his pack and tied his blanket for travel. For a moment longer, he sat motionless on the hill, letting the new day wash over him.

What was his next landmark? He reopened his pack and pulled out the scrap of sheep's hide that served as his map. An unnamed black dot sat close to the abbey on the line of the road, which Magnus supposed was a village somewhere ahead, then a rather large blank space marked as desert. Beyond that, a larger dot marked as San Pedro, and a short distance beyond that an X for the town of Santa Inés and General Tun's fortress. When he'd first looked at the map, the desert space hadn't looked so large. Now it seemed much more forbidding.

He would complete his task. He ate one of the apples Brother Bernardo had given him, and descended to the road.

CHAPTER FOUR

Walking was something Magnus had taken for granted, the way to get from one place to another in the course of a day's work. This was different, though, when walking was itself the day's work. As a task, it demanded little attention, and changes in his surroundings along the road were too slow to hold his interest. His legs and feet followed their steady rhythm, leaving more hours for him to think than he had thoughts.

By mid-afternoon and with the sun beating down relentlessly, imagining what was happening at the monastery had lost much of its appeal, and in light of his current situation, relevance. Whatever was occurring there grew more distant with each step. Shade and cool water became more enjoyable to contemplate, and although it wasn't helpful to dwell on them too much, he stayed alert for green vegetation indicating where he might find water.

Wherever he did find water, it felt prudent to take a long drink and then top up his waterskin. He had only himself to rely on. He hadn't seen another person all day, a fact that sometimes made him feel exhilarated, but more often lonely and hopeless.

Before dark, Magnus made camp by a tiny spring barely able to maintain a green patch visible from the road. Still, it was fresh, sweet water. Even though he'd done nothing but walk all day, he ached in unusual places, especially his ankles. His rucksack still held two apples and a hardening remainder of bread, but he was too miserable to eat.

It seemed the last threads of connection to the monastery had frayed, leaving him desolate and vulnerable. As he held his waterskin to catch the spring's trickle, he felt more alone than he could bear—like a lost fawn in a strange forest, not knowing where its mother was, or wolves, or a good place to hide. He longed to hear a friendly voice, or see a smile he could trust. A shoulder he could clasp in good faith.

"Please," he called out, close to tears. "Someone talk to me."

The silent gnarled olive tree nearby offered no relief to his melancholy. It seemed alone, too—the last living tree among the dead stumps of whatever abandoned orchard had once grown here.

As he stared at the stars, a brooding sorrow washed through him. He was just passing through, and didn't belong here. Or anywhere, it seemed. "Everyone should belong somewhere," he murmured to the night sky, which he knew wouldn't answer. It never had.

He scolded himself for his self-pity and unrolled his blanket. As he set his rucksack as his pillow, he had to wipe his eyes in spite of his self-reproach. Somewhere nearby, an owl screeched, reminding him he was not entirely alone. Besides, he carried a sacred relic. His obligation to it, he told himself, was a kind of belonging. That was something, and it would have to suffice for now.

Magnus slept, and dreamed San Sarvras searched for him among voluptuous scarlet clouds that curled and pressed warm against his body everywhere. The saint, naked and unmarked by the torture of his martyrdom, caught him by the arm near a flower-laden spring, where he promised they would be together forever. They embraced and fell to earth laughing, their limbs tangling in glorious pleasure.

The dream stayed with him after he woke, clouding his sense of what was real in time and place. For a moment, he had to think before he remembered this was his third day traveling. With his knife, he carved two little notches on his walking staff, one for each night on the road. Then he took a stone to dig out a little basin below the spring's outlet so thirsty animals and travelers might drink more easily.

It felt good to provide for others he'd never meet—an act of service to others, if not belonging. When he was finished, he held his hands over the spring, wanting to bless and protect it but not knowing the right words. He settled for a moment of gratitude and good wishes for its future. A trickle of happiness rose up in him, as if an artesian spring flowed from him into the water below his hands.

A strong male voice Magnus didn't recognize sounded behind him. *I am the path of your happiness.*

Magnus wheeled, his heart pounding. There was no one there.

I am the path of your happiness, the voice repeated, again from behind. He spun back to face the spring.

I am the path of your happiness, the disembodied voice said again. *Your joy, your pleasure, your belonging. Listen. Listen, and open yourself to me.*

Magnus turned slowly in a full circle. Nobody. He ought to feel afraid—or at least wary. But to his surprise, he didn't. He trembled with excitement, a longing that made him hot with need. "Who are you?" He shook his head. "What are you?"

I am the path of your happiness. Again the voice sounded like it was behind him.

Then Magnus knew. Slowly, reverently, he shrugged off his rucksack and opened it. He reached down to the bottom and took out the box, holding it in both hands. "It's you, isn't it?"

There was no reply, but a shivering warmth filled his hands. "It is you," he whispered. "I know it." With shaking fingers, he lifted the lid of the box and stared at the little reliquary. It was so small. How could it be a path to anyone's happiness? How could it be anything to him other than this object he'd promised to deliver to General Tun?

No, he was being silly. He closed the lid. This was nothing more than sentimental imagination, a wisp remaining from his dream. Yet his heart pounded to believe. He would give anything for a path to real happiness. Anything.

A sharp spark of defiance ignited in his chest. What if he chose to believe the voice? He could if he wanted to. All his life, people had called him gullible. But here in this wilderness, if the voice never spoke to him again, no one was here to laugh at him. No one would even know. He would simply carry on, deliver this thing to the general and escort Brother Calmas back to the monastery as promised. He risked nothing. But if the voice was real! If it was real, then happiness, everything he had ever ached for, was possible.

I am your path of happiness. The voice was softer, farther away. Was it waning? He needed to say something before it disappeared altogether.

He took a deep breath and opened the box again. The morning sunlight glinted off the glass, filling his eyes until there was nothing anywhere but glittering light. He angled the box so he could see again. "Thank you," he said, slowly filling with the solemn knowledge he was forging an unbreakable agreement. "Yes. Please be my path of happiness."

Nothing happened. Magnus laughed at himself as he returned the box to his rucksack. What had he expected? That the heavens might open to a celestial choir? That San Sarvras himself might appear, healed of his hideous mutilations, wrap him in his arms as if he were still in his dream, and give him unending happiness forever? He laughed at himself again, more gently this time, and gathered up his belongings. He looked back at the spring, content with what he had done, and turned to the road.

All morning, Magnus pondered what it might mean if the relic truly was his path to happiness. Several times he asked it questions, but got no answers. What if the voice was merely delirium from being in the sun too long? What if the voice spoke true? What might his happiness look like? Was it wrong to want happiness? Was that too selfish? It sounded so selfish as to be un-Christian. But it didn't feel selfish at all. The contract he'd made with the voice felt simple, solid, and good.

Chapter Five

Day after day, the road wore on. The unrelenting sun beat down.

Though Magnus was used to working in the fields all day, he learned to begin his trek before the sun rose and then seek a place of shade to wait out the sun at its highest before resuming his journey, making camp only when there was barely enough light to choose a good place to sleep.

By the fifth day, he forgot to pray with his brothers at the monastery. When he noticed, it no longer seemed so important. He walked on, praying in his own way, feeling liberated instead of alone. He carved little notches on his staff each morning as a kind of prayer as he watched the sun rise. He would have begged for food, but there was no one to beg from.

A little after midday on the sixth day, he noticed smoke hanging in the air far ahead of him, but it was approaching sunset before he stood in front of a dilapidated smithy. It was no more than a shed open on two sides at the edge of what appeared to be an equally bedraggled village. A man stood with his back to the road, hammering as he shaped something on the anvil.

Magnus approached, ready to shout to him over the noise, but a shiver of caution made him wait silently at a distance. The smith stopped hammering and plunged the hot iron into a tub of water, the sharp hiss softening to a sigh rising in a cloud of steam.

"Good day to you, friend," Magnus called out. "Will you tell me what village this is?"

The man stiffened and turned slowly, hammer slightly raised. His face and posture relaxed as he took in Magnus's robes. "This is Vera Cruz." His voice sounded as worn and tired as the village looked. "Last stop before the desert, if you're headed west."

"I am. I hope for shelter and food before I go farther."

The blacksmith glanced at the sky. "Father Damario will be at the church now, hearing confession before Mass. First street on your right. He's the one you'll want to talk to about that."

"Thank you for your kindness. A blessing upon you and your forge."

The smith raised his hammer in acknowledgment and turned back to his work.

Without directions, Magnus would have missed the church, which had no spire, no bell tower to navigate by. It was a rough, squat adobe building set as if it had turned its back to worldly life, forcing Magnus to walk along its side and through the graveyard to get to the weathered east-facing door, which stood half open to Jerusalem.

Father Damario's kind, worn face, patched cassock, and slow, arthritic hands seemed to match his church well. Yes, he could give Magnus food and shelter for the night, and perhaps more: he'd heard a merchant was leaving for San Jose in the morning. He might be willing to provide a faster way across the desert.

In the morning, Magnus eagerly followed the priest's directions to an inn, where he found a man harnessing his donkey to a cart.

"Good day to you, kind sir!" said Magnus. "Father Damario suggested you might be traveling west across the desert, and that a ride with you might be possible."

The man's face brightened. "Yes, indeed I am traveling west, and I'd be glad for the company of a man of God, for the desert is not a friendly place. I trust you have your own food and drink? I have only enough for my donkey and me."

Magnus was about to thank him for his generosity when he heard a shout behind him. *No!*

He turned, but there was no one there. The voice had to belong to the relic, but he didn't want it to. "Surely getting across the desert more quickly would be a good thing?" he muttered, hoping the merchant didn't notice.

The voice—unmistakably the relic's—came again, so loud it made Magnus flinch. *No!*

"But—"

No. The voice was insistent, but softer, farther away. Again Magnus became afraid the relic might abandon him if he ignored it. He took a deep breath, letting it out slowly. Barely risen, the sun blazed from a cloudless sky, already hot enough to make the skin on his neck prickle. Who knew how many more days it would take to cross the desert on foot? But if the relic was his path to happiness, he had to listen to its guidance, didn't he?

If.

On the other hand, a path to happiness wasn't important if he died of thirst on the road.

"Who are you talking to?" The merchant's smile had disappeared, and caution glinted in his canny narrowed eyes.

Magnus tried to laugh, embarrassed, but the sound that came out was weak. "I argue with myself sometimes," he said. "Predictably, I always lose. I thank you for your offer, but I must make my journey on foot."

The merchant looked both surprised and a little relieved. "As you must, then. I wish you good fortune." He climbed onto his cart, released the brake and gave the reins a snap. Torn, Magnus watched the cart roll down the street toward the open road.

It wasn't too late to call out and run after the merchant. Only a madman would follow voices in his head to choose crossing the desert on foot over an offer to travel in a cart. But that's what he'd just done. Therefore, he must be mad. He might pay for his madness with his life.

"Are you sure about this?" he whispered to the relic. No answer came.

Magnus sighed bitterly. Why should one? The relic had already spoken, and begun to fade at his hesitation. What was the point of arguing? He'd asked for its guidance and made an agreement. Either he would honor his agreement or not.

Resigned, he made his way to the village fountain. He took long pulls from his waterskin, waiting as a stableboy filled his buckets. At least he'd start with as much water as he could.

By the time he got to the road, the merchant's cart had already disappeared over a rise. He could have been sitting in that cart, riding through the wasteland in relative ease. He spent the rest of the day alternately railing at the relic, which remained silent, or himself, for being a fool to hope for happiness. He argued with himself as to whether he was mad to believe the relic might actually guide him to happiness. As the sun lowered, he gave up his anger in favor of tenuous hope he'd done the right thing.

That evening, he found a thicket of scrawny bushes just off the road, leaning over a patch made green by a seeping spring. It was good enough for a night's rest. He put out his bedroll and stretched out on his back with a groan. The stars pushed down on him as if pinning him to the ground, demanding his attention.

Doubts tried to come creeping back, but he banished them to silence. He'd already made his choice. The rest was speculation. He'd obeyed the voice and refused the merchant's offer, so here he was, resting his aching feet by the road, the merchant and his cart long gone. He reminded himself that regret was a form of self-pity. He lost himself in the stars until he fell asleep.

Magnus woke before sunrise to see a brown hare nibbling on the grass at the spring. He watched. It was so soft and alert, its movements delicate, yet it endured somehow in this harsh wilderness. He lay still until it hopped away. He arose, somehow encouraged, lighter, without being able to say why.

The afternoon sun made the air above the road ripple and dance. It was time to seek shelter. He scanned the sides of the road ahead until it disappeared over a hill. No usable shade anywhere. In the distance, he noticed dark birds circling. Perhaps they watched animals drawn to water beneath them. Where there was water, there was sure to be shade. Hope quickened his pace.

But when he arrived, there was no spring and no shade—only the wreckage of the merchant's donkey cart, and his bloating corpse. Magnus crossed himself, then shouted at the vultures, driving them back into the air. He approached slowly and stood for a moment, staring at the ravaged body. His own could have been lying there as well.

Bandits must have ambushed the merchant and taken the donkey. He hadn't even learned the merchant's name. Should he bury him? Why wouldn't they have taken the cart? In the endless heavy brush stretching away from the road, the cart would probably be more trouble than it was worth. The donkey, however...

I am your path of happiness. The voice sounded so loud Magnus jumped as if a robber had crept up behind him.

"You saved my life," he said to the relic in his rucksack, shivering more at the certain knowledge than the sight of death before him. The relic's voice was real.

I will teach you happiness.

"Thank you." Magnus wanted to learn happiness, especially the happiness of living long enough to find where he belonged. "Teach me."

He erected a makeshift shelter with the remains of the cart and the merchant's cloak, well away from the body. Crouching in its shade, Magnus sipped his water and pondered his situation.

Take what you need. Water. Clothing. Take his shoes. Do not stay here tonight.

Magnus frowned. Was that not wrong to do? Thou shalt not steal. He might be committing another kind of robbery, but passive and perhaps even more macabre. Grave robbing.

No.

In spite of his misgivings, Magnus knew he'd be a fool to argue with the voice that had just saved his life.

When the heat of the day broke, he chased the birds away again, and collected the merchant's hat. He took the waterskin and gathered up the cloak. The shoes were far too small for him to wear, but maybe he could use the leather to fix the ones he had.

He didn't trust the water in the skin, so he poured it out onto the ground while saying a prayer for the merchant's soul. He donned the hat, organized his new belongings as best he could, and struck out on the road again. He imagined he could feel the relic, lying in its box at the bottom of his pack, watching over him. For the first time in days, he felt... comforted.

CHAPTER SIX

H e would not have survived without a second waterskin.

By the tenth day, Magnus had learned to make friends with hunger, and to take tiny sips of water even when he was so thirsty his head spun. He was not alone; the relic was with him. He told the relic what he saw. He talked to the waterskin sometimes, thanking it instead of taking a drink. He learned to scrape the spines off cactus, and eat small pieces of the fleshy lobes to moisten his mouth.

Even though the road wore on, it also held occasional surprises. Sometimes he was startled into joy by the beauty of tiny things—the spark of a quartz rock catching the sun just right, or the song of a meadowlark. Magnus shared his excitement and wonder with the relic, even though its voice hadn't spoken to him since the day he'd found the merchant's body.

Something taller than the brush beside the road caught his attention. A tree! Or what remained of a tree. He stopped to wonder at the naked dignity of it: lightning-struck, charred, deformed and exquisite, yet little more than a broken stump. A single limb, crooked and undaunted, rose from the shattered trunk. From it, two smaller branches stretched out to bear a few leaves.

See. The relic's voice startled Magnus, but he didn't jump this time.

Can you see that tree is happy? Never compare happiness. Your happiness begins when you love the world.

Look, and you will see happiness.

Magnus practiced. He tried to be more observant, looking for happiness, even if the relic stayed silent when he asked if he was practicing the right way. Every day was a puzzle uninterested in finding a solution.

The air, stirred by a steady breeze from the southeast, blew hot and dry. On most afternoons, clouds built, usually bringing thunder but rarely any rain. Magnus learned to smell the rain before the first drops hit the ground. Even a light spattering in the dust would unlock the scent of earth and sage and rabbit brush, making him drunk with it. It was exhilarating.

His sandals broke every few days. To repair them, he used pieces of the merchant's shoes, and even his sheepskin map cut into strips. He learned how to make braided twine from yucca leaves scraped until all that was left were the long white veins. Were they happy to be part of his shoe repair? He hoped so.

One morning, Magnus was so hungry he ate a large chunk of a cactus he hadn't seen before. It made him queasy and lightheaded. As he walked, he heard the relic whisper to him.

See. This desert is happy. It is part of the original garden, planted eastward in Eden. Do not let its appearance trick you. It is all beauty.

He stopped in the middle of the dusty road and looked again, believing with all his heart. In a sudden burst of glory, God's pleasure in tiny things poured out to him from every pebble and thistle, taking him into a rapture so fierce it lit a bonfire in his chest. It spiraled upward, even to the drifting vulture which had followed him for over a day. The horizon turned slowly even though he stood still. Like Adam, Magnus stood in the midst of the Garden. He walked on, burning and joyous, in praise greater than any prayer could hold.

That night, he couldn't take even a sip of water without retching. Shivering, parched, and weak, he asked the relic if he was going to die.

Not yet, whispered the relic. *Not yet.*

Magnus prayed it was right as he slid into a fevered sleep.

On the twentieth day, two days since he'd last eaten, he sat resting to ease the cramps in his legs. He was tired. His feet bled. One waterskin was empty; the other was nearly empty. The relic had been silent for days. The road steadily climbed a hill that seemed to go on forever. He had to stop often, just to summon his will and his breath. His body whispered to him that, soon, will and breath would not be enough to make him stand again. But he had a little water yet. He'd continue until it was gone. He'd made a promise.

A breeze startled him with the smell of water, and his whole body came alert. He sniffed again—nothing but dust. He was imagining things. His mind had come untethered, running off into wishes. The scent came again, flowing around him, cool and sweet.

No, this was no delirium. The breeze lifted him to his feet. He tried to walk faster, but couldn't. Slowly, so slowly, he made his way to the crest of the hill, gasping and staggering.

CHAPTER SEVEN

Below him, nestled in a wide, gentle valley spread the largest town he'd seen since he left the monastery. A river wound through it, a glittering silver ribbon, lined on either side with the varied greens of fields and trees. So impossibly, overwhelmingly green! He'd forgotten how many greens could exist in one place. There would be people. And food.

From the simple map he'd memorized in the first days of his journey, he knew this would be San Pedro. A croaking sob broke from his throat and he wept, though he had no tears to shed. He leaned on his staff, his body shaking with relief. And gratitude. He was saved.

Fields spread out before him, full of promise and plenty. Barges plied the river. Twin spires rose from the center of the town—a substantial church. Prayerfully, he gave himself to the prospect of abundant fresh water. He would beg in the square for a meal and perhaps shelter at the church for the night. In celebration, he drank the last two swallows from his waterskin. He started walking, his steps charged with relief and hope.

As he entered the town, the same wordless belonging that sometimes had enveloped him in the wilderness took him again, filling him. He knew, and was known. It was as if he had lived in this town all his life, even though he'd never been here before. Such peace. What was this mysterious communion without need of a host?

Maybe it was only the smell of the river, remembered from child-hood, but every lane, every house and tree had a familiar sparkling density—some simple realness, a durable significance that spoke to him. He crossed himself.

He made his way toward the spires, where there would be a square. Where there would be a fountain. In no time at all, he stood before the church, which sat like a mother hen watching placidly over the brood of houses clustered around her.

At the fountain, he forced himself to take tiny sips from only one cupped hand at first, fighting the urge to fill his waterskins right away. He chided himself gently for his lack of trust—the fountain was not going to run dry this afternoon. The coolness of the water spread in his belly like a blessing. He took a longer drink, and like a child, he let his hands play in the basin. Clear, cool, sweet water. Life. Bliss. A miracle. His face stung when he rinsed himself in preparation to enter the church.

But before he could mount the steps, the manse, a small stone house attached to the church, called to him. Paint cracked and peeled away in crumbling flakes from the weathered window boxes full of geraniums on either side of the door. Magnus stared at them, trans-fixed, as if pulled into the blaze of orange-red against the whitewashed stone. He plunged his face into the flowers' soft petals and breathed in their pungent smell. He drew his thumb along the rough edge of the window box in a caress, feeling a kinship so strong it made his heart pound.

He felt old whispers, the mingled procession of all the lives that had taken their turns at the hearth inside. Those lives had filled the cottage stones with their stories, their meaning, a meaning he could feel but never learn. A story about belonging he couldn't quite hear. It felt sacred.

The church door swung open smoothly to his pull. Inside, dim stillness enfolded him in familiar peace as he made obeisance, removed his pack, and knelt to pray. It seemed strange to not be moving—strange and welcome. Magnus lost himself in a wordless prayer of gratitude. He'd survived.

"Welcome to San Agericus, traveling brother," came a warm voice, drawing him from his prayers. Magnus opened his eyes to see a priest, white-haired and a little bent with age, leaning on the pew in front of him, his brown weathered face lit by a gentle smile.

"Thank you, Father," he replied. "Your fountain saved my life."

The priest chuckled. "You must have come to us by the desert road, then."

Magnus nodded, only now surprised he'd survived the journey. "I travel from the abbey at San Fortunatus to the chapel of General Tun. I beg for food and a place to sleep if you are able to give it. In return, I gladly offer what labor I am capable of. But I must add that you'll get better work out of me after I eat something, as I've had no food for days, and I'm a little weak at present."

"What is your name, pilgrim?"

"Magnus."

"Well met, Brother Magnus. I'm Father Bartolo. This is my parish. You're more than welcome to our hospitality such as it is." He turned his head away, still smiling. "We will gladly give you food and find shelter for you, but... perhaps first you might wish to bathe?"

Magnus laughed with awkward relief. "Your hospitality is more than I could hope for, Father. I'm sure my presence will be less of a burden once I've washed."

\#

Later, after Magnus had washed and Father Bartolo had gently tended to the raw places on his feet, they sat at a modest table in the stone manse next to the church. Before them spread supper served by the housekeeper: a loaf of bread and a meat stew, fragrant with rosemary. After a prayer from Father Bartolo, they ate in silence until they were almost finished.

Father Bartolo lifted the serving bowl. "Would you care for more? Miranda always makes plenty."

"It's gluttonous of me to admit I would, but I dare not. At present, my stomach is not used to holding much." The stew sat warm and satisfying in Magnus's belly. "This is the finest meal I've had since I began my journey."

Father Bartolo chuckled. "I can tell by watching you eat that you're no glutton." He carved himself another piece of bread. "You've traveled a long way from San Fortunatus. May I inquire as to the nature of your journey?"

Magnus looked down at the table to think. Its dark wood bore countless scars and stains, but had been faithfully oiled. Durable. Cared for. It glowed in the candlelight.

Secrecy had not been one of his instructions. Besides, surely he could speak freely to a parish priest. "I bear a holy relic, a gift from the Lord Abbot to General Tun, in exchange for the release of a friar who the general holds captive. A kind of ransom, I suppose."

Father Bartolo's brows knit, but he chewed in silence for a long time.

Finally, he spoke again, his tone more serious. "Forgive me for pressing further, but this relic—is it the Mantle of San Sarvras?

Magnus almost choked on his sip of water. "How could you have guessed that?"

Father Bartolo's smile was thin, joyless. "Your Abbot offered this same gift to our parish not two years ago as enticement to align with San Fortunatus instead of the Diocese of Santa Teresa. I inquired into the legitimacy of the Mantle. A conclave of archbishops ruled it was not a true relic but an old forgery. That ruling came twenty years ago." Father Bartolo shrugged. "We chose not to accept your Abbot's gift."

Magnus struggled to breathe while his thoughts darted in every direction. He studied the bowl in front of him. He had to make sense of this. He knew both the Abbot and Father Xavier had lied to him—he'd seen their lizard faces. Could the archbishops have been wrong?

But the Mantle itself—how could it be false?

"I know so little of such things, but it *is* sacred, I know it. I've felt... a presence. Its blessing aided me greatly as I carried it. I believe it saved my life. That can't be only my imagination—it's not that good."

"I suggest that speaks more to your own devotion than to the object itself," said Father Bartolo gently. "But I would never deny your claim. Perhaps your belief is more powerful than the thing believed in. As we in service to God know very well, it often is."

Magnus gazed at Father Bartolo, grateful for his respect. His face had not become a lizard's. He was speaking truth. Magnus closed his eyes, his head suddenly too full of contrary thoughts, far too many. He needed silence to make sense of them. But part of what sense he needed came to him quickly and unsought.

They knew.

The Lord Abbot and Father Xavier knew the relic had been discredited. That was their lie. A cold anger took him. They had used him, deliberately sending him out to perform an act of deception, every bit as false as Father Xavier's accusations against him.

Perhaps they had not expected him to return, or even survive his mission. He nearly hadn't.

General Tun lived no more than three days' journey from Santa Teresa. If Father Bartolo knew the Mantle had been discredited, then surely General Tun, as devout as the Lord Abbot had claimed he was, must also know. How might the general respond to the insult of the Abbot's false gift?

He thought back to his audience with the Lord Abbot. Yes. Father Xavier had simply wanted to get rid of him, nothing more. That was why he'd said, "Should you return" through his smiling lizard lips. Maybe he hoped Magnus would die. They didn't care at all if the general received their gift. They didn't care if he released Brother Calmas.

Their betrayal bit deep. He was nothing but a gullible junior monk. Magnus's eyes stung with shame. He blew out a sharp breath to soften his humiliation. Gullible, yes, but he knew what they did not—the Mantle had bestowed very real blessings upon him for carrying it. It had saved his life at least twice. It had shown him beauty and happiness. Of that, he had no doubt.

In his prayers tonight, he would ask for help to forgive the Abbot and Father Xavier. Tonight, and as many other nights as it might take. Right now, it felt as though it would take many. His trust, his very faith had been exploited, exactly as Father Xavier had used his body.

"I'm sorry to be the bearer of such unwelcome news," Father Bartolo said, placing a gnarled hand gently on his. "This must be painful for you. You are welcome to stay with us for a while if you wish. Or longer—we would find a place for you in the parish if you chose to stay."

The town had seemed familiar, and welcoming. Father Bartolo seemed to be a good man. Maybe Magnus should simply join the ordered procession of life here, so similar to the procession of life the church afforded anywhere. But the Mantle in his rucksack, sitting on the floor beside him, told him his journey was not over.

"Thank you," he said, part of him wishing he could stay forever. "A few days, perhaps. To regain my strength, and repair my shoes." He couldn't think farther ahead than that. "And to pray for guidance."

"You are welcome here. I mean that."

"Your kindness moves me deeply. Thank you." Magnus tried to banish the bitterness of Father Xavier's betrayal, but it wouldn't budge. It sat in his chest, heavy and cold. "But regardless of the relic's provenance, I will finish my task," he said after a while. "I made a promise."

As soon as he'd said the words, a new clarity seized him. His promise was not to the Lord Abbot, but to the Mantle itself. It *wanted* him to take it to the general. His heart became so light and free he thought it might float out of his body.

Some ray of wisdom shone through him, surprising him. Not his own, but it still set him free of his doubt. He smiled at Father Bartolo as his sadness melted away. "Besides, I cannot answer for the faith of others, only my own. I will keep my word."

CHAPTER EIGHT

S lowly, the tower of the general's stronghold rose from behind a hill, long before Magnus could see anything else of the town of Santa Inés. He quickened his stride, caught up in new urgency. After so many trials on the road, it was as if his body knew this part of his ordeal was nearly over.

His repaired sandal had come apart again, but the garrison would have leather, a cobbler's bench, and tools. If he could use them, he'd do a better repair this time. He would also ask to rest for a few days before he and Brother Calmas began their return to the abbey.

The abbey. His stomach went cold, bitter when he thought of the place, as it had ever since Father Bartolo's revelations a week ago. He didn't want to go back. What was there to go back to? Lies and hypocrisy he'd surely have to confront, followed by inevitable expulsion. He would simply deliver Brother Calmus as promised, and leave.

A wicked thought slithered into his heart: he could leave right now, before he took another step. Keep the Mantle for himself and just disappear. No one would know. If Father Xavier inquired as to why Brother Calmus hadn't returned, he would learn that Magnus had never arrived at the fortress. He'd be satisfied Magnus had died in the desert. He could keep the Mantle, and other men's schemes be damned. Like a grass fire, the idea swept through him, making him shiver hot and wild.

Just as quickly, the fire died out. In that same conversation with Father Bartolo, he'd realized that his obligation was to the Mantle, not to anyone at the monastery. The Mantle *wanted* to be taken to the general.

If he stole away like a thief, he would break his promise to the Mantle. Even if no one else knew or cared, Magnus would know he hadn't kept his word. The Mantle would know. He couldn't live with that. Besides, Calmus would still be the general's prisoner.

So just as he couldn't stay in San Pedro, he couldn't change course now. He had to present his sacred charge to the general in good faith. That was what the Mantle wanted, and he owed it his very life.

The high street of Santa Inés bustled with colorful traffic. Loud voices and sweet wood smoke filled the air, overwhelming him after so many days of solitude. The street led past the church and directly on toward General Tun's looming stronghold. Magnus was tempted to pause at a bakery to beg for a piece of bread, but strong in his new resolve, he pressed on without stopping even at the church. The sounds and smells of village life slowly faded as he followed the road out of the town, past tidy farms with stone-fenced fields and up a long, gently rising slope.

As Magnus approached the fortress gate, the low sun stretched the high wall's shadow out toward him, promising him... loss.

Whatever the Mantle was, he would never see it or walk in its grace again. It was hubris to think he had any right to it beyond this journey, but he knew he would feel bereft after giving it up. Even now, his throat ached against tears which would surely come later.

Regardless, he was grateful at having been its courier. He'd borne it for nearly a month, and it had changed him into a better man. Happier and more brave, he realized—he'd survived an ordeal, and somehow no longer felt so vulnerable in the world at large.

These changes were the Mantle's doing, he was certain of it. It had shown him at least a hint of belonging in the world, something he had prayed for but until now never found, not even in the monastery. Maybe it was done showing him his path to happiness, but it didn't feel like it. Surely there was more to happiness than this.

He fell to his knees at the side of the road. He took off his pack and drew out the box. He had to see it once more, touch it before... it lay on its velvet bed, coruscate in sunlight so bright it illuminated flaws in the roughly cut glass and pits in the metalwork. It was beautiful, and it was holy, no matter what anyone else might claim.

Magnus began to weep, not caring that his tears landed on it.

In an act of sheer will, he forced himself to close the box and put it away.

As he pushed himself to his feet and continued on, his thoughts darkened. If General Tun agreed to the Lord Abbot's bargain, he would no doubt add the Mantle to his collection in a private chapel no more than a handful of people ever entered. It rankled that so few would see it then.

If Magnus had his way, he would build a beautiful shrine for it—open to all, where as many as wished could come to receive its blessing. That would never be. But he couldn't let go of the vision. It felt... ordained, even though it was nothing but his personal desire. But what if it wasn't?

The general must already know the Mantle had long been discredited. What then? He wouldn't want it. Even better. Magnus could keep it then. Yes, let other men think whatever suited them. Magnus knew the truth of it. In a flash of wickedness, he hoped the general would refuse to accept it. He was unworthy to touch it, let alone to be its keeper.

Magnus would gladly fail in his mission if it meant the Mantle could somehow have its own place of honor. It was a beautiful vision, but the relic wanted to be delivered to the general, and Magnus would not betray what the relic wanted.

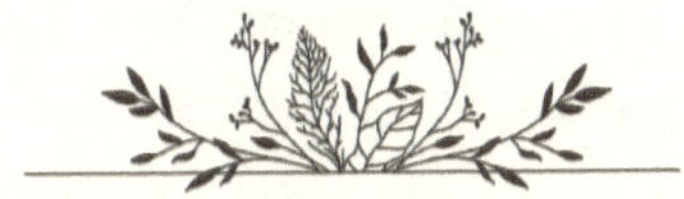

He pounded the heavy iron knocker hanging on the wicket gate, and waited.

After a moment, the panel on the grilled hatch slid sideways. "State your purpose," a rough voice ordered.

"Greetings from the Abbey of San Fortunatus. I deliver a gift from the Lord Abbot to General Tun."

From the other side of the door, noises of a bar being lifted were followed by the clank of an iron latch. The wicket opened. "Step in."

Magnus crossed the threshold into a chamber that could hold no more than six men standing. There was no changing course now. The heavily armed guard slammed and barred the wicket behind him. There was no furniture, not even a stool. It felt like a cell for a prisoner. But the Mantle had led him here. That was enough.

"Wait here." The guard opened a small door on the opposite wall, went through, closed and barred it from the other side, and left Magnus on his own. What dim light there was filtered through a large murder hole in the wooden ceiling. Footsteps above made the boards creak. Magnus sat cross-legged on the cool stone floor, leaning his back against the wall, glad for the rest.

He was nearly asleep when the inner door clanked open, revealing a different guard, this one in a more colorful uniform. "Come."

His escort marched him across the bailey into the keep and then upstairs to what Magnus guessed would be the general's headquarters.

The stairs led to a long, high-ceilinged chamber, richly appointed with tapestries and carpets. More than a dozen armed men stood along the walls. Magnus was hauled roughly toward a low barrier at the far end, set in front of a dais like a chancel rail. On the dais, in a raised chair as magnificent as the Lord Abbot's throne sat a stocky man dressed in a blood red tunic adorned with a blue sash and gold ornaments. A large sunburst medallion hung from a ribbon around his neck.

"Kneel," ordered his escort, striking the back of Magnus's knees with his scabbard, forcing him down. "Wait for His Excellency to give you permission to speak."

Magnus began to sweat at the physical blow. The soldier would slice him open at a single command, without hesitation.

General Tun scowled at Magnus, then at the guard. "What's this?"

"Greetings, General. I—" Magnus began.

The soldier cuffed the back of his head. "He wasn't speaking to you." He brought his fist sharply to his chest in salute, and lowered his head. "Your Excellency, this man says he has a gift for you."

"Does he, indeed." Tun drummed his fingers on the arm of his chair for a moment. He fixed Magnus with a cold stare. "Speak."

A chill passed across Magnus's shoulders as his fear left him. He felt a deep calm. The Mantle still watched over him. He was here to deliver the sacred gift, and that's what he would do.

He cleared his throat. "Greetings, General—"

Another blow landed on the back of his head. Harder, this time. "Address him as Your Excellency."

Being struck hurt more in its intention than the blow itself. Magnus took a steadying breath and began again. "Greetings, Your Excellency.

I bear a gift from the Lord Abbot of San Fortunatus to gain the release of Friar Calmas and his return to our abbey."

"And what is this gift you bear, so valuable that I would consider depriving myself of a fine artisan who thrives under my patronage?"

"Our Lord Abbot offers the Mantle of San Sarvras, Your Excellency. It bears the tears of his martyrdom, and I'm told it has healed many."

General Tun barked out a harsh guffaw. "Do you really believe that?"

"Yes, Your Excellency. I do."

"Then you're a fool. Are you aware that the Church discredited your trinket many years ago?"

"I learned this only days ago, while on my journey. Nevertheless, I still believe it is a sacred artifact."

"Why?" The general leaned forward on his throne, sounding truly curious.

"I have carried it this month-long journey from the abbey and across the desert," Magnus said. "I have often felt its blessing, its guidance, its protection. It twice saved my life in the desert so that I might deliver it to you."

"Bah. Then you are a fool many times over. I shall enumerate."

He held up a finger. "One. The Church dismissed it as a fraud years ago, yet you openly refuse to accept its ruling. In fact, you claim it performed miracles and saved your life."

He raised a second finger. "Two. The Church's decision in this matter is common knowledge. Yet you believe somehow your Abbot and your Prior didn't already know it was worthless when they sent you on your way."

He lifted a third finger. "You believe that I provide Friar Calmas my hospitality in defiance of your abbey, and that your Prior wants me to return him."

He sat back in his throne. "Whose idea, do you think," he said in a voice thick with scorn, "was it to host the good friar here? None other than your very own Father Xavier. Four times a year, he sends me a stipend to keep him here. That he sends you with this so-called gift tells me he wants me to make sure you never return to San Fortunatus. Perhaps I should accommodate his wish."

The general's face had not turned into a lizard's. He believed what he was saying was true. Magnus closed his eyes against sudden dizziness. How many layers were there to Father Xavier's iniquity? It didn't matter anymore. These were noxious intrigues belonging to other men, and he wanted no part of them.

Still, he couldn't give up. Discredited even by the Church, the Mantle deserved respect. He was honor-bound to speak the truth. The general was the fool here, but he would give him another chance.

"All that may be true, Your Excellency, although I know nothing of your last point." He looked up at the man, surprised that he felt pity for him, and lifted his hands to beg. "Excellency, please accept this sacred gift. With my whole heart, I swear before God it is sacred."

The general was silent for a while. "Then that makes you not only a lunatic fool, but a dangerous one, rejecting the wisdom of the Church. Perhaps a heretic. But I am an open-minded man. You can show me the healing power of this precious relic."

He beckoned a soldier from the wall. "Step forward. Remove your armor." The man paled, but obeyed. The general signaled for another. "Break his arm," he ordered, tilting his head toward the first man.

The soldier led his unresisting comrade toward the rail in front of the dais, seized the man's arm, and smashed it over the narrow wooden beam. The victim shouted in pain but stood before his general sweating and shaking, his forearm now bent at a hideous new angle, swelling and turning purple.

Shocked by the general's casual violence, Magnus fought to not vomit.

The general stared down at Magnus, who still knelt at the rail. "Now use that thing to heal my loyal man."

Magnus was too shocked to protest. That wasn't how the relic healed people, he was certain. This wasn't a fair test. He hastily reached into his pack and drew out the Mantle, already praying that it might restore the soldier's arm. He clutched it to his chest and listened for the slightest whisper, but the relic was silent. He steadied his breath, closed his eyes, and begged it to perform a miracle.

Nothing. Nothing but the wounded man's ragged breathing.

Magnus opened his eyes. He passed the relic slowly over the man's arm. He held it against the man's forehead. Nothing. He'd failed. Worse, he'd caused an innocent man to suffer. Stricken, he looked up at the general. He could hear Father Xavier laughing at him.

"Take my valiant man to the infirmary," Tun ordered, without looking away from Magnus.

"We have one more test for people like this man, don't we?" the general asked, his voice raised. "We throw them off the tower, and if their belief be true, angels catch them before they hit the ground." He looked around again, as if expecting the soldiers to enjoy his wit. Each one laughed a little too heartily, a little too long.

The general turned again to Magnus. "In your case, we'll see if your precious trinket saves you." He shrugged. "Or angels, either way. So far, every man has hit the ground exactly the same, and not got up again."

He signaled to the guards. "Let's take a look at this fool's treasure."

A soldier snatched the Mantle from Magnus's hands, raising it for the general to see.

"Good. Tie it around his neck," he ordered. "We want to make sure he doesn't lose it on his way down."

Magnus was too numb to resist as one of the soldiers secured the Mantle around his neck on a leather thong. He was a dead man. To his surprise, he felt more relief than fear. Death solved all his problems. Maybe that was the happiness the relic wanted for him.

"Very well," he heard the general say. "Take him to the tower and let him fly."

Magnus was roughly dragged to his feet and force-marched out of the chamber to a chorus of jeers and laughter.

CHAPTER NINE

Magnus couldn't see much past the soldier in front of him on the narrow turning stairway or past the two close behind him with short swords drawn, so he focused on the worn stone steps directly under his feet. They seemed to go on forever. He swallowed against a wry chuckle. Even with all his problems about to be solved, he wasn't in a particular hurry to get to the top.

It occurred to him that he should pray to prepare for his death, but each prayer he began felt empty, and he couldn't finish.

He'd done his best. He touched the relic hanging against his chest. For reasons of its own, it had wanted to be delivered to the general, and he'd done his part.

Its sweet calm spread through him. Where had its presence been when he'd needed to heal the soldier? Had he betrayed the Mantle somehow? Not that he could see. Abandoning his mission to stay in San Pedro would have been betrayal. Lying to the general to save his life would have been betrayal. He'd done his best. At least he wouldn't die having betrayed the relic. That was a kind of happiness, he supposed. Just not the one he'd hoped for.

The lead soldier pushed up against a trap door and it creaked open. Sunlight and a fresh, sharp breeze flowed in. They'd arrived. They took the last steps onto the parapet. Magnus closed his eyes and lifted his face to the sun, opening himself to the life around him. Its whispered songs poured into him—a benediction of tender, poignant beauty given before dying. Not only beauty, but oddly also anticipation. A kind of welcome. Was this the happiness the Mantle had promised? It certainly wasn't what he'd expected.

The breeze was surprisingly strong, buffeting his face. It tugged at his cowl. Maybe his life would just flow into the wind, the trees, and the animals when he died. That seemed far more attractive to him now than getting stuck in the Church's version of afterlife.

One of the soldiers behind him prodded Magnus with the tip of his sword. "Will you jump, or do we have to throw you?"

Magnus turned to face him, feeling curiously settled. "This isn't my choice. You'll have to do it."

"As you wish." The soldier behind him hooked his hands under Magnus's arms and pulled back. Another grabbed his ankles and lifted. They carried him to the edge of the parapet. Twice they swung him back and forth to gain momentum, and on the third, they let go.

Magnus looked up. He watched the soldiers on the parapet shrink. He felt the sun warm on his face. A large bird crossed his vision. A vulture? Then with a sharp shock that took his breath, there was nothing.

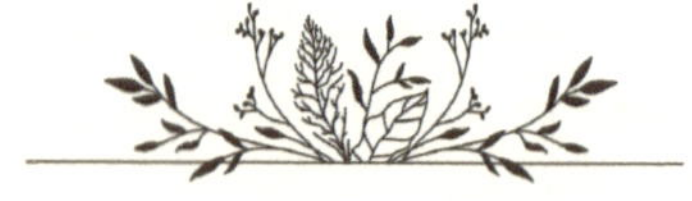

He couldn't tell if his eyes were open. He couldn't see anything but darkness. He felt no pain. He felt nothing. Maybe he was breathing. Maybe he was entombed.

An owl called nearby, so he wasn't entombed—he could hear. He remembered how to open his eyes. There. Stars, shining above the tower. There should be a waxing moon, if he wasn't dead. He tried to turn his head. Still no pain. There was the swelling moon, yellow, serene. A cloud drifted in front of it. The owl called again. He must be alive.

He felt for the relic. It lay against his chest. He closed his hand around it, and flooded with relief, gratitude. He must be alive. If he was, the Mantle had saved him yet again. It was still with him.

He tried to move his legs. Yes. He rolled tentatively onto his side, braced for agony that never came. He sat up. A breeze brushed against his face. He looked down at his hands. Even in moonlight, he could see the last of the blackened nail on his thumb. Miraculously, he was alive, and even more miraculously, unhurt. The relic's gift, without doubt. A very welcome gift. He hadn't been eager to die.

He took a deep breath and surveyed his surroundings. He sat on a rocky slope that dropped away from the castle wall behind him. Below him a rutted oxcart path with grasses lumpy and thick between the tracks ran along the edge of a forest.

What should he do now? He'd lain here unconscious for hours. If they'd bothered to look, General Tun's men would have thought him dead.

Word of Magnus's execution would eventually get back to the abbey. Not that it mattered now. Father Xavier had got everything he wanted from his scheme—to be rid of Magnus without appearing responsible, and to keep Brother Calmas here for purposes Magnus didn't care to know. He would never go back to San Fortunatus now. Even if Brother Calmas had wanted to return to the monastery, Magnus no longer had reason to care. He had fulfilled his promise.

Yesterday he had argued with himself about keeping the relic. Now the memory made him laugh. He'd escaped all the intrigues in a way even better than he had imagined. He'd kept his word. He was alive, but dead to the world that had known him. He had no responsibilities, no ties, no plan, no resources, nothing anyone wanted—not even the sacred treasure hanging around his neck. He was alive, but he didn't exist.

He could walk back to San Pedro, but that would take nearly a week. Maybe he'd do that eventually, to join Father Bartolo in his quiet parish work. But perhaps not. No, that was habit speaking. The prospect of living in service to the Church that had spawned so many betrayals and lies had lost the appeal it had held for him even a day ago. Before he'd been executed for keeping his word.

Besides, if he returned to San Pedro, then Father Bartolo would know he was alive. Word might eventually reach the wrong people. Before making any decisions, he needed time to think. He needed to eat. And he was tired. So tired.

He took off his rucksack and found the relic's box, broken badly in his landing. He carefully took the Mantle from around his neck and put it inside, wrapping the leather thong around the box to hold the sides together. He'd repair it when he could. But while it was dark, he needed to put the fortress behind him and find a sheltering tree or some other place to sleep. He stood, shouldered his pack, and carefully picked his way down to the path in the moonlight. He walked until a field called to him. He climbed into a field of alfalfa and made his bed against a stone wall.

Magnus woke from tangled, heavy dreams to jubilant birdsong calling for the sun. He lay still for a while, letting his last dream dissipate, breathing in the rich smell of alfalfa in bloom, gazing at the pale purple sky. This was sweeter than mornings at the monastery. He ought to rise, and... ought what? He laughed aloud, knowing it was mere habit prodding him. He had nowhere he ought to go, and nothing he ought to do. It was a little disturbing, to be without an "ought to" to follow.

His last dream had been about that, feeling he was late, that he'd forgotten where he was supposed to go and no one would remind him, but if he thought about it hard enough, he'd suddenly remember and have to get moving in a hurry.

He sat up and leaned against the meadow's stone fence, letting his gaze drift across the field. He was in no hurry at all. For the moment, he'd stay right where he was and enjoy the sunrise.

He pulled the Mantle's box out of his rucksack and placed it on his lap. Yesterday, it had given him a new life. How else could he have survived such a fall? He needed to acknowledge that somehow. He pondered while the sun broke over the horizon's rim and all the colors of the field shouted for joy as they caught fire.

Then he knew. With the same reverent welcome the fields had given the sun, he opened the box and hung the Mantle around his neck. He put the box back in his pack and leaned his head back against the wall, satisfied. And then not so satisfied. Something still wasn't right. He looked at his chest, where the relic and his large wooden crucifix hung.

No, he couldn't.

Surely not that. It would be sacrilege, renunciation. But a gentle swell in his chest, warm and sweet, told him it might be renunciation, but not sacrilege. The relic was sacred. He took a deep breath and let it out. Then another. He slowly lifted the crucifix from his neck, kissed it, and placed it with trembling hands in his pack next to the broken box.

What had he done? For a moment, he panicked, feeling lost and cut off. Perhaps even damned. He started to retrieve it from his rucksack, but the terror passed. He wasn't lost or empty. He had an entirely new life. He might not know yet where he should go or what he should do, but he wasn't lost. Content, he tied up his bedroll and shouldered his pack just as he had for so many days, this time unsure of what road he should follow.

He laughed aloud at the empty road in front of him. Now that he was dead and had no one to order him about, what did he, Magnus, want to do? He had no idea. That surprised him. Besides being hungry and wanting to eat, he'd take time to find out what he wanted. That felt very right.

With a tangy sprig of alfalfa in his mouth, he set himself in the middle of the road, ready to go... somewhere. He touched the Mantle, silently asking it to show him which way to go, then turned in a slow circle. As he turned toward the village of Santa Inés, he felt a warm tug in his chest which melted away as he kept turning. He turned his back on the fortress and faced the village. The warmth in his chest bloomed again. His compass had spoken, and he would follow.

He started walking. He felt different—off-balance, but right. He could feel himself beaming at the world. His footsteps had spring, with his weight on the balls of his feet—even with his flapping sandal. He strode on, alert, relaxed, even confident. He laughed at that, too. His skin tingled. He'd never felt this way before. He was on an adventure. His own.

Chapter Ten

Even though he had walked this same road only the day before, Magnus hadn't actually seen it. He hadn't paid much attention to anything but his own emotional turmoil.

Today he was free, his eyes sharp and quick to take in details and vistas alike. He stopped often, simply to be alive for its own sake, to take pleasure in the beauty around him—the morning sun bathing a meadow of flax in bloom, the voice of a lark tirelessly throwing his song at the sky. When he stopped to gaze at a ewe nursing her lamb, an iridescent dragonfly landed on the drystone fence right beside his hand, and died. It felt like a gift, a message. What was it?

Fascinated, he watched the miraculous colors of its body become dull in mere moments. That was the message. Life was more beautiful exactly because it was both fleeting and eternal at the same time. Embracing both truths, his heart nearly burst from being so unbearably full of joy. He held on to the fence to keep himself upright as the world slowly spun around him in arcs of color and meaning. He was alive.

By the time he reached Santa Inés, Magnus was drunk, euphoric, and in love with everything.

Strangely, people shied away from him as he passed. Some even regarded him with alarm. Yesterday, no one had paid him much attention at all. He'd passed through the town without drawing a glance, let alone suspicion. But now it seemed that, the more he smiled and wished people well, the more disturbed they became.

He was sad that, just as he'd found such happiness, it seemed no one wanted to smile with him. He knew he was a little unkempt from his journey, but he'd cleaned up from the desert in San Pedro. When he asked for a crust of bread at a bakery on the high street, the woman seemed terrified. In a hasty blur, she crossed herself three times and thrust a whole fresh loaf into his hands, telling him to please go away. When he asked at the ostler's for work in exchange for a place to sleep, the man shook his head so sharply that he startled the horse he was leading.

It wasn't until Magnus sat beneath a tree on the village green to eat, looking down at the loaf in his lap, that he noticed the Mantle. Maybe it was a trick of the bright sunlight, but it seemed to glow like a little candle. Perhaps others had seen the beveled glass glinting in the sun and felt afraid. Or perhaps they'd simply thought him mad. He wouldn't apologize for how happy he was, mad or not. Stories of saints suggested the difference between ecstasy and madness was not always clear, although his life was as far from sainthood as one could get.

He shook his head, laughing softly at himself. What an apparition he must have seemed! If he were the baker, and one morning some wild-haired unwashed monk came into his shop, radiant with unbearable joy and wearing a strange bright object instead of a crucifix, he'd feel uneasy, too.

Still, raising suspicion was the last thing he wanted to do, so he tucked the relic inside his tunic. He broke open the bread, still warm in the center, and happily breathed in the rising mist. He tore off a chunk—it was delicious. After half a dozen mouthfuls, he made himself stop and put the rest of it in his pack. He had no idea where his next meal might come from, and the remainder would make at least two more if need be.

He leaned back against the tree, wanting to doze, but the sense of urgency he'd felt yesterday returned. Like a persistent itch he couldn't reach, it wouldn't let him keep his eyes closed, as if he was supposed to be going somewhere. After a while, he gave up trying to rest and made his way across the green to a road intersecting with the high street. Again he turned slowly, asking his compass to tell him which way to travel. This time, it urged him away from the town and down a smaller road.

He'd walked no more than a mile or two when the blissful feeling of being one with everything enveloped him in a cloud. He could feel his body lift and relax into it, as if he floated with the current in a river.

As he crested a hill, he saw a stand of trees off the road, just ahead and to his right. A wisp of smoke rose behind them. The pull in his chest intensified—that was where he was going. Someone was calling to him. He had to find out who.

The lane branching from the road was little more than a foot path, nearly hidden by tall grass, wildflowers, and even an occasional wild rosebush. Birds sang all around him. As soon as he stepped onto the path, a large crow he hadn't noticed squawked at him from an overhanging branch, then followed him noisily, flapping from branch to branch and calling out as Magnus walked. The overgrown path led him to the edge of a garden. Beyond the garden stood a ramshackle house.

At first glance, the garden seemed wild and untidy, but as he stood still with the relic thrumming against his chest, he began to feel intention in it—whimsical, enchanting, wise. The path divided, and he took the one that looked like it led to the house. With a desultory *grak*, the crow flew past him to perch on the roof above the door, its head bobbing purple-black in the sunlight.

The house was odd, too, as if cobbled together from several different buildings, one weathered part now propping up what was left of another. He knocked on the door. While he waited, he turned to look again at the vibrant tumult of the garden. A few plants were familiar, but most were strange to him. Butterflies, bumblebees, and dragonflies darted all around.

The door creaked open behind him. "What do you want?"

He turned to a short gray-haired woman peering through the partially opened doorway, looking wary. "Your garden is beautiful."

"I know."

Magnus held back a chuckle. "Of course you do," he said, smiling. He took a deep breath and started over. "My name is Magnus. I was a brother at the Abbey of San Fortunatus. I'm not sure what I am now. I felt led here. I'm hoping I could provide labor in return for shelter and food while I pray for guidance as to what I should do next. I'm good at farm work. I love caring for animals."

"Why don't you know what to do?"

He shivered and felt urged to tell her the truth. Some of it, at least. "I was sent from the abbey to deliver a gift to General Tun." He shrugged. "It didn't go as I expected. I can't return to the monastery, so I'm looking for board in return for work."

"Hmph. You're lucky to be alive, then."

"Yes, I am. They meant to execute me, and I'm still not sure how they didn't. I really don't know what to do now."

The woman in the doorway shook her head firmly. "If the general is looking for you, you can't stay here. You'd bring trouble I don't need."

"They're not. They think I'm already dead."

She studied him with her brow furrowed, then nodded. "Not at all what I was expecting when I cast for a helper, but you'll do. I've got plenty of work for you, that's for sure. But I can't have you wearing those church clothes here. I'm a witch, and people come to me for healing and charms. Don't want them to get confused. My name is Zoya."

A witch. How could someone he'd always been told was evil create such a wonderful garden? He looked around again. Maybe he shouldn't stay. In addition to its beauty, he now felt danger in it, as if imps might leap out from behind an unpruned shrub to carry him off.

His teachers at the monastery had seldom addressed the matter directly, but all the faithful knew witches were dangerous and anathema. Maybe he should turn and leave. Still, the Mantle—his compass now—had guided him here. He was no expert in witchcraft, but he felt no evil at all in Zoya, in fact, just the opposite. Could a witch be good? The same beauty he'd discovered on the desert road and in front of the little stone cottage back in San Pedro sparkled everywhere he looked.

"Church clothes?" He fingered the hooded cloak worn by brothers who hadn't yet taken their solemn vows. It was all he had. "I have no other clothing but this habit I wear."

Something sparked behind Zoya's eyes, then she threw her head back and laughed so hard and long that she had to lean against the door frame. After she caught her breath, she beamed at Magnus, her eyes still bright with laughter. "Oh, that was a good one. You probably don't see the humor in it, but I hope one day you can."

Still amused by the joke Magnus didn't care to understand, she chuckled and muttered to herself as she stepped out, pulling the door shut behind her. The crow hopped down to her shoulder as she limped toward him, leaning on a walking stick with each step.

"I think my nephew left some clothes here on his last visit. You're bigger in the shoulders than he is and taller, but you can start with them. I won't always cook for you, but you're welcome to whatever I have."

The crow hunched down on her shoulder and made a rattling sound which made him nervous. Something about witches and pets. Yes, familiars. He cleared his throat. "Is that crow your... familiar?"

"Midnight?" She smiled as the bird dug under a wing. "Only when he wants to be. Follow me. I'll show you where you'll sleep." She jabbed him playfully in the shoulder. "And where you can escape your old habit."

Her gentle poke staggered him and nearly made him cry out for another. The last affectionate touch he could remember had been Brother Benn's goodbye hug in the pigsty over a month ago. Given how much trouble it had brought him, he hadn't thought of missing physical touch. Now he was hungry for it.

But he was making too much of this. Zoya's touch was merely a fleeting gesture with no expectation behind it at all, simply one person to another—freely given, freely received. A gift.

Still, he wanted to give something back. "After I change, perhaps you'll show me where I can get to work."

Zoya studied his face for a moment, as if she had heard his thoughts. She nodded, apparently in approval. "All in good time. First you clean up and get into some decent clothes. Then I'll take you on a little walkabout."

It felt good to be clean, but it felt even better to know exactly where he would bathe next time he needed to. As he dressed, he decided to keep wearing the Mantle so he could feel its direction more clearly, as well as to protect himself from witchcraft, if the need arose. To be discreet, though, he tucked it inside his shirt as before. There was no need to provoke curiosity.

He hadn't worn trousers since entering the monastery over two years ago. Uncomfortable, he tugged at the drawstring; Zoya was right. The shirt was tight in the shoulders. But if he left the closing string untied at the throat, he could move freely enough. The sleeves were too short, but he would roll them up anyway, just to protect them from work damage. These clothes were borrowed, after all, and belonged to her nephew. He glanced at his monk's habit, now folded at the foot of his pallet. He hadn't noticed how threadbare it had become.

Magnus touched the relic inside the shirt for reassurance. It lay warm against his skin. It seemed content. He tugged at the shirt's hem and his waistband, trying to make them fit more comfortably. He felt naked wearing these. Maybe even a little disloyal, dressed in worldly clothes. He didn't know what to make of that, except that it didn't feel right. He went outside to meet Zoya.

"That's much better," she said, squinting as she studied him.

"Is it? These feel strange on me."

"Of course they do," she said, scoffing. "You've been hiding inside that awful robe, I could tell. Come. We'll go see the animals first." She turned away, limping down a path. Her accusation stung, even though as soon as she'd said it he knew there was more truth in it than she could know. He followed after.

Zoya showed him her chickens, rabbits, a lone cow for milk, sheep, and pigs. She also had a donkey to pull a decrepit two-wheeled cart with wheels that wobbled. All of the pens were in serious disrepair.

The garden was in better condition, but gradually thickening weeds along the rows told him that by the time Zoya finished one round of weeding, the spot where she had started was overgrown again.

In spite of its shabbiness, the place felt... peaceful. As if it was safe to smile and breathe deeply. Almost as peaceful as the monastery. But unlike the monastery, this farm felt happy as well as peaceful, as though laughter hid in every bush, ready to play catch-me-if-you-can. He liked it, although the playfulness also felt a little dangerous, as if the game had no rules.

From what he saw, it would take a lot of work to get things right again. Everything at the monastery was clean and in solid re-pair—proof of devotion and stewardship. Work was love made man-ifest, after all.

He knew the disrepair wasn't Zoya's fault. Merely hauling buckets of water to the garden would be a difficult task for someone with a bad leg. She needed his help, Magnus realized with quiet satisfaction. He liked that, too. There was nowhere else he had to be, and it would feel good to have animals to care for again. If only she weren't a witch. How could a witch be happy or make this place happy? That belied all the Church teachings. But he wasn't beholden to those teachings anymore. He'd given his loyalty to the relic, his compass.

Zoya led him to the shed that her nephew Nuri used as a shop when he came to visit. He wasn't skilled at carpentry, she said, but did what he could whenever he was here, which had helped to keep the farm going after she hurt her hip. A rusty saw hung from a peg on the wall.

Magnus found a mallet and chisel on the bench, and a short hank of old rope.

"Aside from the daily chores, I think gates and fences should be my first repairs," Magnus said as they left the shed. "I'm eager to start. We'll need more materials soon. Do you barter?"

"At the market, every Saturn's day. You'll have to come with me when you know what we need."

We. It was an enchanting word. To his surprise, his chest hurt. Magnus rubbed at the pain, and bumped against the relic. "There's enough to start," he said, "but soon we'll need more rope, a hide to cut into strips for hinges, some nails, and some split rails. Although we can do without, a second bucket would make watering the garden much more efficient. What do you trade?"

Zoya snorted. "What do you think? I'm a witch. My services. Charms, remedies, potions, healing work. And I teach. Folks come out here if they need something more, but I do good trade at the market. I bring eggs or produce if I have extra. People like them. I have two students at the moment. You'll meet them tomorrow."

His stomach twisted at her reminder that his labor would support witchcraft. But the relic had given him this new life and had led him here. It rested warm and untroubled against his chest. Wasn't that indication enough? He'd wear it every day for protection as well as guidance, he decided, and stay alert for telltale signs of wickedness.

After an afternoon of weeding and a simple meal with Zoya eaten in silence, Magnus returned to his room, feeling completely at peace. He found a hole in the plaster above his pallet and worked a short twig into it. He hung the relic—his compass-protector—on it, to watch over him as he slept, just as a crucifix had hung over his bed in the monastery. He touched it once more, already eager to put it on in the morning.

Chapter Eleven

The next day, Zoya's students, two young sisters, Magdalena and Paloma, came laughing arm in arm along the path from the road. They froze when they saw Magnus, and hugged each other more tightly. Even when Zoya introduced him to them, their smiles were timid. After several visits, however, they waved cheerfully before disappearing with Zoya.

At first, Magnus preferred not to think much about what they were doing, even though it seemed the air sparkled with happiness by the time they left. Whatever they did, the relic remained silent, seemingly unconcerned. Since the relic didn't seem to care, Magnus tried to follow its example and relaxed his vigilance against signs of their wickedness. When he thought about it, he didn't really know what to look for anyway. After all, he'd been at the monastery for a long time, and it had proven to be home to more wickedness than he might ever find here.

As the weeks passed, he happily threw himself into farm work. The pleasure of staying in one place day after day grew into the deeper satisfaction of taking root, settling into the life and rhythm of the land itself. He wanted roots. Having roots was a good form of belonging.

In contrast to his weeks on the road, a day now became much too small a period to measure the progress of his work, and he rediscovered the satisfaction in having work which remained unfinished at sunset. The partially weeded row was still there in the morning. The broken fence rail and the gate—still tied shut with fraying, crusty rope—seemed patient with him as he took care of them one by one.

Except his memories of his moments of ecstatic revelation, other details of his journey across the desert to the fortress, and then to Zoya's farm seemed to drift farther and farther away from him by the day, like bright yellow leaves on a slow-moving river. But Father Xavier's smug treachery, the silent betrayal of his monastery brethren, and even the general's mercurial cruelty lay cold and heavy on the bottom of that slow-moving river, unchanged.

He prayed nightly before hanging the Mantle above his bed and asked that if he were supposed to do something other than work on the farm, he be shown when to go and where. He happily took its silence for his answer.

As time stretched out at the pace of vegetables growing, he found himself wondering what else he wanted. In those self-indulgent moments, he discovered he wanted to stay—he felt more at peace than he had in a long time. That was a new enough experience that he still braced himself after his prayers asking for guidance, and felt a rush of relief when the relic remained silent. It was almost as if it was asleep, and he was happy to let it slumber. Yet he wore it every day without fail, feeling defenseless without it.

Every Saturn's day, he harnessed the donkey, whose name was Bray, and helped Zoya load her cart for market. In addition to her sack of remedies and charms tucked securely under the seat, there would be a straw-lined box for eggs, small willow-branch cages for chickens or rabbits, as well as bundles of herbs or baskets of other produce. She would ride off with Midnight perched on her shoulder, and Magnus would apply himself to his chores until she returned at sunset.

One market day, she came back with a shirt and trousers that fit him. When he protested, she just laughed and said that Nuri should get his clothes back before Magnus wore them to rags.

"Why don't you come with me next market day?" she asked as he carried provisions into the house. "Once in a while you might meet a nice young man to be with."

Magnus nearly dropped the sack of flour he held. "I don't want—" he started, before he could think. He didn't mind that Zoya knew he liked men. He scrambled through his thoughts to find honest words to deny... what?

"Never mind. Just a thought," Zoya murmured, looking sad. She tugged firmly on the sack of flour until his fingers finally let go. "It's not important right now."

As he lay in bed later that night, Zoya's surprising suggestion returned to him like a ghost, haunting him. What did he want to avoid? Sex? No. He'd always liked that—far too much, truth be told. Being used without respect? Certainly. He would never agree to that again.

But there was something else, even deeper, something he did want and was afraid to want. He hadn't ever named it—safer not to think of it at all. But her suggestion had wakened a soft, terrible longing. He was lonely. He ached for companionship, and shared tenderness, and secret laughter. He didn't think he'd find that at market day. He'd wanted to tell her that, but his mouth wouldn't work. His galloping heart had called out to the Mantle for some kind of help, but he didn't even know what kind. It had hung silent and cool against his skin.

More weeks crawled by. One night at dinner, Magnus paused over his bowl. "I'm sorry to say that the repairs haven't proceeded as quickly as I had hoped. They will likely take the rest of the summer, and maybe into the autumn to complete. I'm very sorry."

Zoya stared at him for a moment. "Why do you think you should be doing more than you are?" Her face furrowed into disgust. "That church of yours fills people with so much guilt. No place for that here."

"I just want to earn my keep," he said, feeling defensive. "I feel I should be doing more."

Zoya frowned. "I see what you do. It's more than enough, even if you don't think so."

"I want to. I want to feel I belong."

Her face softened into a sad smile. "And you won't belong unless you sacrifice yourself in labor?" She shook her head. "You don't earn belonging. You discover it, wake up to it after it's already happened. You'll know. There's much more joy in belonging than just earning your keep. You're worth more than your keep."

His chest ached as if he were about to burst into tears. He wanted to agree, but the meaning of Zoya's words remained just out of reach, a mystery. Was he worthy of more?

Zoya patted his arm. "There's hope for you, I can feel it. We'll see."

The next morning, Magnus heard horrible screeches coming from the rabbit hutches and ran to see what was wrong. One of the slats in the hutch floor, rotted by years of urine, had given way, and had trapped their most fertile doe by the hind leg. She was frantic, making her awful sound, jerking her bleeding leg back and forth against the broken slat, her flesh torn wide to expose bone and tendon. He didn't want to look any closer. Heavy salt saliva ran along his tongue. He was going to throw up.

Sing!

Magnus startled and nearly looked behind him. For the first time since the desert, the relic's voice called to him clearly. "Thank you," he murmured, so grateful his vision blurred with tears.

He began to sing in little more than a whisper, something made up of whatever notes came to him. Under his shirt, the relic warmed, pulsing to his song. The doe quieted. He slowly reached in, and as gently as he could, freed her leg and lifted her out. Holding her along his forearm and caressing her ears down along her trembling body, he hurried to find Zoya. To Magnus's relief, she immediately took over, cleaning the wound, applying a salve, and binding it closed with a clean rag.

"Go see what you can do about the hutch," she ordered. "I'll keep her with me while you do."

Magnus didn't know anything about healing. Grateful to be sent on a different task, he pulled out the broken slat and the ones on either side of it, which were almost as bad. He cut some willow branches and wove them into a makeshift patch.

The next morning, Zoya startled him as he sang a children's nursery rhyme to the injured doe, feeding her weeds freshly pulled from the garden.

He began to make a joke of his sentimental silliness, but she held up a hand to silence him, her eyes fixed on the animal as if she were listening. After a while, she simply nodded solemnly, patted Magnus's arm, and went on to the chicken coop to collect eggs. That evening, Zoya made a sumptuous dinner of cabbage, chicken, and wild mushrooms for them both.

After they'd finished and he'd helped her clean up, Magnus was about to say thank you and good night when Zoya motioned for him to sit down at the table again. Confused, he sat. This hadn't happened before. She'd just said she wasn't unhappy with his work. Maybe she'd changed her mind. He didn't want to leave the farm.

When they were settled, she lit a candle and sat for a moment, gazing into the flame. He waited for her to begin, trying not to anticipate bad news.

"When you're in the garden, do you ever hear the plants talking?"

At first, Magnus wasn't sure he'd heard her right. Whatever he'd expected, it hadn't been this. He took a moment to collect his thoughts. "Yes. Often. Or at least I believe I do."

"Tell me what you believe."

"When I was a boy, I imagined I could feel the trees talking to each other." His childhood longing welled up in a thorny ache as he watched a trickle of tallow spill like tears down the side of the candle and harden into bumps. "Other plants, too, but especially the trees. I always wanted to join in, but didn't know how. So I just listened. And pretended."

"And now?" Zoya's voice was like a coaxing stroke on his cheek.

"Not more than whispers, really. But I... there's a harmony here. My trek to the general's fortress took just over a month. For most of that time, I walked alone across harsh wilderness." Magnus wondered how much he should say about carrying the Mantle. "The journey changed me." He could feel his ears heat. "It made me... more open. Connected me to everything. The desert was beautiful, in a way I didn't like. I can't explain it very well."

"Hmm." Zoya studied her knobby fingers for a moment, then reached into a pocket and drew out what looked like an old stick, smooth and shiny from handling. "This might help. Hold this and try again."

As soon as Magnus closed his hand around it, the relic woke, warm and vibrating against his chest, and his desert ecstasy returned. Before he could pick them, words flew out of his heart like a flock of birds startled from a tree.

"I broke open like a ripe fruit, everything inside me spread glistening and soft to the sun. So much beauty all around, too much. Fierce and naked. Sometimes painful but always sweet. Sometimes so joyful I couldn't bear it. I haven't really recovered, and I don't think I want to. Sometimes I just—I go into some different place, blending with the life of everything around me, and I feel like it's home. Then I come back and it's like it never happened. I feel lonely and sad then. I want more of being home."

Zoya sat quietly for a while, then held out her hand asking for the return of her stick. She stuffed it back into her clothing and sniffed. "That's good. Do you want me to teach you more about the ways of creatures and plants?"

"Yes!" He beamed at her. The relic vibrated against his skin, as eager as he was. "Can we start tomorrow?"

"Tonight." She leaned over to blow out the candle. "I'll take you to the spring. Best you meet it first at night."

She got up and limped to the door before Magnus remembered to close his mouth and stand. She turned and beckoned. "Come. The moon is nearly full. A good night to start."

Chapter Twelve

Magnus followed Zoya along the path past the house but then away from the well toward a wall of wild bushes. She stopped at the edge and turned to him. "I don't want you coming here without me until I give you permission," she said.

"I promise."

"You must be sky-clad. Take off your clothes and wait here." She slipped between bushes and disappeared.

Remove clothing? This wasn't at all what he'd expected, and it made him nervous. Magnus took off his sandals slowly, wondering if he'd agreed to her offer of teaching too quickly. The grass was soft and cool beneath his feet. He took off his trousers and shirt, folding them carefully, laying them on a branch above his shoes. Sweat ran down his back and sides as if he'd been working in the sun for hours.

Zoya reappeared, and held back a branch. "Welcome to my sacred spring," she said softly, and then abruptly held up her hand. "You're welcome here as a man, but your church is not. Take that thing off your neck."

What was he doing? Could he subject himself to a witch's instruction without his compass? "I can't. This is sacred to me, but it's neither sacred nor important to the church. In fact, I haven't thought much about the church at all since I got here."

"What is that thing you have around your neck, then?"

"It's... my compass." Magnus closed his hand around it. He needed it with him. "Although the church doesn't care about it," he said, "it's saved my life more than once. It's sacred to me."

What might change her mind? "It led me to you."

"Hmph." Zoya studied his face for a while in the silver moonlight. "Well, take it off for tonight anyway. Maybe it won't be a hindrance later on, but I expect you have more to let go of than to learn. I won't waste my time tangled in religious foolishness."

"It's my protection and my guide," he said, pressing it to his chest. "I'd be lost without it."

"Do you trust me?"

"I'm afraid."

"Sensible. Do you trust that I mean you no harm?"

He knew her well enough for that, even if she was a witch. "Yes."

Zoya nodded solemnly. "Good. I swear to you that no harm will come to you while you are with me here at my sacred spring. Leave it with your things. You'll see."

For some reason, Magnus felt like a little boy about to be beaten. He wanted to run away, but the grass was cool and soft beneath his feet, holding him in place. The breeze whispered through the leaves, cooling him, telling him there was no danger here. It swirled around him, urging him forward. The relic itself seemed untroubled as he lifted it from his neck and laid it carefully on his shirt. He couldn't let go.

"Trust. Just a little more," Zoya murmured in a voice that was like the breeze urging him forward.

Magnus lifted his hand, but one finger seemed stuck to the relic. Silently, he begged it again for a sign. It slept. He stepped away, feeling lost and eager at the same time. Something unknown waited for him just behind Zoya.

"Hold your hands out to me. I need to sanctify you before you come to the spring." She dipped a finger in the little jar she held and touched his palms, his chest, and his forehead.

"Good," she said briskly. "Now you can come in." Again she held aside the branches behind her, beckoning him to follow.

He felt the threshold before he saw it. He walked through a thick invisible curtain into a tiny world, lively, peaceful, full. At its center was a little pool, black and smooth in the moonlight.

"Sit at the edge facing the water," Zoya said, pointing. She sat on the other side of the pool facing him. "Now we can begin. Tonight, all we'll do is use intention to connect with the life around us."

Magnus shivered as a gust of air swirled up around him, cool and quick, a caress.

Zoya lifted her hands to the moon, palms open and up. "Open yourself to the air moving on your skin, to the moonlight on your neck, to all the growing things around you. The grass underneath you. The bushes and trees bearing witness to our presence and respectful intention."

The leaves rattled, at once familiar and strange. For a moment, the breeze brought the comforting smell of the animal pens. He relaxed into that.

"Now kneel forward so you can put your hands in the water. Both of them. Not too far in, just so your fingers can enjoy the mud. Dig them in, like roots."

The water was warmer than he expected.

"Now imagine your fingers are roots, perhaps from one of these bushes. Feel how everything, simply by being itself, fits with everything else. Water. Mud. Roots pulling water and mud together into green life."

Magnus pushed his fingertips deeper into the bottom and stared at the dark water encircling his arms. This wasn't at all like his moments on the road, which had come upon him unbidden. This required something of him first. Maybe he needed to be wearing the Mantle to do this right. "I don't feel much of anything."

"You may be trying too hard. Let yourself become broken open again. Just like you described earlier."

He was naked, and he didn't have the Mantle. He was so vulnerable. This was a dangerous way to be broken open. "I don't feel anything."

Zoya didn't say anything at all for what seemed a long time. "Remember when I said you don't earn belonging, but rather discover it? I can feel you trying to connect as if you had to earn it. You already belong to everything here. You couldn't change that even if you wanted to. Reach out. Connect because you already belong."

"Sorry." Magnus took a deep breath and let it out slowly. Not wanting to meet her gaze, he closed his eyes. He couldn't.

"Let's try another way, maybe better for you. Breathe out slowly, out through your fingertips. Just push your breath out through your fingers. Feel them tingle as you send your breath out through them. Then breathe in through them, cool and sweet. Focus on your intention, not results."

His fingers did tingle. So did his chest, just as if the Mantle hung there, speaking to him. "Yes, I think I feel that."

"Good. Now just open yourself to that flow back and forth. Don't try to make it stronger, just notice what it is. Give yourself to the rhythm of it."

He nodded to show he heard. Nothing happened.

"You're too tense. Chasing results, I expect, and you've forgotten to breathe."

"Sorry."

"There's nothing for you to be sorry about. You're already more connected than you know. Just follow your breath, in... and out. Set aside your ideas of what you want to feel. Just follow your breath. Give... and take, no separation, just like when you are with a good lover."

Magnus jerked his arms partway out of the water, and his eyes shot open.

Zoya sighed. "Oh. That's what that barrier was. You don't know how. I wondered. It does feel like you hold that part of yourself away from the sacred world."

"Does that matter?" How could he explain how afraid he was of losing himself in another, how badly he wanted to do it anyway, sacred and free?

"With magic, you can't stay separate, an observer. You must enter the dance unconditionally. A fish can't hold itself back from the river. Being part of the vast family of living things is the root of my craft. I can't teach you if you're not able to share yourself. Understanding the magic of plants is not just taking and using, but sharing and giving, too."

Was she saying he was stingy, or worse, lazy? "My daily labor is a gift." Even he could hear the defensiveness in his voice.

"Don't be so touchy. That's not what I'm talking about. Anyone can work hard without ever giving from his inner self."

"I don't understand."

"You were sharing your innermost self when you sang to the rabbits."

"But that was just a silly song."

"Bah. It was a song. You sang. You gave of yourself."

"It didn't mean anything."

Zoya stiffened. "How dare you?" she snapped. "It meant every-thing." She shook her head, sighed, and rubbed her knees. "I can't teach you much until we find a way past your resistance. I need to think about how."

"I'm sorry."

"Being sorry means nothing. Let's finish up. Before you take your hands out of the water, thank the spring, and say thank you to the living things all around you."

He swallowed against bitterness. He hated failure. "I'd like to try again, when I can."

"Oh, we will. You already do everything I'm asking, you just don't know how to do it on purpose. When you do it by accident, you have a moment of rapture. When you can do it as a conscious choice, it will bring you powerful magic."

Magnus deserved her rebuke. He silently said thank you to the water, the air, and the green life all around him, then followed Zoya out. He'd failed so completely she hadn't even bothered to be angry.

He lifted the relic from where it rested on his shirt and put it around his neck. Its warmth against his chest was sweet relief as he pulled on his shirt, trousers, and finally his sandals. He walked with Zoya as far as the door to his room, where he managed to not apologize to her again and went inside without even saying goodnight.

His room was stuffy from being closed up all day, so he took off his shirt again and opened the window. He thought again about what Zoya had said about being an observer. It was true. Except in his ecstatic experiences of oneness in the desert and sometimes in the garden or with the animals, his habit was to watch—especially with people—while feeling he had to be careful, had to understand, that if he wasn't alert, something bad might happen. He wanted to change, to be part of the flow of life. He wanted to share in things happening instead of just watching them happen. A dance, she'd called it. He wanted to dance.

He undressed and began to hang the Mantle on its twig in the wall. After being deprived of it once already, he wasn't ready to part from it so soon. He needed its comfort. He lay down on his bed, holding it to his chest. "I never want to be separated from you again, no matter what else happens," he murmured as he drifted off to sleep.

He dreamed of flying, and his chest burned hot with the wild joy of it.

Chapter Thirteen

Magnus was flying. His chest burned. Everything was too hot, too bright. He opened his eyes. He wasn't flying. The ceiling spun slowly above him. He was in bed. The sun blazed through his window. He should have been up and working long ago. So much to do.

He rolled onto his side, sick and aching as if he'd been drinking all night. He rubbed at a soreness in his chest, yelping in pain as he hit a bump on his breastbone. His hand came away bloody. He looked down to see the relic half-sunk into his flesh, his flesh swollen and scarlet and seeping blood all around it. He gaped at it, struggling to overcome his fear. It was digging into his body. If it hit his heart, it would kill him. He tried to pull it out until his trembling fingers became too slick with blood to keep a grip. It didn't budge.

He asked the Mantle what was happening. Nothing. Had it turned on him? Should he keep trying to pull it out? Should he leave it alone? What did this mean? Was he going to die? Zoya might know. Fighting his dizziness, he managed to stand, shivering and shaking, thirsty and weak and fever-frantic.

He nearly fell over as he pulled on pants, and staggered out the door. He found Zoya carrying water from the well to the garden—that had been his chore since his arrival. He called out her name, his voice high and sharp as a frightened child's.

She put down the bucket and turned to him, her face alert as soon as she saw the bleeding wound in his chest. "What is this?"

"I don't know. My compass. I went to sleep with it, and now it's digging into my body. I'm afraid it might—"

"Go back to your room," Zoya waved her hand brusquely. "I'll fetch some materials."

As he lurched his way back to his room like a drunkard, Magnus tried to pray. He couldn't hold any of the old chants in his head for long enough to sing even a single line. Out of habit, he asked the Mantle for help. For a heartbeat or two, it burned even hotter in his chest, and the pain eased a little. The door to his room warped back and forth. He fumbled with the latch as it jumped up and down, playing tricks on him. He stumbled in.

Zoya rapped at the open door, carrying a basket cradled at one elbow. "Stop pacing and lie down so I can get a better look."

"I can't. My legs are on fire. They twitch. Arms, too. Burning all over."

"Let me help." She guided him to the bed and pushed gently until he sat. The room leapt and swung sideways as he lay down. "I might vomit," he said, part apology, part warning.

"Calm, calm." She pulled out the worn stick she'd had him hold the night before, circling it over his torso as she hummed softly.

His heart was pounding, but he could breathe again. He could focus a little. His legs and arms no longer spasmed, only prickled. Afraid, comforted, and hopeful, he watched Zoya work.

"Well, this is a surprise," she said cheerfully. "Never seen anything like it. But my casting tells me we're not to interfere or pry it out. It's going to do whatever it's going to do. I can keep the wound from getting infected, though, and nurse you through this. I'm told it's going to get worse before it gets better."

She reached into her bundle and opened a clay jar, dipping her fingers in and drawing out what looked like a dollop of thick sludge. It stank of sulfur and rotting things.

Zoya laughed at his snort of disgust. "This won't hurt, but the smell does take some getting used to." She applied it to his chest in gentle circles, building a thick layer of the stuff across the whole opening. "This is the beginning of a new life for you, and you might be sick for a time. While it changes you."

"It is?" He couldn't find the right words. "Thank you."

"This leather string hanging out—we need to cut that off as close to the skin as we can, but the thing itself? It's going to be part of you now. I get the impression you asked for this."

"I did?" Magnus blinked to make his eyes focus on her face, but his vision wouldn't hold. Everything he looked at was haloed in sparkling light. He struggled to remember. "Maybe. No, yes. I did. Last night. No separation."

Zoya rummaged in her bundle again, poured something into a cup, then held his head up and put it to his lips. "Drink this. It will help you sleep for a while."

Magnus gagged at the first sip, but drank until the cup was empty.

"There," Zoya murmured. "Rest."

Magnus was alone, naked, traveling in a desert again. Not alone. Voices murmured all around him, but he couldn't see anybody. Zoya's crow Midnight appeared, squawking and flapping in circles around him.

The bird's scolding made his whole head hurt. The sun beat down mercilessly, unbearably hot. He had no water.

Midnight landed on his shoulder, talons digging into his bare shoulder. "You need to find shade before you cook," the bird said in his scratchy voice, his beak poking Magnus's ear.

"That hurts," Magnus complained. "And we're in a desert. Do you see any shade? I don't."

Midnight's voice became a silky whisper. "You don't have to go on, you know. You could rest here for a while. You're probably tired."

He was tired. Bone-weary. He shielded his eyes to check the sun. "I'd be dead before nightfall."

"Yes," said Midnight gently. "That is a choice you can make here."

Magnus thought about it for a while. He thought he heard music, but it was only the searing wind. "I want to keep going. Something's waiting for me."

Midnight flapped to the ground by Magnus's feet. He pecked at the dry ground, and a puddle appeared. "This is a door to Mistress Zoya's spring," he said, his voice scratchy again. "Jump in."

Magnus crouched down and stuck his hand flat in the puddle. It barely covered his knuckles. "I could stand in this, and it wouldn't even wet my ankles."

"You have to jump in, otherwise you'll get stuck before you get there." Midnight returned to Magnus's shoulder, the dig of his talons oddly reassuring. "I'll go with you so you don't get lost."

He puffed out his neck feathers into an iridescent ruff and hunched down. "Back up a bit and take a run at it. You'll do better that way."

It was a little irritating to be ordered around by a bird, but Magnus didn't want to stay in the desert heat. He reached up to hold Midnight against his neck, backed up a few paces, ran toward the puddle, and jumped.

The water was cool and clear as it closed over his head. Magnus wanted to laugh, but they were underwater. They kept sinking down until the surface was only a faint circle of light far above them.

Quickly now, Midnight's voice sounded in his head. *You can't stay here too long or you'll die.*

For some reason, the thought amused Magnus. He didn't even feel short of air. *I'm not in a hurry. This is nice.*

Not for long, trust me. We need to keep moving. This way. Midnight spread his wings and began to beat through the water, dragging Magnus forward by the shoulder. A pillared archway appeared ahead of them, rough and green-black in the faint light.

I'll leave you once you're in the grotto. Make your way up to the surface as fast as you can.

Magnus was going to object, but Midnight had already disappeared. His chest began to burn with need for air. He struggled toward the dot of light above him. It was so far away. Nearly... impossible. When he broke surface, he was not in the spring. He was thrashing around in his bed, gasping, giddy with searing pain and dripping fever sweat.

Midnight seemed to float above his head. *There you are, finally. You took longer than you should have.*

Magnus wanted to laugh and make a joke but managed only to cough and then wince at the pain. A hot knife was splitting his chest open. The Mantle. He tried to look down at it, but he couldn't lift his head. He couldn't move his arms or legs at all. Maybe he was dying in spite of his choice.

Half-formed thoughts circled slowly around him, like wary animals, just out of reach. "What's happening?" he managed to groan.

Zoya's voice floated across the room to him. "You travel on your adventure, Magnus. Long way to go yet, but we're with you." She leaned over him with a cup and lifted his head. "Drink more of this, as much as you can, and then some water."

By the time he'd finished, he was panting from the effort. Zoya wiped his brow with a wet cloth that was so cool and sweet he had to groan again. "Sleep again, now," she murmured. "That's the best thing you can do. Let your adventure take you wherever you're supposed to go. We'll watch over you."

"Thank you." Magnus closed his eyes and tumbled into roiling darkness.

After a while, the darkness eased, giving way to soft half-light. Magnus found himself sitting against the trunk of a large tree. The smooth cool bark felt good against the bare skin of his back. He was naked again. It didn't seem to matter, though, because there was no one else around except for Midnight, perched on his shoulder and pecking vigorously at the hole in his chest.

"You're always pecking at me," Magnus said, annoyed. "It hurts."

The crow stopped and swiveled his head to look up at Magnus, a shred of pink tissue stuck to his bill. "That may be," he said airily, "but it's necessary. I have to get this leather string out of you. It's already causing infection."

Magnus looked down to see his stomach and thighs dotted with snippets of leather and bits of bloody skin. "Can't you just pull it out all in one piece?" He complained. "I'd rather just get it over with."

"If you wish," said Midnight, sounding aggrieved. "I thought it would be easier on you if I did it in pieces. But let's try your way. Put your forearm across your lap so I can stand on it. Give me a better angle."

Magnus did as he was told. The crow settled himself on his arm and stretched up, grasping the thong in his beak and pulling. Nothing happened.

"Can I help?"

"Let me dig around the string a little more," the bird said. "That will give you something to grab."

Magnus tried not to watch while Midnight dug around the leather thong, sending ragged bits of his flesh flying as he worked. He concentrated on his breathing.

"Very well," Midnight said cheerfully. "Let's see if that gives you enough to pull on before this thing takes root in you."

Magnus grasped the end of the leather between his thumb and forefinger and pulled outward. He could feel the whole length of it scrape against his insides as it began to slide out of his body like a long worm. He felt sick to his stomach. Hand over hand, he continued to pull it out. He hadn't remembered it being this long.

Midnight grabbed hold with his beak. "Here, let me help." They pulled together, and with a sudden rush, the last of it slithered out, followed by a rivulet of black blood and pus. The leather stank like a dead animal's carcass.

"You need to clean that up right away."

"What with?"

Midnight puffed out his neck feathers. "How should I know? Use your imagination." He took off, flapping heavily into the woods.

Magnus stood, feeling much better now that the festering leather was out. He noticed a creek just down a mossy bank. He walked over, bent down, and washed off his chest. The water was so cold it stung.

Once he'd washed it clean, he could see more clearly what was happening. The inflamed, puckered skin had nearly closed over the relic, which now sat in an ugly hump against his breastbone. The skin all around it, twisted and red, looked like the burn scar Brother Ignatius carried on his leg after a pot of hot oil had spilled in the monastery kitchen.

If nothing else, Magnus decided, this was a lesson about vanity. People had often told him he was beautiful. He must have been proud, too proud of his body even if he was the only person he tolerated admiring it. It was still hubris. Perhaps the worst, most secret kind.

He touched the skin at the relic's edge. It was tender but no longer as painful. A clear liquid seeped from it, but there was no more pus. In a while, he would wash it here in the creek again.

Someone was singing. Magnus looked up from his chest to see a beautiful man kneeling on the other bank, washing clothes in the creek. "What are you doing here?" Magnus asked him. "You're intruding on my ordeal."

The man didn't seem to hear him. He was lovely. Lithe, with long dark hair. His eyes were so wise. Youthful. But his voice... it was exquisite, magical.

For a while, he listened as the man scrubbed clothes against a rock in rhythm with his singing. He seemed content, even happy in his task. Eventually, Magnus became too tired to stay by the creek. He got up to lean against his tree again.

He nestled on the ground between two large roots and leaned against the trunk. It felt like the most comfortable chair he'd ever sat in. A winged ant, red-and-black-bodied, landed on the back of his hand. It looked terribly familiar, but Magnus couldn't remember where he'd seen it.

"I'm done with my wings," the ant said cheerfully, "so I'm giving them to you. Use them well. They'll help you find your mate, as they helped me find mine. Once you've joined with your mate, you won't need them anymore. Pass them on, if you like. Or not."

Then Magnus remembered. The ant on his foot while he waited to see the Lord Abbott. "Thank you," he said, overcome with reverence. "I don't know how to fly, but I'll do my best." The ant climbed up onto his chest, crawling along the margin of the closing flesh, and wriggled once. As if clipped, its wings fell and melted into his skin. That seemed odd to him, but what did he know? The ant had given him a sacred gift, that much he knew. His vision blurred with tears as he watched the ant drop to the ground and disappear under the curl of a stiff brown leaf.

A wave of fatigue washed over him. He leaned back against the trunk of the tree and toppled backwards, down into the trunk where the roots began to spread out into the ground—or perhaps the other way around, where they left the ground to join the trunk. Magnus couldn't decide which, but it didn't seem to matter.

The darkness was sweet and gentle, wrapping him in a cool welcome.

At first, the voices were so soft he barely noticed them, just the faintest of whispers. But as he listened, they became more distinct. The trees were talking to each other through their roots, through the ground, with their trunks and branches resonating like musical instruments. It was a wonder—music so rich and graceful Magnus began to weep at the beauty.

"We've been talking," one voice said, getting stronger, "my family and I." It was as if the voices circled close around him. "We don't think Magnus is a very good name for you. Would you like a different one?"

Magnus laughed. "Honestly, I've never liked it much, either," he said. "The Prior gave it to me when I entered the monastery. I wanted to belong, so I took it."

"Would you like us to give you a new one?"

"Yes, please. I'd much rather have a new one from all of you."

"Very well. Please give us some time. We don't like to do things in a hurry."

"I'm happy to wait. I've got nowhere else to go."

"Yes, you do, but not just yet. Let my sap be part of your healing." The voice seemed to part his lips. He tasted strange honey.

Magnus lost track of time. It seemed as though he grew longer, sap-slow in the darkness, suspended in sleep yet awake enough to feel the comfort of the tree he was in as well as the murmuring presence of its kin all around.

The rustling whispers became louder, more rhythmic. "We're back," the tree announced. "After some deliberation, we think you should be called Mateo. How does that sound to you?"

The name landed in his heart, solid and warm. "It's exactly right. It feels lighter. Happier. Which is what I want to be. Thank you."

"You have to go now. I'll give you a push, but you have to lean forward and ask to go back into the world."

"May I come back sometime, just to visit?"

"Yes, of course. We'd be delighted to have you amongst us again."

Mateo leaned forward, tumbling upward into daylight.

His face was wet. Was he crying? He didn't feel sad. Maybe he was too happy at having a new name. His hand was strangely heavy, but he managed to lift it to his face and rub the moisture off his cheek.

"Hello, Magnus. Welcome back," said a male voice he didn't recognize.

He opened his eyes, but they didn't focus for a moment. A man bent over him, smiling, as beautiful as an angel. After a puzzled moment, Mateo recognized him. "You were washing clothes in my creek, but you wouldn't talk to me then," he said. "Hello."

Zoya appeared next to the man's shoulder. "I thought today might be the day. You've journeyed far, and for a while, I wasn't sure you'd find your way back. Well done."

"The trees helped me," he said as the angel lifted his head and put a cup to his lips. The liquid didn't stink. He gulped it down.

"Easy, Magnus," he said, taking the cup away. "Just a little at a time at first. We don't want it coming back up."

"The trees gave me a better name. I'm Mateo now."

"Oh, that makes so much sense!" Zoya clapped her hands. "How could you not come back reborn?"

"That's a beautiful name," the angel murmured, wiping Mateo's forehead with a cool cloth. "Good to meet you, Mateo. I'm Nuri. I've been helping my aunt take care of the farm." His smile reached into Mateo everywhere. "And you."

Chapter Fourteen

For days, Nuri fed him, brought him drink, sat with him, washed him, and sang to him. Even though he was too weak to stand without help, Mateo still felt embarrassed when Nuri washed his backside and took out the chamber pot, but Nuri just laughed. As his fever subsided and he gained strength, Mateo was able to stay awake longer and carry short conversations.

He learned that Nuri made his way as a traveling musician. He'd sing in taverns, in market squares—wherever people would listen and a few might throw coins in his hat. Endless stories of his travels and exploits made Mateo alternately laugh or gasp in amazement. He'd never encountered such wit and charm, and didn't really care whether the stories were embellished or not. Mateo just loved listening to Nuri's enchanting voice, watching his face as he told them.

Most of all, he loved listening to Nuri sing. His voice was agile, as sweet and rich as honey. It was satisfying in some way that Mateo couldn't explain, as if it touched something important but too elusive to name.

Nuri's repertoire seemed inexhaustible with a song for every occasion, every topic they discussed. And he was observant. Nuri always noticed when Mateo tired, which happened quickly and often. He would pick up his guitar and say, "That reminds me of a song." Then his nimble fingers would dance across the frets and Mateo would usually fall asleep before the song was over.

Mateo craved his company more than food, and Nuri seemed perfectly happy to spend hours with him every day. He washed Mateo's face and applied one of Zoya's many ointments to the knot of red scar tissue, which rose in a twisted lump on his chest like a misshapen rosebud that would never bloom. Mateo confided that he thought it made him ugly, but Nuri insisted it was a thing of beauty to be proud of—a mark from the gods.

His touch was always tender and sometimes playful when feeding him, and occasionally even affectionate. In his entire life, and under all three of his names, Mateo had never experienced such generous, innocent intimacy; such guileless generosity. It watered a dry place in his heart.

One evening, Nuri asked him about love, and his lovers. Instead of freezing in shame as Magnus would have done, Mateo took Nuri's hand, lifted it to his lips, and confessed that, while he'd had plenty of sex, he'd never been in love; that his discouragement had driven him to hide in the monastery, where sex was coerced and even less loving than before.

Sitting on the edge of Mateo's bed and holding his hand, Nuri smiled. His face was beatific in the candlelight. He didn't say anything for a long time, then he leaned forward and gently kissed Mateo's temple. "Perhaps now that can change," he whispered, his breath a caress against his ear. "You deserve love." Mateo hoped that was true.

Nuri sat back, picked up his guitar and began a ballad, never taking his eyes off Mateo. The song told the story of a beautiful young maiden who, while walking one day along the beach, came upon a merman.

The merman told her that, since she had surprised him sitting on his rock where humans might find him, he could grant her three wishes before the sun set.

The maiden quickly asked for true love, but the merman said that he couldn't give her that—only because she already had it in her heart, ready to give to someone else.

She then asked for happiness, and the merman told her no one can give that to you, either—you can give it only to yourself, not even to those you love truly. The maiden sat on the beach for a while in silence, staring at the merman, wondering at his wisdom and his beauty.

Finally, as the sun was about to set, she told the merman her third wish: to join him, to live with him in the ocean for as long as she could. He smiled and granted her wish, to frolic together among the waves forever.

When the song was over, Nuri carefully put down his instrument, made Mateo drink a sip of water before applying salve to his cracked lips, kissed him again, unhurried and sensual this time, and bade him goodnight. Almost before the door closed, Mateo fell deeply asleep, his dreams rolling in waves, to the long slow chant of the sea.

Chapter Fifteen

The next morning, Mateo told Zoya and Nuri he wanted to get up and that he felt strong enough for a short walk. After a brief survey with her twisted stick, Zoya agreed.

"What do you have in mind?" Nuri asked as he helped Mateo put on a fresh shirt.

"Not much," Mateo said. "Perhaps just around the garden." He felt his ears heat with embarrassment. "Maybe a little farther, so I can say hello to the animals. I've missed them."

Nuri beamed. "That sounds like an excellent walk to me," he said. "As long as we take our time."

Being vertical for longer than it took to get to the chamber pot was strange. Mateo lurched and flung an arm around Nuri's neck before they got to the door. "My balance is… off. Do you mind me leaning on you like this?"

"Lean as much as you need to. I'm right here." Nuri wrapped an arm around Mateo's waist and opened the door. "You're lucky I'm shorter than you. We fit together well."

"Mmm." Content, Mateo spread his hand against Nuri's chest to keep from swaying. "I agree."

Stepping outside, Mateo flinched at the fierce sunlight. "Too bright, can't see. Let me get used to it before we move." He shaded his eyes. "How long have I been in that room?"

"Zoya didn't say. Since before I arrived. I've been here ten days, I think. I haven't counted. I never do." Nuri gave Mateo a squeeze, drew in a deep breath, and let it out slowly. "Take your time. We have nothing to prove."

"What did you say?"

"I said, take your time. We have nothing to prove."

"No, right after that."

"I didn't say anything."

"I hear voices. So many. I don't understand what they're saying."

"Are you sure you should be out here?"

"Yes, yes, yes." Mateo stiffened, then slumped forward. "Nuri, let me sit down. This is marvelous! I can feel them. All of them. It's like music, just like Zoya said."

Nuri helped him sit. "I should get Zoya."

"Yes," he gasped. "She should know. Tell her I can hear them now."

Mateo collapsed onto his back as the world surged and swirled around him. Everything breathed. The soil chanted. Every plant sang. In and out, just like Zoya had described that night at her spring. Life opening. Twisting, reaching, spreading. Closing. Rising, falling, curling, drying, dying. Giving, turning, taking. Dancing. Resting. Insects. Animals. Birds wheeling in their dance above. Rivers of wind herding tumbling clouds under stars unseen. He heard-felt them all, vibrating in his flesh, his cousins. This was his family—he was home. He couldn't bear the glory of it. He spread his arms and let the voices take him, pulling him down, up, stretching him in all directions at once, vibrating. He had to join them, and share in their vast music. He could dance with them forever.

"Mateo." Someone was calling to him. Zoya. He opened his eyes and blinked, spilling tears. He was so happy.

Nuri leaned in over her shoulder, looking worried. Mateo beamed up at him.

"We need to get you inside," Zoya said. "Lift your arms."

Mateo reached for Nuri, gasping at the startling, intricate beauty of his touch. Then he went dancing again.

The voices grew distant. Mateo noticed he was lying fully dressed on top of his bed. He gazed up at Zoya, feeling butterfly-soft with wonder. His whole body hummed. "It is just as you said. Everything. In and out, breathing. Beautiful."

Zoya wiped his cheek, beaming. "Yes: beautiful. I'm so happy for you, Mateo. This is a great milestone." She patted his chest, avoiding the lump of scar. "Your journey is breaking you open. This is good. But you must learn to listen with more control or you'll go mad, and that would be a waste."

"I'm lucky you can teach me, then. I want to learn."

"I can't teach you my magic, not now." She pointed at his chest. "You're walking too different a path from mine. But I can support, even guide, maybe. But I would do you harm, now, trying to teach you my ways."

"Then how—"

"Our ways will cross well and often, I promise. We'll always meet in the dance of nature, I'm sure of it."

He looked away and studied the ceiling's cracked plaster. Might she abandon him? "What should I do?"

"Learn to listen with intent, with focus. I think you became overwhelmed because you weren't expecting what you felt. Now you know. You must learn how to not be so taken by surprise. To focus with purpose. Take Nuri with you whenever you go outside, at least for a while. He can keep you grounded."

He looked at Nuri. "Would you?"

"Of course. You can even come with me while I do chores some-times. This will be an adventure for all of us. I can't wait to see what happens now that you know more of what to expect. Rest now. We'll try again tomorrow."

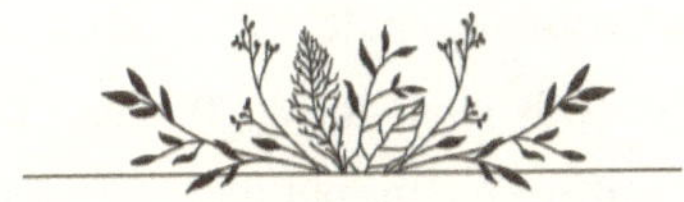

Mateo staggered and grabbed Nuri's shoulder. "It's like learning to walk again," he said, feeling apologetic. "I don't know how to put my feet down. Every time I take a step, the voices come shooting up my legs all the way into my... whatever the relic is now. In my chest." The lumpy scar itched, and he rubbed it. "My new heart. When I take a step, it feels like I'm stepping on something delicate, like an egg I could crush."

"Delicate?" Nuri murmured as he held Mateo's arm around his neck. "Delicate, perhaps, but surely not fragile."

"I've been so careless," Mateo muttered, mostly to himself. "I must be more reverent, more respectful of where I'm walking. So enormous and alive. So sacred. I could never have imagined before now."

"Maybe this is what Zoya meant when she talked about letting nature strengthen you."

"Maybe. It's like fire, though. I'm... afraid to let it all the way in. It feels hot, like it might burn me up."

"She warned against resisting it, too, didn't she? She said to stay in the flow—breathing it in, and then breathing it out."

"That's what I'm trying to do, but it's so intense. When it comes up my thighs, I feel like I'll turn into a torch. Or explode." Mateo stopped for a moment, eyes closed. "It feels like it wants to come up through me and out the top of my head. Give me a minute so I can try that. Breathing in through my feet. Oh. And then up... to give it away. Give it away through the crown of my head. Oh. Let me lean on you, I need to take my shoes off. This is holy ground."

He planted his bare feet on the path. The hard-packed dirt was warm and smooth, welcoming. He lifted his arms above his head, as far as he could reach, with his hands open to the sun. "Like a fountain."

His feet began to tingle, and the pulsing music spiraled up through his bones. He looked at Nuri in awe. "Yes, giving it away. So simple."

"I'm a fountain!" he shouted. His whole body shivered and shook. Wild jubilation came bubbling up through the soles of his feet along with the earth's song, and he hurled his shouts and laughter into the sky in exultation, in triumph. "A fountain! A fountain!"

Zoya hurried around the corner, Midnight flapping beside her. "What's all this noise about?"

He could hear and see, but the swirling current held Mateo captive, and he couldn't answer.

"It seems Mateo's become a fountain of earth music," Nuri said, laughing. "Isn't he beautiful? But I can't tell you more. You'll have to ask him when he comes back to us."

Zoya stepped close to Mateo and waved her hand in front of his face. His eyes wouldn't follow. "He can't do too much of this at a time or his awakening will kill him." She drew out her stick and pointed it at him, murmuring something.

Mateo's face snapped sideways as if he'd been slapped. He blinked hard and labored to focus on Zoya. It took a moment before he could speak. "You saved me, I think. I was going wild inside and didn't know how to get back. Midnight, hello."

He turned to Nuri. "I've been having the most extraordinary time," he said dreamily, rubbing his chest. "My relic claimed me, gave me a new heart. The trees gave me a new name. I'm... I'm new. You sing to me and I lean on you. I can be a fountain, taking and giving. I love being a fountain."

He stumbled to Nuri and wrapped his arms around him clumsily, nuzzling into his neck. "I love leaning on you. I love everything, but especially you, my beautiful angel Nuri. Maybe I'm somebody else now, I'm not sure. I think I should lie down for a while. Will you rest with me? Just for a little while, maybe. As a favor. If you don't mind."

Nuri chuckled and gently stroked Mateo's hair. "I don't mind lying down with you," he said, drawing Mateo's arm around so they stood side by side. He gave his aunt a knowing smile. "I don't mind at all."

That evening, Mateo was able to join Zoya and Nuri at the dinner table. Zoya had prepared a rabbit pie with root vegetables and soft cheese made from sheep's milk, accented with sage and lavender. Sitting here with them felt like a new beginning.

His hands shook as he took his first bites. He chewed slowly. "This is delicious," he said, pointing to his bowl, "but I can't eat all this."

"Let me help." Nuri reached over and retrieved half. He smirked as he lazily licked the thick sauce off both sides of his spoon before sliding the whole spoon into his mouth, closing his lips around it. He whimpered as he pulled it out slowly and licked his lips. "Does that help?"

"Um, yes. No." Mateo's cheeks burned as he shifted in his chair to make room for his arousal. Nuri winked and tucked into his dinner.

"Don't tease him at the table, Nuri. He's still convalescing." Zoya covered the remainder of the pie and carried it to the counter. "There'll be plenty of time for that later."

Mateo surprised himself by laughing and not feeling a flicker of shame. "I certainly hope so." He was a different man, free to celebrate his body without guile. He liked what he'd become. He stood to help clean up, if he could manage.

He cleared his throat. "Zoya, I want to build a shrine somewhere. To honor my new state, I suppose. I had a vision of it in one of my fevers."

She turned to him with a frown. "Not some church thing, though. Can't have that here where people come for my help. If they want that kind of help, they can stay in town and go to a church."

"No, not a church thing at all," Mateo said, almost as amused as insulted. "I don't feel any obligation to the church the way Magnus did, and even he wasn't all that committed. And Magnus is gone now. But come to think of it, even he imagined a shrine for the Mantle where people could come for healing. On the road to the fortress."

He pulled in a deep breath and let it out, pleased by the confirming glow he felt in his chest, understanding afresh how stifling that old burden had been. He gave a gentle chuckle. "I think I belong to the Church of the Trees now."

Zoya nodded her approval. "In that case, yes, I'd welcome that. Just not close to my spring."

"Absolutely not. What I saw in my vision was near the well somewhere. Much more open to the public." He brushed his hand over the lump in his chest. "I hope that in time I can help people with healing. Or something. I don't really know what, but I need to do something with what I've been given. Help people, somehow."

For what seemed like a long time, Zoya stood still, said nothing, and stared at Mateo as if she'd never seen him before. "Yes," she said finally. "I think that's right. Near the well would be fine. Tomorrow morning, let's take a look together."

Then Nuri walked him back to his room, shepherding him inside and settling him on the bed. He took off Mateo's shoes and helped him out of his clothes, then stood, pulling his own shirt over his head.

Mateo watched, fascinated, aroused, and a little nervous. "What are you doing?" he asked, even though he already knew, and the knowledge was lightning in his veins.

"I'm going to make good my spoon-promise at dinner," he said with a smile. "I know you remember."

Mateo smiled back, happily. "I do remember."

Nuri took his time untying the cord cinching his trousers. "I'm going to make sure you never forget."

Later, when all was quiet and the moon shone softly through the little window, Mateo drew his thumb across Nuri's lips. "Thank you," he whispered. "Please stay. I want you to stay."

Nuri curled into him. "Stay? Do you mean tonight?"

"Tonight, yes. Longer. I don't know when you intend to leave. Stay a long time. I know I have no right to ask. Harvest is nearly upon us, and I don't know how useful I'll be to Zoya."

With a playful frown, Nuri swatted his shoulder. "Just for Zoya and the harvest?"

Mateo kissed Nuri's hair. "No, but I wanted the most persuasive argument I could mount."

"I've never stayed that long before. But you don't need an argument at all." Nuri licked the hollow of Mateo's throat. "I want to stay. With you."

He rolled, pressing his back against Mateo's chest, wrapping himself in his arms. "And with Zoya, of course. I'll be glad to help with harvest, too. But to be clear, I'm staying to be with you." He gave a sleepy sigh. "In the great kitchen of the gods, you're an adventure on the boil, Mateo. I love adventure. And you. We'll build your shrine together."

Chapter Sixteen

Mateo startled awake as Nuri stirred against him, solid and warm. He'd never slept through the night with a man before, had never wanted to. He liked it. But the sun had risen, and today would be his first to help with chores since the relic took him.

He eased himself out of bed as gently as he could, but Nuri grunted, rubbed his eyes, and rolled onto his side facing him as Mateo pulled on trousers.

"I like watching you get dressed," Nuri said after a while. "I should do it often."

"You should get up, too," Mateo said, wishing he could climb back into bed. "Zoya is likely already up and busy."

When they got to the kitchen, they found bread and cheese set out under a cloth on the table. Nuri made tea.

Their intimacy, soft and rich, hung like a thick substance in the air between them, a gentle cloud caressing every motion, charging it with deeper meaning. Every glance or touch shivered with their shared awareness.

Nuri sat next to him and nudged his shoulder. "Everything seems different this morning, doesn't it?" Nuri cut another piece of cheese and placed it on Mateo's plate.

Mateo nodded, savoring the feeling. "It does. Like the air between us is another part of our bodies. We touch even when we're not touching. I've never experienced it before. Have you?"

"Not often. Sometimes. It's a mystery of good sex, somehow. It doesn't last, though. That's kind of sad, but sometimes merciful, too." Nuri put down his knife, turning to face Mateo. "With you, I'd like it to last as long as possible."

Mateo stroked Nuri's cheek, leaned in for a kiss. A heavy thump at the door cut it short.

Zoya appeared, her basket filled with carrots, their long lacy tops hanging in a graceful cascade over the side. "I'm going to need at least one of you to come with me to market tomorrow," she said, breathing heavily. "There's more produce than I can manage on my own, and it's time to take a few chickens as well as eggs."

"We'll both come," said Mateo, looking to Nuri for his agreement. "We also need things you shouldn't have to carry. We need new slats for the bottom of the rabbit hutches."

"I didn't get to that," Nuri said, a note of apology in his voice. "I didn't do anything about repairs without you. I managed to clean pens, water, feed, and weed, and that was about all."

"Pah. That's plenty. You were busy tending to more important needs than rabbit hutches." Zoya emptied her basket onto a shelf in the pantry. "I dug out some potatoes and onions for tomorrow. They're in piles at the foot of the rows. Can one of you bring them in?" She poured more water into the teapot. "I need to sit for a moment before we go looking for the right spot for your shrine, or whatever you have in mind."

"I know I've needed a lot of your time and attention." Mateo rubbed his chest. The scarred lump still felt strange to touch, even through his shirt. "I would never have survived this without you both, I'm certain."

"The farm got by." Zoya pointed at him with a mischievous grin. "*This,* as you call it, is by far the most interesting thing I've seen in many years, and I can assure you your journey's far from over. I'm curious to see what comes next."

Nuri picked up the empty basket and gave Mateo a smirk. "Gathering potatoes and onions come next, don't you think?"

"When I was Magnus, I had a vision of a shrine that anyone might come to for a blessing from the relic," Mateo said, holding Nuri's hand. "And here we are, about to build it. It's a marvel."

He took a deep breath and laughed. "But strangely funny, too—nothing like I had imagined. I never imagined it would claim and inhabit a human like it has. I feel like maybe I'm its first shrine."

"Maybe that had to happen first," Zoya said tenderly. Midnight appeared from somewhere and settled on Zoya's shoulder, pecking affectionately at her ear. When they got to the well, Zoya stopped and turned to Mateo, eyebrows raised, not saying anything.

He looked around, feeling unsure. He'd come to this place countless times, drawing buckets of water for the garden, for the kitchen, and for bathing. Now it was as if he'd never seen it.

"The first time I used this as a compass," Mateo said with a finger on his chest, "it led me to you. I stood in the middle of the road and turned until I felt its pull. That's the direction I followed, through the village and then to your farm. Do you think I should try that?"

Zoya made a sour face. "We could stumble around for days doing that. You want to be a healer. So treat this as if someone is asking for your help. Open your vision a bit. Look for the lines of flow in the earth, just as you would in someone's body. Where they go, where they cross in a good way, where they might be tangled or blocked."

Mateo took a deep breath, closed his eyes, and relaxed, reaching to the scars on his chest, asking to see more. An answering surge of warmth filled him, and he opened his eyes.

Every plant and rock, every leaf glowed with its own halo. Below them, bright lines of life shimmered through the soil. Below those, wider, slower rivers of power sang, like glowing roads on a map he didn't recognize. And below them... he couldn't. Shouldn't. It was too holy, and he hadn't been invited. He dropped to his knees, covering his face with his hands.

Nuri's arms wrapped around him, drawing him upright, bringing him back to the regular world.

Zoya was saying something soothing about one step at a time. He steadied himself against Nuri's shoulder. What would Mateo do without him? He'd never needed anyone like this. But something in him understood already. It wasn't much of a mystery. He turned his attention to Zoya.

"So did you see the big earth-lines?" she asked. "Not the shallow little ones at the surface. Those are for other work."

Mateo hung on to Nuri's shoulders. "Yes. I went deeper, too, but it felt like trespassing, as if I had to be invited."

"Hm. Wise of you. Good. So look again, this time with more focused intent. Form a question. Keep your eyes open. Where do you see the earth-lines?"

Mateo stared at the ground in front of him, asking to be shown the right place for his shrine, and felt his vision softening. A line emerged, silver-gold in the dark brown dirt. He pointed to it. "There's one here," he said. "It runs out from the well toward those trees. Then there are two others—no, three—running through the well. Is that why the well was built here?"

Zoya laughed. "The well was always here. But yes, that's why wise ones dug the hole there long ago. Now stay focused on your purpose." She squinted at an ash tree close by. "Do you see there where another line crosses the one near your feet?"

"Yes. Why is it a different color?"

"That doesn't matter right now. But you might make that crossing your spot. What do you have in mind?"

"In my vision, I saw a cairn of stones, about my height, maybe less, with a place to sit next to it. But it mainly had a feeling. Enclosed and safe, like a house but without walls or a roof."

"Hmm. Interesting." Zoya stared at him thoughtfully. "And an altar?"

"Maybe a small one. Nothing big."

"I can see it!" Nuri exclaimed, spreading his arms. "It's perfect! The cairn would be the fireplace of your house, and the seat would be there, next to the hearth. The altar would be like a mantelpiece. We could place a stone at each corner of the house, just to mark the space. It wouldn't have to be big at all."

Mateo turned to him, stunned. "You see it better than I did. You made more sense of it, too." He hugged Nuri, and lifted him off his feet. He kissed his neck as he reluctantly put him back down.

Nuri laughed and straightened his shirt. "No magic on my part, I assure you. Metaphor is a basic skill for poets and musicians, is all."

Zoya wagged a finger at her nephew, but she was smiling. "Don't disrespect the gift, boy. It *is* a form of magic, and a powerful one. I see it now, too. This is a fine vision. Good will come of it."

Together, they fanned out into the bush beyond the ash tree to find points defining the corners of the house, laughing. While the area was larger than they expected, no house they'd ever seen had such odd shape.

Zoya stood at the narrowest point, near the well, staring at the space. Mateo joined her. "Did we get it right?"

"Yes. This is good. I wouldn't have seen this on my own."

Nuri joined them and slid his arm around Mateo's waist. "Something the three of us created together. That feels important to me. Like a new home for us."

"We'll find out as we go," Zoya said. "That's all we need. Will you start on the cairn today?"

Mateo shook his head. "No. The day after tomorrow, I expect. Market day is tomorrow, and we have plenty to do to get ready for that. Besides, we've already finished the hardest work. Now all I have to do is arrange some stones."

"We," Nuri corrected, pinching Mateo's side, making him yelp. "You and I will arrange the stones. Together."

Chapter Seventeen

By the time the sun had cleared the horizon, they were already on the road toward town. The cart was so laden with produce that Nuri and Mateo agreed it would be unfair to Bray for them to ride in the cart. Walking alongside as Zoya drove suited Mateo better than riding, anyway, as he could steady or push the cart as it navigated ruts and potholes. Nuri had slung his guitar over his back and shared story after story of performing in countless town squares, sleeping wherever he could.

"It's a hard way to live year-round," he said. "Cold as they are in dead of winter, stables are far better than a side-street doorway. I'd miss it, though, if I didn't entertain folks at least once in a while."

"You would," said Zoya, voice firm and solemn. "You have bard magic in your blood."

Mateo shivered. He didn't know exactly what bard magic might be. He knew Nuri's voice had helped heal him, helped keep him in this world. But now he saw it might also have a price. Was this why Nuri kept wandering from place to place? The thought of his Nuri huddled in a doorway while a bitter wind chewed through his clothing was an offense to everything good.

"When I was in the desert," he said, pushing his disgust aside, "I had no choice but to sleep in the open. I think you had it harder, knowing there were people nearby, warm and comfortable in their homes. Seeing warm light shining from behind their shutters. It would be hard for me to not despair, I think."

"Sometimes it was," Nuri said, giving him a joyless smile. "Though if I was desperate, I could usually find a warm bed when I had to."

Mateo knew what he meant. He didn't mind, and smiled back to tell him so.

"Mostly," Nuri said, breaking the brief silence that followed. "I made my way to milder climes for winter. One thing I don't miss is having to move from place to place to stay fed." He caught Mateo's eye and held it with a grin. "Although that's the least of the reasons I love staying on Zoya's farm."

When they arrived at the square, Nuri took Bray to the stables, and Mateo maneuvered the cart into a good space where it would get afternoon shade. Zoya arranged the vegetables and animals in the bed of the cart but left her potions and salves discreetly covered by a cloth. When she saw the question in Mateo's eyes, she said she had no good reason to invite trouble. The people who would buy her wares already knew about them, that it was safer not to display them to those who didn't.

Since Nuri enjoyed bargaining more than Mateo did, Zoya sent him off to the potter to buy more small clay jars, a sack of flour from the miller, a tanned cowhide, and some rope. A few villagers stopped to talk quietly with Zoya, and went away with a jar of salve or an object Mateo didn't recognize. He began to feel restless, and a little guilty as well. He wasn't needed here. He should have gone with Nuri.

There was a sudden drop in noise across the square as half a dozen armed soldiers appeared. They strolled among the stalls and barrows as if they were shopping. Zoya clutched Mateo's arm. "Tun's men," she murmured. "Don't watch them, or even make eye contact. Pretend you don't see them. Let them take whatever they want."

"Do they always do this?"

"Especially around harvest time. They tell the tax collector who seems to have had a good year."

"Like us."

"Yes. Now make yourself unremarkable."

"I am always unremarkable."

Zoya stopped arranging the carrots and scowled at him. "You insult my Nuri, who would never love an unremarkable man." Her scowl deepened as she chewed on her lip. "This is a dangerous lie you insist on telling yourself. Embrace your power and your beauty. Now sit down. Don't look up until they've passed."

Cheeks burning at the rebuke, Mateo sat against the cart's wheel and stared at the cobblestones between his feet.

Somewhere nearby, a woman yelped in alarm, followed by crashes and angry shouts. Mateo looked up to see a large calf bolting through the square and dragging its lead behind it, knocking over barrows and upsetting piles of market goods, headed directly for him. Without a thought, he leapt to his feet and seized the halter as the confused animal tried to push past. *STOP*, he silently ordered the steer, using the halter to pull its head to the side and break its momentum. To his surprise, it quieted immediately. As he gathered up the animal's tether, a young woman ran up to him, wiping away angry tears.

He held out the rope to her, keeping a grip on the halter. "Does he belong to you?"

She nodded. "I'm so sorry. Yes. Thank you." She took the lead from him. "I was tying him to the post when a soldier grabbed my... grabbed me. I was so startled I cried out and dropped the lead." She looked back at the mess her animal had caused, and sighed.

"Let me help you put things right. I'd be glad to have something to do."

"Help would be welcome. Thank you."

When he returned to Zoya's cart, she glared at him and pressed her lips into a hard line, then ignored him completely. Was she angry that he'd helped the girl? She couldn't be.

Eventually, Nuri returned with their supplies. By then, their chickens and rabbits had sold, as had most of the produce. But to further sour the day, two of the soldiers stopped by Zoya's cart and took half the apples she had traded for chickens. Mateo sat off to the side and pretending to be asleep, calling himself a coward even though he knew that's what she wanted.

Nuri must have felt the chill in the air right away. His smile faded as he glanced at Zoya and then raised an eyebrow at Mateo, who shrugged and shook his head.

Nuri seemed to not care as he checked the tuning on his guitar. He put his hat upside down on the cobbles in front of him and began to play. As always, passersby gathered to listen, and afterwards moved on with smiles on their faces. Occasionally a coin landed in the hat.

Although he would never tire of Nuri's music, Mateo found the afternoon dragged slowly. He hated the feeling of being out of joint with Zoya, who seemed to have forgotten he was there. It was a relief when the market began to close down, and he could load their supplies into the cart while Nuri fetched Bray.

They made their way out of the village without a word. At first, Nuri whistled a tune as he walked alongside the cart, but he soon fell silent. Steadying the cart from the other side, Mateo retreated into himself, waiting for Zoya to start scolding him or saying whatever she had to say. He'd never liked arguments, and it felt like a bad one was coming.

Zoya finally cleared her throat and turned to Mateo. She still frowned, but her eyes had become kind again. "You don't see how you make yourself stand out, Mateo. You are too nice, too good. You must grow up from being a good little boy who just wants everyone around him to be happy. That's fine for a little boy, but it's a kind of selfishness in adults. For all our sakes, you have to grow into being a good man who understands how to be good wisely. You'll never be able to keep enough people happy that you can be comfortable."

Was that true? Was he just a nice little boy in a man's body? That was insulting. Nuri would never love just a nice boy. But something in what Zoya said rang true, something he didn't want to look at, and it hurt to hear the words.

He took a deep breath. "In the past, I've been accused of being too kind to even be a farmer. I don't understand why that isn't enough. Kindness costs nothing."

"That's not true," Zoya snapped, her voice more harsh than he'd ever heard before. "Unwise kindness can cost you everything. It seems I have to remind you of your old church's martyred saints. All good people, no doubt, but they were like little children who didn't understand the world. I'm not saying you should be unkind. But you must learn how to be kind in ways that fit wisely with your circumstances."

He swallowed against his anger but it wouldn't stay down. "So helping that girl with her cow and helping to restore some of the damage it caused was unwise?" He looked to Nuri for some clue, but the set of his jaw reminded him that he hadn't seen what happened.

Zoya shrugged. "Maybe, maybe not. Time will tell. But you took a big risk today, acting so openly in a way that could have been interpreted as a rebuke of Tun's soldiers."

When she looked at Mateo again, her eyes were sad and afraid. "If those soldiers had taken offense at what you did, that could spell trouble not only for you but for Nuri and me, too."

"What should I have done, then? Nothing? What would you have done?"

"I don't know." Zoya's voice was small and afraid. "But I felt something dangerous in the air. I'm asking you to be careful, for all our sakes."

Mateo's chest hurt, and he wanted to cry, but he knew that would just make things worse. Everyone kept telling him what could go wrong. He would try to be more careful, of course, and try to think of more than the immediate need before acting. But he couldn't bear to live constantly thinking about what might go wrong. Maybe he was just stupid. He knew he wasn't clever like Nuri, or Zoya. He was just a farm boy who liked helping people.

But that wasn't the whole truth. What if he was somehow hiding in helping people, in being good? What if he did have to grow in some kind of wisdom he didn't yet possess? Maybe the relic required that. It was a frightening thought.

He smiled at Zoya, asking for some new kind of courage. Courage to be wise, perhaps. The relic vibrated deep in his chest in answer. Some heavy weight fell from him, leaving him more agile, stronger. "I know I don't understand what you're saying yet, but I want to. And I'll be more careful."

Chapter Eighteen

The afternoon sun slanted through the trees onto Mateo's back, still hot but gentler now. He pondered the piles of stone he and Nuri had gathered, wishing he were more skilled at dry stone work. He wanted this altar to outlive him.

They had managed to lay the first dozen courses of the cairn, which was turning out to be more of a low, thick wall than a pillar. Along the way, they'd learned to wedge small stones between larger ones to stabilize and level them, having fun debating how to combine the shapes to finally arrive at what they wanted.

Now it was time for the slab of flagstone they'd found, setting it so one edge would stick out from the front of the cairn to form the mantel-altar surface. Securing it with irregular stone without breaking the mantelpiece was going to be a challenge. Maybe... yes, first a bed of the smallest pebbles they could find underneath the slab, to distribute its weight as evenly as possible.

Nuri appeared with a load of fieldstone in the piece of canvas they were using as a carrier.

"You're trying to do too much at a time," Mateo scolded, taking the canvas and dumping the stones onto the ground. He kissed Nuri to soften his words. "I don't want you hurting yourself."

"Want to do my share, that's all." Nuri kissed him back. "We should probably stop for the day soon, anyway. I'm tired, and we still have animals to feed."

"Yes, soon. But first let me show you my idea for the mantelpiece. We level off the top of what we have, then spread out even smaller stones on top so the weight of the flagstone is distributed well. Maybe haul some from the river when we can. Tomorrow is market day."

"Even better, there's nearly a cartload of gravel behind the chicken coop. You probably haven't been out there since I bartered for it with one of the quarrymen."

"That would have cost a lot. What did you barter? Zoya's services?"

"No." Nuri looked away.

"Whose, then?"

Nuri didn't answer right away. "Mine. He was a complete gentleman about it, fortunately, and surprisingly gentle. It was his proposition, but I thought the gravel might come in useful for paths. Or something."

"Oh." Mateo understood all too well what he meant. A brief flash of anger stung him. The thought of another man's flesh inside Nuri made his whole body hurt. How had he provided those services? On his knees, those pale green eyes looking up, wide and vulnerable? Or hands braced against a tree, his trousers around his ankles, his long dark hair swinging in rhythm with the thrusts, hiding his face altogether? Mateo scolded himself. He had no right to be offended, given his sexual duties in the monastery.

"You were somewhere far away on your fever journey at that point." Nuri's voice was tentative, pleading. He took Mateo's hand. "We had no idea whether you were going to wake up again." He touched Mateo's cheek, looking hopeful. "And I hadn't fallen in love with you yet. I wouldn't make a trade like that now."

Mateo drew him into his arms, kissing his hair. "No need to explain yourself to me. We've both survived by doing what we must, and sometimes it's not easy. I hadn't fallen in love with you yet, either. Hadn't even met you, or I'm sure I would have the moment I saw you."

Nuri burrowed against Mateo's chest. "You're not angry? I've made trades like that often enough to be called a whore. I probably deserve it."

Mateo kissed Nuri's hair again. "Nothing to be angry about. I've already told you about Father Xavier." Mateo slowly stroked along Nuri's spine. "And you know, without my many nights whoring myself to him, I wouldn't be here now. He sent me away to get rid of a whore he'd tired of, and now here we are in this wonderful place. How could I possibly object to being here with you? I'm happier here than I've ever been."

Nuri laughed against Mateo's chest. "Good."

Mateo held him tight, stunned by the truth of what he'd just said. The relic had promised to be his path to happiness, and here he was. Happier than he could have imagined. He kissed Nuri's hair with a contented sigh.

"Are you happy?" he asked, his face still buried in Nuri's hair.

"Yes. More than I've ever been. So happy."

They took care of the animals together, their contentment quiet and soft. When they came in for dinner, they found the table spread, but Zoya had eaten and gone. They ate, then put dinner away. They made tender love in their moonlit room. Still not ready for sleep, they lay face to face, touching, whispering.

Nuri drew a finger along one tendon of Mateo's throat. "You make me feel clean and new again. Thank you."

"You've made me new, too, you know. Saved my life, I'm pretty sure. Maybe we've saved each other."

"Mmm." Nuri turned, his back against Mateo's chest and snuggled in, pulling Mateo's arm around him and holding it under his own. "I like that version of our story." He pulled Mateo's arm tighter. "Let's keep it."

When their other chores finally allowed, Mateo and Nuri carried a load of gravel to the shrine and began working it into the existing stones, creating a more even surface for the flagstone mantel. Then Mateo dragged the thick slab over and wrestled it up onto the top of the cairn, shifting it different ways until they could see which placement was best.

"Let me lift it up again," Mateo said, "while you make sure the bed underneath it is still right." He took a deep breath, and grunted it out as he lifted.

Nuri poked a finger at something, then added a little more gravel. He nodded at Mateo. "Ready."

Mateo set it back in place with a huff. "It still wobbles. I'll lift it up again while you pack more gravel in at the back."

"Are you going to be able to hold it like that for a while? I'm not sure how long it will take."

"I can hold it. Most of the weight's on the cairn now. Take your time. It's important we get this right." Nuri filled, adjusted, and poked around. "Good." Mateo tilted his head toward the left. "Maybe some more there, too?"

Nuri thumbed beads of sweat from Mateo's face "I'll be as quick as I can. Aren't you getting tired?"

"I can manage."

Eventually, Nuri stood back and nodded. "I think you can let go now. The slab seems stable."

"Good. I could do with some shade and a drink of water."

They sat side by side against a tree trunk, holding hands, quiet and intimate, sharing a cup Nuri had fetched from the house and filled several times at the well.

When they returned to the cairn, Mateo studied where they'd left off, trying to figure out what they needed to do next. Nuri squatted down to look at the underside of the flagstone. "It looks like there's a large gap here. Does that matter?" He steadied himself against the edge of the shelf to get closer.

"Be careful," Mateo began. "If the hole is too large—"

Nuri's scream drowned out the sharp clack of tumbling stone.

"Nuri!" Mateo dashed over, fearing the worst. It was worse than the worst. The flagstone had settled directly on Nuri's fingers. Mateo lifted the slab away, and Nuri cried out again, his face pale and waxy, eyes glazed with pain. Two fingers were already swollen and turning dark. The thumb and first two fingers bent sideways at hideous angles.

Mateo helped him back to the tree where they'd just been sitting so peacefully. Nuri turned his head away. "Is it bad? I can't look. It's my playing hand. Oh, gods, it hurts."

"It's bad, I won't lie to you. The bones aren't right." Mateo kissed Nuri's temple. "I'll get Zoya."

"No," Nuri whimpered. "Don't leave me. You can heal me. You." His eyes darted back and forth, unfocused. "You want to be a healer," he gasped, with a horrible grin. "I'm your first supplicant at the shrine."

"But I don't—"

"Yes, you do. Call on your thing. Compass."

"What if I can't... Nuri, I'm afraid I won't—"

"Just say it out loud."

"Say what?"

"'I can heal you, Nuri.' Say the words out loud. You can. Oh, gods, it hurts."

Mateo took a deep breath, wrestling with doubt, banishing it for Nuri's sake. "I can heal you. Here, give me your hand." Mateo rested Nuri's hand in his. His lovely, elegant fingers were swollen as thick and purple as blood sausages. So much blood. He tried to think. Zoya had said something. He could find the lines of flow in someone's body. Where they might be tangled or blocked. Or broken. He turned inward, asking the relic for sight and guidance to heal.

His vision shifted. Yes, there were the lines, clear and whole in Nuri's arm and palm, dark and broken in the thumb and fingers. So many pieces. He opened himself and prayed with a desperation he'd never felt before. *Please use me to heal this man. Let these lines be restored to wholeness. Let the pieces fit again as they did this morning, nerve and bone, blood and tissue, so he can play again.*

Heat blossomed in his chest, and he groaned in wordless relief, grateful to feel the relic's answering power. It flowed down his arms, burned out of his eyes, streamed out on his breath, and poured into the wounded fingers. Nuri cried out and slumped against him, unconscious. Mateo knew it was a mercy.

The lines lit up with a different color, more yellow, and began to pulse and pull. Pulse. Pull. *May these lines be drawn back into wholeness. Let the pieces fit again as before—bone and blood, nerve and tissue. May his beautiful fingers be restored, agile, to play music again without pain or stiffness. Use me to this purpose, I pray.*

Chapter Nineteen

Concentrating on the line fragments in Nuri's hand with consuming ferocity, Mateo didn't notice Zoya's arrival until she was crouching beside him, her face grim.

"Let's get him into the house," she said. "Your bed."

Mateo gathered Nuri into his arms, got to his knees, and labored onto his feet. He looked at Zoya, feeling uncertain as his body screamed with Nuri's pain. "His thumb. Fingers." He said the words aloud, not because she couldn't see for herself, but because he was summoning courage to acknowledge the horror lurking behind the injury.

"I know," she said, her voice gentle. "I see you've already begun a healing. That's good." She put a reassuring hand on Mateo's shoulder. "To the house now."

Nuri squirmed in his arms. He whimpered but didn't wake. His forehead was dotted with sweat. Mateo wanted to hurry, but he was afraid he'd stumble. The path seemed impossibly long. Finally, they arranged Nuri on the bed and covered his legs with a blanket.

"Resume your healing," Zoya ordered. "He needs to sleep, especially through this worst part, realigning the bones."

"Can you take over? I have no idea if I'll do it right."

"No, you've already begun. It's yours to do. Follow your guidance. I'll help."

She hurried to the door, and Mateo shivered against a sudden fear. "Where are you going?"

"To get supplies. It's better if he doesn't wake up for a while. And he needs strength. I'll be but a moment."

Mateo watched her leave, feeling a rush of terror. What if something happened that he didn't know how to take care of? The vision of Nuri's beautiful hand caught between the rocks returned, and he squeezed his eyes shut as he remembered Nuri's scream. If only he had lifted the slab away fully... No. He knew he could get lost in the pain and remorse, but he refused. Nuri needed him present. He opened his eyes.

He put his hand to his chest and asked to see the lines again, and for healing. His chest heated, his vision shifted, and he *saw*.

The lines in the crushed fingers had dulled again. He could tell that wasn't good. He put one hand on Nuri's elbow, where the lines were bright and whole, and put his other at the tips of the damaged fingers. A fierce jolt of connection shot between his hands, making him wince. Nuri cried out, even though he was still unconscious. Mateo leaned over to kiss his shoulder and focused again on the broken, dull lines. A deep calm settled over him as the fire in his chest rose and flowed out again.

Pulse. Pull. Pulse. Pull. A slow, heavy swing developed, flowing into Nuri's right hand and seemingly traveling on beyond his shoulder, only to flow back down Nuri's arm and into Mateo's hand. Flowing out past his hand to who-knew-where before returning.

Connecting. Yes. Whatever was being connected was steady, and right. Alive. True. The fragmented lines brightened, and began to shimmer.

He wanted to talk to the lines. He stared at them as a question formed behind his eyes. *Are you willing to connect?*

Not yet, they said. *Give us more.*

Time?

More fire.

He reached to the relic. *The lines want more fire. Please let it come.* A surge came rushing, Mateo's hands felt like he'd set them on the kitchen stove. He refused to move. *As much as he needs.*

He lost himself in the effort to hold still and let the fire come.

Mateo heard Zoya come into the room, but he couldn't bring himself to look up.

"I brought some tea for us as well as remedies for Nuri," she said. "He's in shock, and it's better if he sleeps as long as possible. Just a few drops of this will do it."

"Good," Mateo whispered. "I'd help, but I can't stop what I'm doing. I don't think I could move my hands even if I wanted to."

"Don't try." She dragged a chair toward the bed and sat near Nuri's feet. "May I join you from here?"

"You know what he needs better than I do."

Zoya pulled out her stick, whispered something, and pointed it at her nephew. After a while, she nodded and returned the stick to her pocket. "I've never seen this kind of healing before." She got up from her chair. "I don't think you need my help. Not sure I know how I *would* help. Whatever you're doing is different from how I work, so I'll make you tea and give Nuri his drops."

It was hard for Mateo to concentrate on the flow between his hands while talking, but he had to ask. "But he's healing, isn't he?"

"Yes. Keep doing whatever it is you're doing. It's working. Do what you can."

Zoya nursed a half-dozen drops of a dark liquid between Nuri's lips, followed by a dribble of water. She held the mug of tea up for Mateo to take a few sips, patted his shoulder, and left.

In the quiet, Mateo turned his attention again to his burning hands. A thought came to him that his hands weren't what was important, so he looked for the pulse between them. It swelled and continued, as deep and sweet as slow music. He willed his vision to show him the light-lines in Nuri's hand. Still fragmented, but brighter, stronger. They seemed to shiver in response to the shifting pulse.

A quiet knowing rose in him. All he had to do was maintain the pulse, and the fragments would knit back together. Even as the knowledge came, one fragment shifted to connect with another, sparking as they joined. His heart lifted, and he breathed into the pulse, adding to its momentum.

Mateo had no idea how much time had passed before Zoya returned, although he could see it was still daylight. She put a tray on the table.

"Do you feel any progress?" she asked.

"Yes. The lines have begun to knit. Maybe the bones, but I'm not sure." Mateo didn't look up. "See what you think."

Zoya sat at Nuri's feet again and drew out her stick. A moment passed before she nodded. "This is moving quickly. Why don't you rest for a bit? It'd do you good."

"I can't. Not yet, anyway. Not until... I don't know. I think I have to wait for a sign that it's time to rest."

"I'll feed you, then. You need to keep up your strength if you're to help him." She returned to the table, and a soft clatter of pottery sounded behind him. A fork holding a piece of meat appeared in front of his face, and he opened his mouth.

She was right: he needed to eat. He chewed and swallowed. "Thank you. Oh, that's good. Maybe more?"

"Hmpf. As if I would stop at only one while you heal my Nuri. Well, our Nuri, now, I suppose. He belongs to you, too, now. I have water or tea for you after you've eaten what you want." She put another chunk in front of him. "You know, you'll have to take at least a nature break at some point."

"Not yet. Not until it feels safe to let go."

"That's well enough, but you have to trust, too. Don't fall into the trap of believing that the healing will fail if you don't constantly manage it. That's a dangerous kind of grandiosity. The healing comes through us, but the healing is greater and more important than the one it comes through."

She was right. Of course she was. He nodded slowly, feeling Zoya's wisdom all the way down his spine. He was an instrument, not the musician, and much less the music. He wouldn't be doing this at all if the relic hadn't taken him. "It still doesn't feel right to let go yet, though. I'll ask for guidance. I know I need plenty."

Zoya patted him on the shoulder again and left.

She returned after sunset to coax more of her drops between Nuri's lips. "No matter what, we'll have to let him wake up after this dose wears off."

"Do you think that's enough to keep him asleep through the night?"

"Easily. May I look again at his healing progress?"

Mateo stretched his neck sideways to make it pop. "Please. Tell me what you think."

She leaned against Mateo's shoulder, holding her stick above Nuri's hand. "This is good," she murmured. "Keep going. I'll come back later."

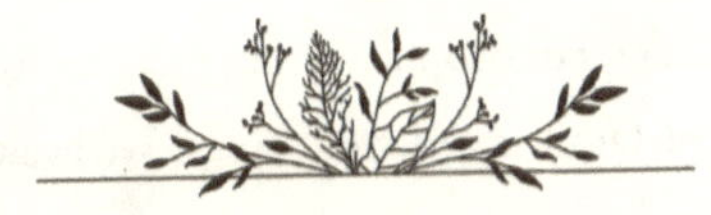

Mateo turned in his chair at a bird call outside and saw that the sky was getting light. His candle had burned out, but he hadn't noticed. Zoya came in and set a platter of bread and cheese on the table next to the dishes from yesterday.

"I see you ate something during the night," she said, picking up the empty plate. "I hope you got outside for some fresh air, too."

"I did, once." Mateo's arms were suddenly heavy, and his shoulders ached. He'd worked through the night. "Would you take another look? I have more hope now."

Zoya put down the plate and drew out her stick, pointing it at her nephew's hand. "This is remarkable. I've never seen bones knit this quickly." Zoya frowned as she put away her stick. "This is good, certainly for Nuri. It's very good. Far better than I had hoped, at first. But for you, there's a warning here, too."

"A warning?"

"I'll take these dishes back, then we'll talk outside."

Mateo stroked Nuri's brow. He seemed deeply asleep. but he still felt hesitant to leave him. No clammy sweat. Skin warm, but not fever-hot. Perhaps this was a good time to rest a little. Mateo stood, stretched, and stepped outside, waiting for Zoya to return. The pre-dawn air, cool and fresh, so soft, enveloped him like a prayer.

Zoya returned, offering Mateo a cup. "Drink this. Not all at once. It's a restorative, so just sips."

Mateo sipped. "You said there was a warning here for me."

"The power moving through you in this healing is astonishing. Dramatic. You need to be careful with it," she said, nodding slowly. "Dramatic healings become dangerous when they draw too much attention to the healer. For people without imagination, such healings seem to disturb the familiar order of things. We healers must learn a particular modesty. For our own safety. A disguise, if you like."

"People would be ungrateful for such a healing?"

"Not the recipient of the healing, necessarily. But others can take offense or become afraid of what happened. Look no further than the stories of your old church. Miracle workers usually got killed."

"So I should do less?"

"No, that would be a betrayal of what's been entrusted to you. But always remember you can't promise outcome. Be grateful for even the smallest change. Just find a way to avoid notoriety as much as you can. Be alert. You'll find the right way."

Mateo stared at the garden, its colors still muted in the pre-dawn light. This was a complication he could never have imagined. Then again, he'd never imagined the relic would be part of his body, or that the relic's power might be able to heal Nuri.

"I'm not the least interested in fame. The idea makes my stomach sour."

"But you're not the problem. Those you heal might cause trouble inadvertently. You'll still have to caution them."

"How can someone hide the fact they've been healed?"

Zoya shook her head. "Not hide. But be discreet. You'll have to start with Nuri, or he might compose a song about you and perform it in the town square. His enthusiasm is charming, but in this case, it might pose a terrible danger to us." She turned to face Mateo, her eyes hard and knowing. "This is for my protection, too, you know. You both can leave this place. I can't. So long as you are here—and I hope you stay a long time—my fate is joined to yours. Maybe even after you leave. These events can bear fruit over and over."

This was a staggering new responsibility. Being bound to the safety of others overwhelmed him, but it felt right. "I'll talk to Nuri, but I think you should, too."

"Why?"

"He'll listen to your advice more readily, I think. You know him better. You're his aunt."

Zoya stared at Mateo for a moment with her lips pursed. "I know him well enough to know he's given away his heart, possibly for the first time in his life. He's made you its keeper. You'd best be kind to it. The worst you could do to him is pretend he hasn't given you his whole heart." She turned away, stopped, looked back at him as if she was going to say more, then limped on toward the house.

Mateo stood motionless in the strengthening light. He knew Nuri loved him, and he knew he loved Nuri. But he hadn't thought more of what that meant. This weight of responsibility was the weight of belonging. It was a good weight. It felt right on his shoulders, in his heart. He was part of a real family now—not like his parents and siblings, who thought nothing of him except whether he brought in money. Not like the monastery where he belonged as long as he did what he was told. He belonged to Nuri and Zoya as surely as they belonged to him: distinct, connected, needing each other.

But it was more even than that. He belonged to the very ground he stood on, and the rivers of energy flowing below its surface. He knelt, putting his hands in the cool dirt of the garden path, surrendering his old separateness, surrendering to his new belonging, weeping in gratitude at the exquisite bond.

Chapter Twenty

Nuri woke before noon, asking for help to the chamber pot, and laughing with Mateo about the reversal of their roles.

Mateo got him settled again, made him drink some water, and resumed his healing work. Zoya arrived to give Nuri a red-tinted tea to drink, promising him broth later, but no solid food until tomorrow.

Nuri lifted his good hand to Mateo's head. "Do you mind me stroking your hair while you work on me?"

Mateo leaned down for a kiss. "Not at all." He rested his elbows on his knees, hunched over Nuri's arm, following the pulse and pull of the healing. "It feels good."

"Feels good to me, too. Like I'm helping."

Mateo lifted his head to smile. "I'm sure you are."

"Will I be able to play again?" Nuri's whisper was soft as a little rabbit and cautious, as if he braced against the worst news.

"I think so, but I don't know." Mateo had to say more. "I don't know much of anything, but that's my hope."

Nuri fell silent, and Mateo returned his concentration to the slow pulse of energy.

After a while, Nuri spoke again, low but full of certainty. "If you say I will, then I will. But you have to say it aloud."

"How do you know that?"

"I just know. I think it's the way your magic works."

Mateo grunted, not believing. "If there's any magic at work here, it's the relic's doing."

"How can you not see?" Nuri cuffed him gently on the side of the head. "I dare you to separate the relic from your body. You can't, and you know it. You are one thing now, and its magic is yours as much as you belong to the relic."

Mateo put his hand over the knot of scar on his chest, stunned. He'd always thought of the relic as a separate thing. What Nuri said was true in some way he hadn't come to on his own. He stared at his lover, whose certainty and enthusiasm blazed in his eyes like a torch.

"Somehow, your magic has to be put into words for it to work," Nuri said with a shiver. "I have to say it, and then you repeat it, agreeing. Then it happens."

Mateo wanted to agree, then to deny, but couldn't form any words at all. He was on the threshold of something important. Nothing would be the same after he crossed it. Again he felt the call to be bound, to make some deeper promise to the thing in his chest. The relic's magic—the magic—his magic—was waiting for his agreement. A contract he would never be able to revoke.

Mateo adjusted his hands to find a clearer pulse between Nuri's fingers and elbow, then sank his attention into the comforting rhythm. "You believe in me too much."

"I'll believe in your magic enough for both of us until you can believe in it yourself. More than enough. You've been taken by it. You can't escape it. You carry it now. I've seen it. It's easy for me to believe what I can see so clearly."

Mateo's chest heated and sweat prickled his skin. The relic—the magic—demanded his answer right now. This was real, and terrifying. If he said yes, he would become an agent of power he didn't understand and certainly couldn't control. If he said no, Nuri might never play again.

Love made the choice for him. "Very well," he murmured, knowing he was putting his new name on the contract. "Say the words."

Nuri beamed at him, then spoke slowly, with meticulous diction. "With this healing, I will be able to play my music just as well as I could before."

Mateo swallowed hard and looked into Nuri's eyes. "With this healing, you will be able to play your music just as well as you could before."

The heat in his chest exploded, and he cried out in pain and surprise. He knew instinctively he mustn't resist, so he let go, opening himself to it. A searing fire flowed outward from his chest, into his shoulders, down his arms, through his fingers, and into Nuri's damaged hand. A cloud of swirling color rose from it, hiding the bandages from sight. Mateo's hands burned. He wanted to pull away, but he knew he couldn't.

Nuri groaned and began to pant. "Oh, gods. Oh, gods. Oh, gods. It hurts so much, but it's... I don't—" he whimpered and fell back against the wall behind him, unconscious.

Mateo forced himself to breathe in deep, even breaths. He could concentrate on that instead of the screaming pain in his hands.

After what seemed like a long time, something shifted, like a change in the wind at the end of a storm. The furnace in his chest cooled first, then in his shoulders and arms, and finally in his hands. The cloud of colors evaporated. He wiped his forehead and leaned forward on his knees, breathing deep and slow to gather himself.

Zoya burst in and frowned at Nuri slumped against the wall, then looked at Mateo with worry in her eyes. "What happened? I felt a surge of something powerful."

"Either a miraculous healing has taken place or I'm an even bigger fool than I thought. Would you unwrap his bandages? I'm not brave enough to find out for myself which it is."

While Zoya put a pillow behind Nuri's head and carefully unwrapped the bandages, Mateo told her about Nuri's belief in how the relic's magic worked, the feeling of forging a contract with it, and the painful intensity that followed.

Zoya drew the last of the bandages away from Nuri's hand. His elegant long fingers were slender and straight again—no swelling, discoloration, or a single visible trace of the injury remained. With slow, gentle pressures, she curled and straightened Nuri's fingers and thumb, testing the mobility of his knuckles and palm.

A terrible weight fell from Mateo's shoulders. He slumped back, bathed in a flood of relief.

She lowered Nuri's hand to his lap and turned to Mateo, her gaze impassive. "This healing is complete. Perfect. I've never seen anything like it. No scars, even. I dared not hope for half of this."

"It's a miracle." Mateo bowed his head and pressed his hands to the lump on his chest in relief and gratitude. "The relic..." He stopped, remembering the new contract. "It's a marvelous healing."

"Yes." Zoya stroked Nuri's sweat-damp hair from his face. "Let him sleep now. He'll wake soon enough." She stood, looking worried. "Now more than ever, you must be careful with this power," she said firmly. "We'll both have to talk to Nuri to make sure he understands how dangerous miracles can be for the one who channels them."

"Believe me," Mateo said with a grim smile. "I know how trouble can grow from good intentions."

"It's not just good intentions. A lot of folks, including in your old church, are afraid of anything they can't control. Some would rather burn you at the stake than have your healings available to anyone who

asked for them, then claim you as a saint once you were safely dead."
She pointed at Mateo's chest. "All the nonsense you told me about
whether the relic was authentic proves it."

She turned toward the door. "Come to the house. You probably
need to eat something, and we need to talk more."

"I... I'll be there in a moment." He had to watch Nuri for a little
longer in case he awoke confused or in pain. Or perhaps just because
he couldn't bear to leave him yet.

Zoya said nothing as she left, but didn't close the door behind her.

Mateo eased himself onto the bed beside Nuri, stretched out, and
kissed the side of his head. He closed his eyes and let go in another wave
of relief and thanks and tears. His Nuri would make music again. He
touched the scars on his chest, letting out a wordless groan. The relic
had used him to perform a miracle.

A vision came. He stood on some kind of raft or boat, looking at
a receding shore. Everything he'd done, or been, was back there. He
could barely feel it. He turned to look in the direction his raft was
headed. The distant shore wasn't clear, but it was a different place.
He knew that much, even though he didn't know much else. He
knew Nuri and Zoya were there waiting for him and that they would
welcome him ashore. Whatever his journey was, it was taking him in a
good direction.

Zoya was still seated at the table with bread, cheese, and a bowl of
pickled carrots laid out when Mateo came in. Although her plate was
already empty, she held a steaming cup of tea in both hands. She

looked up as Mateo sat, gave her a tremulous smile, and reached for the bread.

"You've been crying. That's good."

"Is it?"

"After such an intense healing and especially for you, yes. Very good."

Mateo carefully cut a thick slice of cheese and spooned pickled carrots and onions onto his plate. "Especially me." He was too empty, too calm to argue, and he knew Zoya had more to say.

"That night at the spring, you startled at my suggestion that you could be intimate with the life around you, giving and taking."

"That's when I was still Magnus. I'm a completely different person now."

"That is true. But there's a difference between intimacy with the glory of magic, and the mystery of being connected deeply to another person. You need both to keep you grounded, balanced. For a while, at least. You have the glory of magic at the moment. But I don't think you have much experience in giving and taking with respect, with love." She shrugged, and took a sip of tea, giving Mateo a hard look over the cup. "I could be wrong."

He shook his head, unable to stop a smile at her invitation to deny it. "No, you're not wrong." He paused, reaching for what he knew he had to say. "But I'm learning. I feel clumsy. First time I've been fond of anyone in a long time. But this... this is different. What I feel for him... I've never felt it before. He knows me, maybe better than I know myself. I'm beginning to know him." He blew out a breath. "It's wonderful, and frightening at the same time."

Zoya nodded and put down her cup. "Good. I'm glad. You need each other." She drew out her stick, turning it slowly in her hand. "So now we must talk about how to stay as unremarkable as possible in the midst of the glory of your magic, so you can protect those you love as well as yourself. We didn't get very far earlier."

From outside came music—Nuri's voice and guitar, notes glittering as bright as a fountain in sunlight. With a joyful shout, Mateo leapt to his feet and rushed out to meet him, with Zoya close behind.

Nuri beamed at them through his singing, his fingers dancing over the frets as the melody lifted and fell. He ended with a dramatic flourish and laughed, wild, drunk. He locked eyes with Mateo. "I can play again! Your magic healed me, just as I said it could."

All through dinner, Nuri would pause from eating and lift his hand into the light of the candle, turning his wrist, spreading his fingers, touching their tips to his thumb, and studying the movement with child-like happiness. Then he would reach across the table and stroke Mateo's face, or draw circles on the table top.

Mateo shared in Nuri's joy without saying much of anything, content just to be included. It seemed Zoya did, too—smiling when Nuri did, nodding gently in understanding whenever he laughed or wiped a tear from his eye.

After they had eaten and cleaned up, Nuri tapped Mateo on the shoulder. "Walk with me?"

"Of course."

Once they were outside, Nuri laced his fingers through Mateo's and laughed. He lifted their joined hands and squeezed. "I laugh because I can do this. First thing on our walk is to visit the shrine."

"Are you sure?" Mateo drew him into his arms.

"Why would I not want to? We're going to finish it." Nuri nuzzled into Mateo's chest. "Perhaps more carefully now, but we still have to finish what we started. Together."

Even in the soft evening light, Mateo could see the dark stains of Nuri's blood on the rocks of the shrine. "I'll wash those stones tomorrow," he said.

"No." Nuri's voice was firm. "I want my blood to be part of what we've built. Let the weather wash away what it will, but some will remain in the hidden places. As long as the shrine stands. I want that."

Mateo shivered at the power of Nuri's words. "Yes."

They stood together in silence as the evening darkened, and bats darted in their ragged patterns against the purple sky.

By the time they strolled into the herb garden in front of the house, still hand in hand, a waxing moon had risen, bathing the plants and paths in pale silver.

"They're happy for us," Nuri said. "They're happy we're here with them. I can feel it."

Mateo nodded, finally surrendering to the fatigue he'd resisted before. He lifted Nuri's hand to his lips. "Yes," he whispered over the knuckles. "I wish I could stay longer, but I'm about to fall asleep standing up. Come to bed when you're ready."

"I'm ready now. I've been selfish. It's my turn to take care of you."

"Again."

"Yes, again. But this is different. It will always be my turn now. I like that."

In the morning, their lovemaking was gentle, full of tender playfulness, a quiet celebration. Afterward, Nuri burrowed into Mateo's side, resting his cheek on Mateo's shoulder and drawing slow circles around the scars on his chest with a restored finger.

Mateo kissed the top of Nuri's head. "You're thinking about something."

"About my good fortune. I'm a little afraid of what that might mean."

Mateo stopped breathing, suddenly wary. "What might it mean?"

"I don't know, except I promise to be circumspect about your magic in public, like Zoya asked. More like feelings. So I get to tell you how I feel right now. You've given me my music back, which is my life. I will never forget." Nuri pulled Mateo's arm around him tighter, lacing their fingers together on his hip. "I'm yours now. For as long as I live."

This was what Zoya was talking about—the mystery of deep connection, both wonderful and frightening. She was right. It was a huge unknown. Mateo lifted their joined hands to his lips. "I belong to you, too."

Nuri made a little humming sound. "Not in the same way, though. Which is why I'm afraid. You belong to your magic first. I can tell."

"But—"

"No." Nuri put their joined fingers against Mateo's lips again. "I understand. I don't mind, even though I'm afraid. I'm willing to share you with your magic for as long as I can, but your magic might well take you away one day, in a future we can't see."

Mateo didn't know what to say, didn't even want to think of the possibility.

"You're squeezing my fingers too hard," Nuri said with laughter in his voice. "We know it's not going to happen tomorrow. And maybe it won't ever. If it does, I'll try to let you go gracefully, but until then, I want us to be inseparable."

For a long time, Mateo stared at the ceiling, already aching at an unknown possibility. "I want us to be inseparable, too," he murmured. "I belong with you."

But Nuri had dozed off. He kissed the top of Nuri's head again, and returned to gazing at the ceiling. His eye caught the stick wedged in the plaster above him, where he'd hung the relic every night, back before... before so much. It no longer served any purpose there. It belonged outside again. He'd take care of it when they got up.

Chapter Twenty-One

"It's beautiful." Nuri leaned his head and back against Mateo's chest, and drew his arms around him. "It feels like our altar has always been here. So simple."

Mateo smiled against Nuri's ear. "It's certainly simple," he said. "No one will accuse us of sophisticated stonework. I was going to say it was kind of ugly, but would serve our purpose anyway."

"Not true!" Nuri reached back to swat Mateo's thigh. "I won't let you say that. Imagine coming across this in the middle of the forest. An altar set among the trees, covered with vines, with shafts of sunlight slanting down through the branches. What a mystery! A crude altar, yes, but so powerful, so alive. Who or what does it serve here in this hidden green sanctuary? What offering should be placed reverently upon it? A poet could stand here all day, entranced."

"That's a beautiful vision, to be sure, but you make this seem like more than it is."

Nuri pursed his lips and made a farting noise. "Open your eyes, love. Look! What part of that vision is not true? Well, the vines have yet to grow, but we can plant them tomorrow. Look how the trees welcome it, cradling it. Listen to all the life around it. See how the sunlight floods down on it through the branches. Feel how our intention and sweat, even our blood and pain, have transformed a pile of rocks into an altar to nature, to healing. It's magic."

He pulled away and turned to face Mateo. "Now you have to say it. It's beautiful, and perfect for us."

Mateo laughed softly. "You're right. I lost sight of all that. It *is* beautiful."

"And perfect for us."

"Yes. And perfect for us." The knotted scar on Mateo's chest burned in agreement, its heat flowering out and down his legs and feet, into the ground. "I needed to be reminded."

"Good. Let's find Zoya and show her what we've made."

Mateo stood quietly while Nuri showed Zoya every detail of their work with child-like enthusiasm. Why did he not feel the same? Something in him resisted and didn't want to acknowledge the importance of what they'd done, but the relic's knot in his chest thrummed happily.

"And then we'll plant vines around it, making it truly belong. Won't that look beautiful?" Nuri crowed, crouching by the corner of the altar, running a finger through the dirt.

"It's good. Very good," Zoya said, smiling, although her voice cracked. Mateo glanced at her in surprise. Was she about to cry? She took Nuri's hand, making him stand up, and beckoned to Mateo. When he approached, she grabbed his hand, too, pulling them both to her chest. "This changes things. Soon, all three of us will belong to this place, not just me."

Mateo watched Midnight strut back and forth across the stone slab, his feathers iridescent in the sunlight. Why did he feel unsettled? What did she mean, soon? He was already happier, more connected here than anywhere else he could remember. "But not yet?"

"Now, too, but it's a growing thing," Zoya said. "Not yet finished." She squeezed his hand. "What you love is where you belong."

Mateo glanced at Nuri, surprised to see tears streaking down his face. He loved Nuri. He knew they belonged to each other. But she'd also meant the land—its life and its magic. And Zoya herself. Hadn't he already found the place he belonged? Did he dare admit there was more work to do, that his belonging wasn't yet complete? What he loved is where he belonged. What he loved was here, but Zoya said it was not yet complete. "I do feel that growing," he said cautiously.

Zoya nodded, still clutching their hands more firmly against her chest. "I know you do. All in good time."

Her warmth evaporated as she dropped their hands and turned. "Now we need to talk about the tax collector. He'll be visiting soon with his soldiers. We should take a walk around, looking at it through his eyes."

Mateo frowned, looking toward the garden. Their garden. His garden. "How much will he take?"

Zoya's answer came hard and flat. "As much or as little as he wants."

Standing at the head of the rows, where he stood a dozen times every day, Mateo tried to look with a stranger's eyes. It was going to be a good crop. For the first time, instead of his usual quiet satisfaction, he felt uneasy about how good everything looked. He scratched the back of his neck. The long rows were clear of weeds, and the plants looked vigorous, promising abundance. Had they worked too hard? He looked at Zoya, full of the dangerous question.

"Now you understand why I wasn't as eager as you were to repair everything right away and make things look pretty," she said.

"I'm so sorry—" he began, but Zoya stopped him.

"It will be alright. They might take more than is fair, but we'll manage. It's in their best interest if we don't starve. They'd get nothing at all next year if we did. Unless someone took the land, of course. But every new moon, I cast to protect this place from being coveted."

Mateo winced. He'd repaired things to show his love for the place. His gratitude. Why did he not see these things for himself? He knew he wasn't stupid, but he also knew he lacked Nuri's agile imagination. It must be that he was still terribly naïve. Or a coward. Sometimes, it felt safer to not see, to not know, to not think. But now he saw it as a false safety. He had to expand the circle of his thinking somehow. He'd ask Nuri to help.

When they reached the hen house and the rabbit hutches, he smiled, relieved, at how crude his repairs had been. He'd leave them that way for as long as he could.

"They usually take a fifth to a third of what we have," Zoya said, leaning heavily on her stick. "They'll come through and make a list of what we have to give them. Then they'll come back a few days later with wagons, expecting that we'll have everything ready for them to take away."

"We don't have to kill and dress the animals, do we?" Nuri asked. Mateo smiled. His clever Nuri always thought ahead.

Zoya shook her head. "No, they'll want them all alive, and they'll butcher them as needed over the winter. They used to make us take care of the animals until they wanted them, but I think it became too difficult to keep track of what they were owed. The paint didn't always last through the winter."

"What paint?" asked Mateo, confused.

"They'll decide not only how many animals, but which ones," Zoya said. "The best, of course. They mark their choices with a daub of paint. Usually red. They'll collect soon after, while the paint is fresh."

Mateo bit his lip to keep from complaining. Some kind of tithe was appropriate, but it was unfair for them to take the best of everything, as if they worked first for the general, and only after for themselves. It wasn't just.

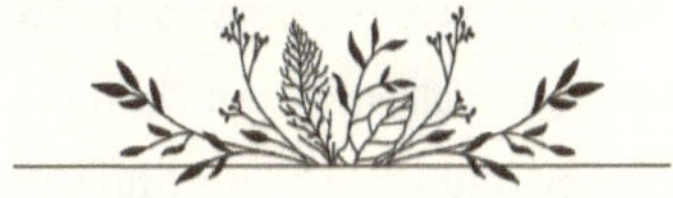

That night, as they lay in bed, bathed in moonlight. Mateo lay on his back, with Nuri curled into his side. He slowly stroked Nuri's long hair, feeling like he was running around in circles in his head.

"You're not sleepy, are you? You stare at the ceiling, which isn't really that interesting. Do you want to make love?" Nuri asked, sliding a thigh over Mateo's leg.

"No. My head is too noisy, and I can't stop it."

"What are you thinking about?"

Mateo sighed and turned his head to kiss Nuri's forehead. "What Zoya said about the farm repairs and the message they might give the tax collector."

Nuri snuggled in closer, waiting. Their tranquil silence stretched on. An owl hooted, answered by another.

Eventually Mateo sighed and rubbed his forehead. "As soon as she said why she hadn't been eager to make the farm look too good, I knew exactly why. But I should have thought of that myself. I hadn't, and I'm angry I hadn't. I just wanted to make the place look beautiful. Loved and cared for. My idea of beautiful. I didn't think once about what that might mean to others, or that danger could inhabit my versions of love and beauty."

"Do you—" Nuri started, but Mateo cut him off with a kiss.

"I need to hear what you have to say, but I've got to get the rest of this out first." He dug around for the right words. "At San Fortunatus, we had a saying: that work was love made manifest. I liked that a lot. I even believed it. I still do, I think. But what should love made manifest look like? I just accepted that everything should be perfectly clean and in perfect repair, as if that were the proof of perfect love. The circle of my vision has been too small, and I seem blind to anything beyond it. I need to think larger, and I don't know how to do that. It's as if something in me doesn't want to see or know. What I do know is that I'm tired of being so stupid."

Nuri bit Mateo's shoulder. Gently, but firm enough to make Mateo yelp in surprise. "You're not stupid. Not by a country mile. Let me puzzle this for a bit."

Mateo went back to staring at the ceiling. It had been plastered with casual sloppiness. He stifled a laugh. In spite of what he'd just told Nuri, here he was, still wanting to make everything look good. For what, or for who? For himself? No, he didn't need it. That was just a cover for pleasing others. Even so, he'd get to fixing that eventually. He'd have to.

"Very well." Nuri kissed the shoulder he'd bitten a moment ago. "First, you're not stupid. You're not allowed to say that again in my hearing. Agreed?"

"I'll do my best."

"Fair. I think your habit goes deep." He tapped Mateo's side. "Look at me so I'll know you hear. You want to do good. Always. It's one of the many things I love about you." He fell silent for a while. "But maybe you've wanted that too much—to be good. Maybe you've simply accepted what other people used as a measure of being good instead of developing your own. Maybe you want to pretend everyone else wants to be good, too—as much as you do, when so many people just don't. Maybe you don't want to think about what people who don't care about being good might do when they take what they want. Or at least try to take it. Maybe you want to trust too much. You believe what people say too easily. That's partly admirable, but it can also be as dangerous to not see as to see."

"Ugh. Zoya's scolded me for that, too," Mateo murmured. He took a deep breath and blew it out toward the messy ceiling. "It stings to hear, but it feels true, too. I've been a child. My head shuts down, somehow. What can I do?"

"It might be something to do with your imagination. Ask your magic. It chose you, so I think it will guide you, too."

"I like that," Mateo said. "Giving my imagination more room. And you're right. I should have thought of asking the relic myself. Thank you."

Nuri kissed Mateo's bite-marked shoulder, snuggled closer, and slipped away into sleep as if he hadn't just peeled away his confusion and laid bare his greatest weakness. And then suggested a way to grow stronger.

Mateo focused on the rhythmic puff of Nuri's breath against his skin, overcome with a flood of affection. Nuri was a miracle. In spite of having led a life without the stability Mateo craved, he was happy. He was wise and quick and free in a way that enchanted Mateo even when he didn't really understand.

He rubbed the knot of scar on his chest and stared at the ceiling. "Please guide me to wise imagination," he murmured. "To see and understand how to be in the world, without becoming cold and cunning like Father Xavier or General Tun."

As if it had been waiting for his words, the relic's fire flowered outward in his chest, filling him, roiling in his belly, and then shooting out through his arms and legs until his toes burned and his lips tingled. Something inside him was burning away like old dry pine needles thrown on a fire. The fire faded, but for a long time, the air around him seemed to sparkle.

When sleep finally took him, his body had become as quick and light as a bird. He dreamt of being the wind it rode.

When Mateo woke, earthbound again but content, Nuri was already gone. He squinted out the window at the angle of the sun. He'd slept much longer than usual. To his surprise, the usual shaming whisper telling him he was lazy never came. He thought about that for a moment. It was gone. That felt important. He liked the secret space in his chest where that whisper used to sit, nestled just behind his heart. Now, it was open space.

All morning, as he cleaned out pens and fed and watered the animals, he felt his new secret space—this bright-shining gift from the relic—fill and overflow like a pond teeming with minnows, playful and free. With every thing he noticed around him, some detail became a minnow, a surprise flashing in the sun, darting with intent he couldn't track before another caught his attention. They seemed to be flashes of curiosity, or the idea behind a thought, carefree and transient—not needing to be permanent, not needing to even be important at all. Each one made him smile.

What did Zoya's protective spells cast over the property actually do? Were the clouds trying to tell him something? Would Nuri like their room if he could paint a wall the color of that butterfly? There were answers somewhere beyond the bright minnows. He could feel them even if he couldn't find them yet. But the minnows themselves were fun. He didn't need to go chasing after the answers.

Never had he been so interested in things he seldom noticed. He'd taken so many things for granted as solid and unchanging, but one could change in a moment, even if only in the way he looked at it. Better yet, he felt lighter for being so playful, and not embarrassed at all for it. He was having fun. It was a strange experience.

By the time Nuri shouted to him to come in for lunch, Mateo's mind was galloping. As he recounted his experiences while they ate, Nuri laughed with him often, as if he usually did these things. Perhaps he had. If so, Mateo was unspeakably happy for him.

"This sounds a lot like what you've told me about your journey when the relic chose you," Nuri mused. "But this time, you are conscious and not close to dying."

"I hadn't thought of that," Mateo said as he crunched on another pickled radish. "It does feel similar. Happier, though. More fun."

The afternoon flew by in moments of humor and wonder as well as sweat. At the monastery, labor was undertaken in piety and meditative silence. Laughing felt like sweet rebellion, and he reveled in it.

As he and Nuri were cleaning up, Zoya dug some coins out of her pouch and handed them to Nuri. "Tomorrow at market, I want the two of you to buy us a ewe lamb. Nothing older than a hogget. We can't barter for it, as farmers already have most of what we offer. Make sure it's healthy. There's word of a coughing sickness that's spreading. Be cautious, and don't pay too much."

Nuri laughed. "Why give me the money? I don't even know what a hogget is, let alone how to buy one."

Zoya closed his hand around the coins. "That's why I'm sending you both. You're the better haggler, and Mateo has a better feel for what to look for in the animal."

"A hogget is just a lamb between its first and second shearing," Mateo said, pulling Nuri into his side and planting a kiss on the top of his head. "It's a northern word, I think. At the monastery, we called them shearlings."

Nuri's eyes danced. "This will be an adventure. I've never haggled for a hogget before."

"Won't buying one now increase what the taxman takes?" Mateo asked.

Zoya's eyes sparkled as she clapped her hands. "Very good! You're learning!" She nodded. "It might, but I don't think so. Every farmer in the area is thinking the same thing, so now is the best time to buy at a good price."

Mateo smiled to himself. He was learning, and Zoya noticed. He could feel himself blush, but he didn't care.

Chapter
Twenty-Two

Before the sun rose the following morning, Mateo and Nuri loaded up the cart with produce, rabbit hides, and chickens, then headed out with Zoya toward town.

The market filled quickly, and Zoya had constant customers for cures and charms as well as for their piles of carrots, cabbage, potatoes, and onions. Quickest to go were the rabbit hides and chickens. During their first lull in trade, Zoya sent Nuri and Mateo off to look for a ewe lamb.

As they were leaving the square for where the larger livestock was on offer, a squad of General Tun's soldiers pulled an old man from his stall where he'd been selling pottery. He cried out for help as they marched him away, but no one protested or even acted as if something unusual was happening at all. Most of the vendors around him didn't even lift their eyes from their goods. Those who did looked away quickly.

Mateo looked around in shock. What had the old man done to deserve this? Several groups of soldiers were patrolling the square, swaggering as if to remind everyone how order was maintained. He must have noticed, but he hadn't given it much thought. His circle of awareness had been far too small.

"There are more soldiers here today," he murmured to Nuri.

Without looking at him, Nuri shook his head and fiddled with his belt. "It's nearly tax time," he muttered to his clothing. "You weren't here last year. The general is flexing his muscles. I doubt the old man the soldiers dragged away really did anything wrong. They pick a target to make a show, bully their victim a little, maybe give him a bruise or two, and let him go. If he's lucky."

"That's hideous," Mateo angrily whispered back.

Nuri stopped Mateo from saying more by grabbing his arm. "I'm glad you noticed the soldiers, but did you also see how other folks pretended not to see what happened? This is how it is here. Why do you think Zoya told you to look unremarkable after that day you helped the girl and her cow? We were lucky. Drawing the notice of the general's men when they're strutting around the market can be very, very dangerous."

"Oh." How foolish he'd been to think Zoya had just scolded him for just helping the girl. With what he'd thought of as a good deed, he'd risked Zoya's wellbeing as well as his own. "I think I finally understand now." But understanding made him even angrier. It shouldn't be this way. It was completely unjust.

They spoke with three different farmers, but only the last one had lambs.

The farmer pulled one out of his makeshift pen, and Nuri began to negotiate the price. The farmer slapped the animal's haunches, declaring the animal's conformation was perfect and that it deserved a high price, since it would be able to give birth to many lambs. The creature broke into a series of wheezing coughs. Mateo put up his hand.

"This animal is sick," he said sternly. "Has it got the coughing sickness?"

"Nothing's wrong with it," the farmer protested, deftly wiping away green mucus from the lamb's snout with his thumb. His face became a lizard's. His cheeks and throat turned an angry scarlet, and a lipless mouth parted to show rows of tiny teeth. "It's in perfect health. All my animals are."

Mateo heated at the obvious lie. "You're trying to sell us a sick animal that might bring disease to our farm." He put his hand on Nuri's forearm. "We're not taking this one."

For an instant, something ugly glinted behind the farmer's eyes, then disappeared. He looked around, his gaze landing on a group of soldiers nearby. "Are you accusing me of fraud?" He shouted, sending his words more to the soldiers than to Mateo. "I'm just a poor farmer struggling to make an honest living. You have no right!"

Before Mateo could respond, the soldiers had gathered around. "What have we here?" the largest of them demanded. "What seems to be the trouble?"

"This man slanders me," the farmer sputtered, his outrage too dramatic to be real. "He snatches bread from my table, claiming this animal is not worth my humble price."

"That's not true, sir," Mateo replied. He turned to the soldier. "He's asking too much for a sick animal."

The soldier gazed thoughtfully at Mateo, his brow furrowed. "You look familiar," he said. "Where have I seen you before?"

The relic jolted in his chest—a warning. "I'm sure you have not," Mateo said quickly, looking down and away. He caught sight of the soldier's forearm hanging by the hilt of his sword. It had been broken and poorly set, healing at an awkward angle. His blood ran cold in recognition. This was the soldier whose arm General Tun had ordered broken to test whether the Lord Abbot's gift had healing powers.

Mateo lifted his hands in surrender. "We mean no trouble. I was only attempting to negotiate. We'll take the animal at his asking price."

"I always tell the truth," the farmer claimed. His triumphant lizard smirk told Mateo he was proud of his lie, a game he played often. "I'm known for it."

Heat flowered in Mateo's chest. The relic was reminding him of something... of how Nuri showed him how his magic worked better when his hand had been crushed. How Nuri had insisted that Mateo had to repeat aloud Nuri's claim that he'd be able to play again.

Mateo gave the farmer a tight smile. This man was about to regret his lies. "Yes. You always tell the truth." The fire spreading through his body seemed to flow out to the farmer, into his mouth, and vanish. The farmer twitched and for a moment looked confused before holding out his hand for payment.

The big soldier stepped closer to Mateo, crowding him, vibrating with menace. His breath stank. "I'm certain I've seen you before, but I can't place you. I will, though, as I think on it." He nodded as if agreeing with himself. "In the meantime, you should know that this man is my cousin. To insult him is to insult me and our clan. Have a care."

"I will, sir. Thank you, sir." Mateo looked to Nuri, who was already dropping coins into the farmer's hand. "We'll take our purchase and be on our way."

As they led the lamb back to the square, Nuri looked over at Mateo. "That soldier did recognize you, didn't he? That's why you changed your tune so quickly, isn't it?"

"Yes. Zoya needs to know, too, so let me tell you both at the same time. We may have a problem."

Nuri gave him a grim nod. "I'll go on ahead and let her know trouble is afoot."

"So," Zoya said as Mateo tied the lamb's lead to the wheel of their cart. "What happened?"

"It seems so long ago. A different life, when I was a monk. Magnus." He let out a breath that he felt he'd held in for far too long. "That life seems to have returned."

Mateo recounted his assignment to deliver the relic to General Tun and the deceit surrounding it; described the general's scorn, ordering the soldier's arm broken as a test of the relic's power; and its terrible silence when he prayed to it for help. It was a relief to tell them how he'd been thrown from the tower and been saved by the relic, how he'd resolved to follow the relic's guidance as the compass to his new life, and how it had led him to Zoya.

"That soldier was the one whose arm was broken for the general's test," Mateo concluded, grateful that Nuri had slipped a hand into his as he spoke. He gave it a little squeeze. "I hope he won't remember me, as I look different. I was terribly thin then from little food and hard travel, and I was dressed in the monastery's habit. I had long hair and a wild beard. But he felt something, and I knew I had to tell you."

Zoya didn't say anything for a while. "Your talisman didn't want its magic to go to the general. It chose you instead. That's very much in our favor." Another long silence ensued.

"I'm thinking I should leave the market early today so I'm not around to help him remember," Mateo said. "Maybe take the lamb back to the farm now. It's not well enough to walk, but I can carry it."

Zoya looked up, smiling at him. "Excellent idea. You're beginning to think more about the world around you." She looked away, pursed her lips, and scowled. "Very good."

At first, the lamb struggled against being carried in Mateo's arms, but it gradually quieted as he sang little songs to it. Eventually, it gave a pathetic bleat and went limp against his chest.

The long walk home gave Mateo plenty of time to think. Too much time. Why had it never occurred to him that someone at General Tun's fortress that fateful day might recognize him now? It made him queasy with dread, as if he'd just remembered a promise he hadn't kept.

He reached inward, asking the relic to be told what to do. He couldn't bear the thought of leaving the farm, Zoya, or most of all, Nuri. But what if that was the only way to protect them? The relic was silent.

He returned his attention to the lamb in his arms. He could feel that it was seriously ill, but surely between what he and Zoya could do, they should be able to save it. But then maybe this was what they'd built the shrine for. He would take it there and ask the relic to show him what to do. After all, it had guided him through the miraculous healing of Nuri's hand.

His heart lifted when the woods around the farm came into view. As soon as he left the road, he set his charge down in the grass along the path to the house, encouraged to see it graze a little. After a while, he picked it up again. When they got to the well, he stopped to fill a bucket and offered some to the lamb in a cupped hand. The little creature seemed thirsty or perhaps even desperate for water.

Mateo wiped his hands on his trousers and scooped up the lamb, which came this time without protest. He stood before the shrine and asked the relic to show him how to proceed. A heavy peace settled on his shoulders and wrapped around his charge as he stood in the hot afternoon sun, as still as a tree. The warm fragrance of the soil rose up around him. He felt pressed downward, so he knelt and buried his face in the lamb's coat, breathing in its rank odor of lanolin and manure. He muttered his thanks as he felt the familiar fire gather in his chest and spread out through his arms. He began to sway on his knees, crooning, giving voice to the pulsations and heat he felt flowing through him.

The little animal bleated and gave a rattling cough, twisting to escape, but Mateo held on. He sang into its neck, feeling something burn away in its body, something that didn't belong. He kept singing until the fire in his chest cooled again. He set the lamb on the ground and dipped both hands into the water, holding them out to it. It drank feverishly, its stubby tail lashing back and forth as if it were nursing. After several more handfuls, it wandered on wobbly legs into the woods to graze.

The relic's powers were more varied than he'd imagined. Mateo stood and touched his chest in thanks. He felt certain that the lamb would thrive. But what about the soldier? Somehow, Mateo knew he'd remember and cause trouble. He'd talk to Nuri, who seemed to understand better than he did how the relic's power worked—striking an agreement in words spoken aloud. Maybe he could negotiate that agreement. No doubt he'd prove a slow student, but he'd ask Nuri to teach him how to bargain.

Nuri was delighted with Mateo's request, saying that bargaining was a game you could win in dozens of different ways if you paid attention and stayed flexible. Mateo listened and practiced, but knew he'd never be half as good as his teacher.

Chapter Twenty-Three

After lunch a handful of days later, Zoya, Nuri, and Mateo stood at the foot of the garden, discussing the afternoon's chores. Midnight darted out of the trees and landed on Zoya's shoulder with a squawk, bobbing his head up and down.

"They're coming," she said. "The tax collectors. They've just left the road."

"What do you want me to do?" asked Nuri.

"Be our charming liaison," Zoya replied. "They already know where everything is, but offer to be their guide. Accompany them, but don't get in their way. Mateo and I will stay out of the way."

Moments later, six men came down the path. Mateo looked them over: General Tun's tax collector, dressed in much finer clothes than the others, came first, with a young clerk at his side. Four soldiers. One of whom was the man who had confronted him in the market last Saturn's day. When his gaze caught Mateo, he smiled, predatory and sure.

Mateo shivered and swallowed against nausea. He'd remembered. But that wasn't what was most important now. That soldier could make trouble for all of them if he wanted to, but it was too late to hide. It would be better to appear indifferent, as Nuri had taught him. He nodded to the soldier in acknowledgment.

"That's the one?" Zoya asked.

"Yes. By his look, he's placed me. I'm so sorry to have brought this trouble to you."

"Go walk with Nuri. He'll have recognized him from the market. It will be a comfort to him if you are together."

Mateo followed the group to the garden, then quietly sidled next to his lover, gently brushing his shoulder. They watched the official and his clerk walk up and down the rows, talking with each other.

"He remembers, doesn't he?" murmured Nuri.

"Yes."

"He means to use that somehow."

"No question. Whatever he intends must not harm the two of you or the farm. His quarrel is with me."

"No difference. If he harms you, he harms us."

"Let's wait until we know what he wants," Mateo whispered. "One thing at a time. I think your lessons in bargaining came at a good time."

The official and his clerk rejoined the group at the foot of the garden and cleared his throat. "One hundred libra potatoes; seventy-five libra onions; sixty libra turnips; fifty libra carrots; fifty libra beetroot; and fifty libra cabbage."

After the clerk entered his assessment into the book, the official turned to Nuri. "As of this week, live-birth animals are banned from being brought to market until all farms are cleansed of this coughing sickness. Nevertheless, if the animals we choose die, you must replace them. Now take us to your livestock."

Nuri led them on, and three of the soldiers followed. One held back. "You," he said, pointing at Mateo with his crooked arm. "I'll have a word with you."

Mateo nodded, bracing himself, asking the relic for help.

The soldier waited until the others were out of hearing range. He turned to Mateo, his eyes red-rimmed, hard and calculating. His face looked puffy. He smelled like he'd had a lot to drink since that day in the town square.

"Since you had that little exchange with my cousin at the market," he said, keeping his voice casual, "he can no longer lie."

"I did nothing to him. He claimed he always told the truth. All I did was agree with him."

"Ah, but there's the problem. He was lying when he said that. For better or worse, he's made something of a career out of telling lies his whole life. He was very good at it. Now, try as he might, he can't do it at all. Word has spread. His neighbors, cuckolded husbands, swindled associates, everyone with a grudge against him, they're all approaching him and asking him questions. And... as fiercely as he's tried to avoid confessing, he's told each of them the truth. All of it."

The soldier looked away and sighed with a hand on the pommel of his sword. "I don't expect him to live out the week, and there's nothing I can do to protect him."

"If you can't, then I certainly can't, either. I'm sorry for the trouble coming to his family, but bearing false witness violates church doctrine." Mateo didn't need to mention he himself no longer felt obliged to doctrine. With or without a church, bearing false witness was still wrong.

The soldier barked out a bitter laugh. "Aye, that's exactly what came to my mind, too. All who serve General Tun have to attend Mass daily, so I'm very, very familiar." He turned to Mateo with a feral grin, sharp and dangerous. "I asked myself, who else might know of such things? And the answer came as clear as day: a priest would know that bit of doctrine right off the top of his head. Or a traveling monk. Maybe a monk who truly believed that some gewgaw he wanted to give the general had mysterious healing powers. A monk who watched my comrades break my arm to see if his gewgaw could bring a miracle and heal me."

The soldier's voice dropped to a quiet growl. "A monk who couldn't put me back together again. A monk who was thrown off the top of the tower, whose body apparently was dragged off in the night into the forest by some wild animal. A monk who, because he failed to heal me, ruined me as one of the general's personal guard. I lost my place. Good pay. Standing. Suddenly I was nothing, a foot soldier who couldn't even wield a sword properly, let alone protect the general."

The soldier drew his sword and shoved the hilt's round pommel up into the hollow under Mateo's jaw. "You owe me my old life back." He snarled. "You owe me that. I don't care how or when, but my cousin will die soon because you've found magic that works. So you can heal me properly now."

"Yes. I can heal you." Mateo felt the relic waken. He could feel the grave import hanging on whatever he said next. Bargaining was exciting. "But there are conditions."

The soldier pushed harder into Mateo's throat. "You are in no position to bargain, monk! With this sickness spreading through the farms, the general is ready to burn a few witches. I could report to him that you survived and practice black magic right under his nose, laughing at him all the while!"

Mateo fought to keep his face calm as a sudden terror seized him. "What's this about burning witches?"

"Ah. You haven't heard. The general consulted the Bishop of Santa Teresa about the livestock sickness spreading across so many farms. He said the plague was the work of witchcraft, and to look for farms without disease. Those would be where the witches lived." The man's smile was smug, cruel. "I'd wager there are no sick animals on this farm, witch. I'd laugh while you burned."

A slow, implacable fire rose in Mateo. This man was so like Father Xavier. Bullies were the same everywhere—never expecting resistance. "And you are in no position to risk losing the only chance you have of restoring your arm. It seems neither of us holds an advantage."

Mateo slowly pushed the man's fisted weapon down from his neck. "So I'll tell you my conditions, and you can decide whether to accept them."

"I'm listening."

"I have only two. First, you must never do or say anything that endangers this farm or those who live here. Second, you must never tell anyone the truth about how your arm healed. If you violate either of these conditions, your arm will revert to its present state, and you will relive the pain of your injury every day for as long as you live."

The soldier hesitated, scowling. "Very well. I agree."

"What is your name?"

"Anselmo."

"Look me in the eye, Anselmo, and say these words exactly: Under the following conditions, you will heal my arm. Then repeat those conditions just as I've given them."

Mateo watched the soldier thinking, searching for a way around the terms, but he eventually nodded. As Anselmo spoke the words, Mateo felt the relic's fire spread through him, ready to flow.

When the soldier stopped, Mateo shook his head. "You left out the consequences. Speak them clearly."

Anselmo's jaw twitched, but he complied.

"Yes," Mateo said when the man finished, feeling the immense weight of the word. "It is just as you say. Under those conditions, I can restore your arm." The relic's fire leapt out of him like a wild animal, pouring itself into the soldier in a flash before disappearing.

Anselmo gasped, let out a cry of surprise or maybe pain, and stilled. A cool breeze blew between them. Anselmo looked down at his arm and scowled. "It hasn't changed."

"It will. Before tomorrow dawns."

"It had better, or I'll be back. And I won't be alone." Anselmo sheathed his sword and strode to his cohort without looking back.

Mateo's heart hammered so hard that he could feel both beats pound against his ribs. Sweat trickled down his back. What had he done? He'd gambled with Zoya's and Nuri's lives as well as his own. But it felt like he'd won. He'd done exactly what Nuri had taught him, framing the negotiation in terms of what Anselmo had wanted, not what he had threatened.

Now the farm and everyone here would be safe so long as the bargain held. He rubbed his throat where the soldier had pressed the hilt of his weapon. Surely Anselmo would keep their agreement. He stood to lose too much of what he wanted if he broke his promise, to say nothing of the daily pain and injury that would ensue if he did.

Mateo waited until Anselmo had rejoined his group before daring to walk over to Nuri. The taxman was still dictating his tally of the animals to be taken while a soldier marked his choices with paint. When every item had been entered, Nuri signed the page in the book. The clerk stamped a copy of their levy and reminded them that the vegetables would be collected in a matter of days, but the animals would remain the farm's responsibility for at least another month. With business finished, the official turned and marched toward the road, followed by his clerk and the soldiers. Anselmo turned and stared at Mateo for a moment, a cold threat, and took his place behind the clerk.

Midnight took off, following the group without a sound. Everyone else stood as if rooted, watching until the last soldier disappeared into the woods between the house and the road.

"Tomorrow, you boys dig up everything they want to take," Zoya said. "If we're not ready for them, they'll dig it up themselves, and I don't want them in our garden, trampling over everything. Make sure you give them more than they entered in the book, so there can be no question about meeting our levy. That would make trouble we don't need."

Two days later, the wagon came for their produce. Anselmo wasn't part of their escort. A clerk weighed each lot, then stamped their page as paid and left for the next farm. But an unsettling air of wrongness hung over them for the rest of the day, making the three of them strange and disconnected from each other. Mateo and Nuri threw themselves into chores as their way of banishing the eeriness, but it didn't seem to make any difference.

That evening after supper, Zoya announced she would be busy in her sanctuary all night and for most of tomorrow, too—putting the farm back together, she said, and she was not to be disturbed for any reason.

When Zoya returned to the house at sunset the following day, the whole place felt right again. In balance. And Nuri and Mateo had supper waiting for her.

Chapter Twenty-Four

"Your lamb has really grown," Nuri said as he and Mateo readied to repair the gate of its pen. "When you first brought it home, it was too weak to break through this."

"My lamb?" Mateo scoffed as he braced himself, arms around the gatepost, ready to fasten a new hinge. "You were the one who paid the farmer, if I recall."

"Mmm. One of the last sales that man would make, as it turned out. You never heard more from the soldier, did you?"

"Anselmo? No." Mateo said. "Lift that end of the gate higher and hold it so I can tighten this strap."

Nuri grunted, doing as he was told. "He's satisfied, then."

"Must be. I haven't seen him on patrol in the market, so maybe he got his old position back."

"Much good may it do him," Nuri said, his voice declaring he didn't mean it. "He ought to—" Before he could finish, his foot slipped in the muck of the pen and he fell backward onto his rump. Seizing the opportunity, the lamb bolted over his splayed legs and darted down the path leading to the garden, kicking its heels, prancing and bucking.

Nuri couldn't stop laughing. Mateo swore. "You think it's funny because you didn't have to catch her last time. This could take me the rest of the day." He touched the knot on his chest and asked for help catching the escapee, already just a bouncing white dot headed for the road.

In a heartbeat, he was beside the lamb, and he scooped it up in his arms. Nuri was right: it had grown. It was definitely heavier than when he'd carried it after its last escape. That was good. Mateo walked back toward the pens, which seemed to take ages. He didn't remember having run so far.

Nuri was standing motionless by the gate with his eyes wide. "You flew," he said, his voice flat. "You flew."

"Surely not. I must have run faster than I expected, though."

"I saw you. You did that thing where you touch your chest for your magic. Then you took off like an arrow to get to the lamb."

"Did I? Come to think of it, I wasn't breathing as hard as I should if I'd been running. I was just... suddenly there."

"You flew, I tell you! My eyesight is good, even when I don't understand what I'm seeing. Yet another gift of your magic. Your power."

Is that true? Mateo silently asked. Shivering warmth spread through him, as if Nuri had strummed a chord full of peace. It was true. He could fly. A power he never could have imagined, let alone asked for. It felt dangerously wonderful.

The flying ant. In his fever dream, he'd been sitting against a tree next to the stream. It had given him its wings. They'd melted into his chest. Now he could feel them as if they spread out behind his pounding heart, flashing in the sunlight with every movement.

"I have to try this again." He touched his chest, asking to take flight. He lifted into the air, hanging motionless well above Nuri's head, higher than the trees. Nuri waved, and Mateo made to wave back, but the motion made him feel sick and dizzy. It was strange to be standing on nothing but air. It was also strange to see the garden and so much of the farm from above—strange and glorious.

Why wasn't he moving? He'd moved so quickly when chasing the lamb... ah. Yes. He'd wanted to fly *toward* something. He imagined the well. That's where he wanted to fly. Faster than a diving falcon, he shot across the vegetable garden, over the front yard, and directly to the well. He stumbled to his knees as he landed in front of it. But the feeling! Swift, clean, as fierce as a knife glinting in sunlight! A silent shout of triumph—sure, unfettered, jubilant. He'd never felt so strong, so full of his own joy. As he stood and brushed off his trousers, Midnight landed on the stone lip of the well, screeching at him, bobbing his head up and down, hackles full, open wings shimmering in the sunlight. Before Mateo could think of something to say to him, Midnight squawked and took off, flying toward the house, no doubt to tell Zoya.

His test was a success. Mateo refocused on where he'd left Nuri by the sheep pen. *Fly.* His vision blurred, and in less than a breath, he stood next to Nuri again. His skin tingled with wild promise as if just before the first lightning of a great storm. He kissed Nuri, exultant. "This is magic beyond anything I could have imagined."

Nuri nodded, more cautious. "This was given to you for a reason. I wonder what that reason is."

"Whatever it is, it's a power I'm obliged to learn to use well. I expect I'll learn the reason as I do."

Precisely but gently, Mateo landed between rows of cabbage and made a dramatic bow. Only Nuri applauded.

"Now you're just showing off," Zoya said, her face set in a scowl. Midnight squawked his agreement from her shoulder.

"I'm celebrating," he replied with a happy shrug. "I landed right where I meant to."

"You fly according to your intention?"

"Yes. That seems to be the key. I need to have a clear thought or destination in mind, otherwise I just float or drift. I scraped against a tree once when I wasn't paying enough attention."

"Truly a powerful gift. And dangerous." Zoya gave a heavy sigh. "I fear for you. For us. If someone sees you—"

"I know," Mateo said. "I'll take care no one does. I finally understand what you've been trying to get me to see."

"I hope so." Zoya's voice was tight and small. "General Tun's priest has already ordered one death by burning. Someone accused a farmer's wife of causing their animals to die of the coughing sickness, and that's all it took. Fear and suspicion are in the air everywhere. I worry, especially now that I have to go away for a while."

Nuri's head whipped around to her. "You're going away? You've never left the farm—that I know of, at least."

Mateo studied Zoya's face, noticing signs of... what, fatigue? Resignation? How would they manage without her, even for a short time? He'd never thought about the possibility that Zoya might not be here—never thought he'd need to. "What can I do to help?"

Zoya's sigh sounded like relief. "I haven't had a chance to renew for a long time. Recently, my caution has often shifted into fear, and that's a sure sign I must regenerate. Now that the two of you are putting down roots here, you can tend the harmony between the land and everything on it while I'm gone. I'll go down into my spring on the new moon. This one is already on the wane, so I leave in less than a fortnight. I'll be gone at least until the next moon rises. I can't tell you more, so don't ask. Midnight will stay behind. He'll be of more help than you might think."

Nuri put his arm around his aunt and kissed the top of her head, displacing Midnight, who flapped his wings twice and resettled on Nuri's free shoulder. "You do what you must. We'll do everything we can."

"Yes. We'll do everything we can." Mateo took a deep breath. The task felt overwhelming. Tend the harmony between the land and the things on it? How did she do that? For a moment, he felt as uncertain as he had back at the monastery when he'd first tended a heifer's birth all on his own. "It's a big responsibility."

"Just love it and pay attention," Zoya said, resting her head against Nuri's shoulder. Mateo had never seen her lean on anyone before.

She stretched out her arm as if putting it around the whole garden. "The land. The life. Just respect it. That's most of it, and you already do that. For the rest, listen. Stay attuned. Be alert to little shifts, especially in the evening, just after the sun sets. You both should walk with me in the evenings until I leave. We'll walk around slowly while you listen with me and learn. Midnight will help, and you'll want guidance from your own magic, too, Mateo. Listen to the voices, and you'll be able to keep the farm safe and strong. It will be hard for you to make a mistake, so long as your intention of stewardship is clear."

Chapter Twenty-Five

Although nothing had changed in the days since Zoya's announcement, Mateo felt an underlying tension in his work, which he eventually recognized as worry about her approaching departure. A sense of urgency. He wanted everything important finished and secured for winter before she left. And he knew that wasn't remotely possible.

They bought a load of hay at the market, but the farmer's wagon was too big to deliver beyond the edge of the road. For a full day, Nuri and Mateo trudged back and forth, pulling their cart along the path to haul the bundles from the road to stack them in the three-sided shed where they could be stored over the winter. They pulled and trimmed the last of the root vegetables and stored them in the dark, cool cellar under the house.

As if the weather had been waiting for them to finish clearing the garden, the day after the last vegetables were in, a line of dark clouds came scudding in, riding a belligerent cold wind. A procession of thunderstorms brought heavy rain for days, drowning fields and turning every road to mud. On their walk around the farm that evening, Zoya asked Nuri and Mateo if they could feel that the land was grateful, even though not everyone would be.

"Our kind must listen with our hearts," she said. "Place more trust in nature's wisdom than appearances or human convenience. Sometimes that is hard to do."

On the eve of the last market day before Zoya's departure, she announced that she would not be coming with them. It wasn't wise to bring charms or remedies to sell, as the rumors and accusations of witchcraft continued to be spread in both parishes of Santa Inés, as if they now competed for the prize of being the most vigilant in weeding out evil.

By morning, the skies had cleared. Mateo and Nuri loaded the cart with chickens and eggs, discussing what the farm might still need for winter—two full hanks of rope, a cowhide, a new hammer, and a better knife from the blacksmith.

The steady rain had turned the road to mire. While Nuri led Bray by the reins, Mateo pushed the cart from behind just to keep the wheels turning. It seemed that all Mateo could do was stare resentfully at the ground, watching his sandal-clad feet sink into the muck, push the cart, and listen to Nuri sing as if mud were a newfound joy. Mateo knew the road was too public to risk using magic to make their slog easier, but he couldn't stop feeling cheated—offended that he couldn't. Then on one particularly sloppy bend in the road, he actually heard his own grumbling. Zoya had just spoken to them about the land being grateful for the rain and how some might object to nature's wisdom when it became inconvenient. She'd been talking to him. He shook his head at his selfishness.

He concentrated on Nuri's singing, and his feet eventually picked up the rhythm. Still, it was a relief when their cart rolled onto village cobblestones and Bray could pull it without their help.

Even though the sun now shone bright, the market square itself seemed wrapped in a cloud of wary gloom. No one called out to attract buyers. There were no livestock sounds or smells since large animals had been banned in an effort to halt spreading the coughing sickness ravaging the farms. Mateo looked around and noticed there were far fewer carts and barrows offering wares. The gaping spaces felt empty as fresh-dug graves.

As they arranged their cart for trading, Nuri nudged his shoulder. "Why so gloomy?"

"Can't you feel it?" Mateo muttered. "This place is tense, afraid. Something bad is about to happen, I'm sure of it."

"Ha. Of course I feel how the place is blanketed in darkness. How could I not? But you can't trick me into agreeing with you, my love, or by power of your magic, something bad will most certainly happen. Instead, you must agree with me: if something bad happens, people who mean no harm will not suffer."

Mateo snorted dismissively. Leave it to Nuri's imagination to turn a simple observation into a guarantee of trouble. "Very well. If something bad happens, all who mean no harm will remain unharmed." To his surprise, a bolt of heat shot from his chest and spread across the square, leaving him trembling and ashamed. He'd nearly set harm in motion, perhaps exposing Zoya and Nuri to it. The very people he loved more than anyone else.

"You see?" Nuri said firmly. "I'll wager you didn't think your magic applied to the words you initiate. That's disrespectful. Magic is always present and always listens. To everything."

Mateo took a deep breath and let a heavy wave of shame wash through him. "You're right. I was careless and could have hurt us or someone else. How did you become so wise as to know this?"

Nuri shook his head and put his hand on Mateo's forearm. "I know because I believe in your magic. I'm not sure you always do, even though I often beg you to. I'm begging again. Be mindful of your power, respect it. And remember—for all our sakes—it is always listening, always ready to act if it chooses to."

His gaze shifted, and he squeezed Mateo's arm. "Just in time. Don't look around yet, but soldiers have arrived, and they have a priest leading them. There's an angry-looking young man beside the priest who looks like he wants trouble."

Mateo slowly turned back to their cart as if to adjust their stack of cabbages. "Harm to those who mean harm," he whispered. He watched the young man, dressed in remarkably fine clothes, point across the square in their general direction. The priest's entourage wove its way purposefully, stopping where a beautiful young woman stood next to her barrow of vegetables.

"That's the witch!" the young man shouted, pointing at the woman. "She's cast a spell of torment upon me. She should burn!" The entire square had fallen silent.

Raising his crucifix, the priest stared at the woman. "Beatriz Calderón, by the perfect power of Christ's blood and before this holy cross, under peril to your immortal soul, can you deny this accusation?"

The woman straightened, smoothed her hands on her skirts, and gazed calmly at the priest. "Father Hidalgo, you know me well. Since my confirmation, I have confessed my sins to you and taken Communion every week. I readily deny this accusation. I do. Are you interested in the truth of this matter?"

Without lowering his crucifix, the priest slowly nodded and pursed his lips as if he was insulted. "Of course, my child," he said, his voice deadly calm. "We always seek the truth wherever it leads, to expose the lies of wickedness."

Barely moving his lips, Mateo whispered, "Yes, Father Hidalgo. You always seek the truth and expose the lies of wickedness." In response, he felt the familiar hot current rise and flow out of his body to envelop the priest, Beatriz, and her accuser.

"Very well, then," said the woman. "The truth is that this man, whose name is Diego Hernán Delgado, covets the farm I inherited last year when my parents died. First, he sought to court me. When I turned him away, he twice threatened to rape me, saying no one else would want me once I was no longer a virgin. He still schemes to force me if he can, but most of all, he wants to steal my land. Now that I have refused him, the easiest way for him to take my farm is to have me burned at the stake as a witch."

Hidalgo turned to the man. "Is this true?"

"She lies! She has bewitched me! She tortures me in my dreams. I can think of nothing but her! I want her punished! She deserves to die in the fire!"

"Ah," murmured Mateo. "You mean her harm through lies of wickedness. Such harm shall come to you instead." He waited to feel the answering surge of magic flow from him and land in the three-some, but nothing seemed to happen.

Mateo turned to Nuri, puzzled. "I don't know if—"

"Trust!" Nuri's whisper was almost a hiss. "And patience. This is far from over. Your magic may sometimes be an instrument of justice, but it is much more than that. Something else is happening, too."

Father Hidalgo stood silent for a moment, looking puzzled. "How much livestock have you lost to the coughing sickness?" he asked Delgado.

"By grace of God, none. I am blessed."

Hidalgo turned to Beatriz. "And you?"

The young woman crossed herself. "I have lost all my sheep, and I had no cattle to begin with. So far, the pigs remain healthy."

Father Hidalgo nodded thoughtfully. "So clearly no use of witchcraft to save your animals." He turned to the soldiers. "No decision shall be made in this matter until my inquiry is complete. In the meantime, I determine neither of these people are under suspicion."

He turned and marched out of the silent square, followed by the soldiers, leaving Beatriz and Delgado angrily facing each other.

Slowly, almost casually, a burly farmer walked up behind Delgado and dropped a heavy hand on his shoulder, murmuring something that Mateo couldn't hear. Perhaps half a dozen other men had turned in Delgado's direction, remaining still and silent. The farmer leaned in to mutter something else, and Delgado startled, quickly looking around at the men. He gave Beatriz a final scowl and nearly ran out of the square.

"What do you suppose that man said to Delgado?" Mateo asked Nuri.

"I couldn't tell you the words," Nuri said with a grim smile. "But I know a threat delivered when I see it."

The atmosphere of the marketplace slowly lightened, and by the time it was time to pack up Mateo could hear an occasional laugh among the people still present.

On the road home, which had dried considerably, Mateo led Bray by walking ahead, holding the reins. Nuri sang, but Mateo hardly noticed. In the market today, he had seen something, learned something so profound and far-reaching that it had changed him before he'd had a chance to ponder it. He had to ponder it now.

He already knew he loved Nuri more than anyone he'd ever loved before. He felt happiest being near him, seeing him smile, hearing him make music, touching him, and listening to his stories. He was a wonder—a wise, resilient man, and beauty poured out of him in everything he did. This was not at all what he had just learned. His revelation was that he couldn't live without him.

Nuri was the other half of his own being. Without him, Mateo would just stumble forward through a barren life, dull as an ox, oblivious and clumsy, unfinished but not knowing what he was missing, praying for the miracle that was Nuri. And here he was, walking beside him, already here. There was no time to pretend otherwise, no time to waste.

So in the middle of the road, still a mile from home, Mateo stopped. Because he was holding Bray's reins, the donkey stopped. Then Nuri stopped and looked at Mateo with eyes full of questions. Mateo took a deep breath and looked around. The road smelled of drying mud. The soft cool air of a late autumn afternoon, spiced with drying leaves, brushed between and around them. From either side of the road, birds called to each other, to the world, to them.

Because he couldn't think of anything else that might serve, Mateo took Nuri's hands and gently wrapped Bray's reins around their clasped hands.

"Nuri," he began, "I have loved you since I met you in my fever dreams. Every day, you show me your light, your beauty. I've loved you more each day since. To say nothing of my respect for the wonder you are." He was crying, and he proudly, carelessly, let his tears drip. "I need you. More than I've ever needed another. Your music, companionship, and most of all, your wisdom. Will you let me bind myself to you, and agree to bind yourself to me?"

With a radiant smile, Nuri leaned up to kiss Mateo and then down to kiss the cracked, mottled leather of the reins Mateo had draped over their hands. "Yes," he said. "Bind yourself to me, and I will bind myself to you. This is good."

In a flash of playfulness, Nuri stepped back a little. "But I have demands." He laughed, and his face softened. "I want to marry you in the air, in moonlight. Take me flying tonight, with Zoya as witness."

CHAPTER TWENTY-SIX

As if neither man could bear to let go, they walked hand in hand, holding Bray's reins between them. Mateo wasn't sure what Nuri was feeling and didn't want to ask, but for him, this road had never felt more like the road home. Without the slightest effort, some shadow had been dispelled from his heart. After all his uncertainty about where he belonged or where his home was, his quandary was finally over. With the shadow gone, he could see and feel more clearly than ever. Even the trees guarding the path to their house, their home, stood out as if he were seeing them for the first time. The late afternoon sun slanted through the branches, illuminating the space between every leaf and twig, lifting everything into a chorus of happiness and depth. The trees wrapped their welcome around them in the tenderest embrace. It was more beautiful than he could possibly imagine on his own. Nuri had helped him see.

They took the harness off Bray, brushed him down, gave him feed and water, then emptied the cart. Nuri hadn't said anything since their betrothal on the road, but his ready smiles radiated happiness. They bathed and donned clean clothes for dinner, eager to share their news.

Zoya wept happily at their announcement, her tears sparkling in the candlelight as Mateo recounted how an ant he had met at the beginning of his journey from the monastery, then again in his fever dreams had given him the gift of flight—and so now he could marry

Nuri in the air. Nuri told of feeling he'd got his life back when Mateo healed him to make music again, the exact moment when he knew he belonged to Mateo as surely as Mateo belonged to his magic. After they'd eaten, she forbade both of them from helping tidy up and instead ordered them to use the hour before moonrise to prepare and to meet at their shrine when they were ready.

Mateo was the first to arrive at the shrine. Nuri and he had built something together that they had laughingly called the Shrine of the Trees. The name now felt more right than ever, and it felt right that he'd arrived before the others. He brushed his hand across the rough slab and mused at how, together, the three of them had found the right place for it, all the labor, Nuri's scream as the rocks crushed his hand, the vigil, and the miracle of his healing. All the music he'd played since. All the music he was yet to play. His beloved Nuri.

Step by step, it was Nuri who had led him into learning the power of the magic that had chosen him, and more importantly, how it worked. With a certainty that raced through his body like fire in a field of dry cornstalks, he knew he needed Nuri in his life as much as he needed water and air.

A soft sound behind him made him turn. Zoya approached with her shoulders wrapped in a gloriously colored shawl he'd never seen before and a tranquil smile illuminating her face. She carried a cloth bag, which she set on the ground beside her.

"Greetings on this blessed evening, Mateo," she said, her voice firm, unhurried, full of elegant priestess power. "My happiness flows to you as a river."

"Thank you. I'm so glad…" Mateo wanted to say something profound, to bow to this powerful wise woman who had opened his life to more beauty than he could imagine, let alone hold. He lowered his head. "Do you think it would be appropriate for me to take off my clothes?" he asked. "They don't feel right."

Zoya laughed softly. "By all means. Remember that I made you come sky-clad that first night you entered my spring? Clothing can be too cumbersome for magic."

As Mateo laid his carefully-folded clothes on the shrine, he heard Nuri approach. He turned to welcome him, and stopped breathing. Nuri stood next to Zoya. He was a vision of lithe beauty in a soft white tunic tied at one shoulder. A garland of wildflowers hung around his neck. He'd wound more flowers into his hair and held even more in his hands. Mateo knew those were for him.

Nuri walked to him, graceful, happy, open, strong. "I'm glad to see you dressed up for the occasion." He reached out, his hands full of beauty. "These are for you, my love, my mate. Bend down a little so I can decorate you properly."

Mateo felt the brush of the garland dropping onto his neck and then the strange poke of flower stems going into his hair. He stared at the hollow of Nuri's throat, stilled by the tender precision of his deft fingers as they worked.

"There," said Nuri, stepping back a bit, admiring the effect. "Perfect." He took another step back and reached for the knot of his tunic, untying it, letting it fall to the ground.

Mateo wanted to shout his promises, to promise him everything, yet had nothing left to promise that he had not already given to this man. His words came out heavy and thick with emotion. "I love you, and I will never leave you." The relic's fire woke, wrapping around them. Mateo spread his arms open in invitation.

"I know." Nuri smiled and stepped into his embrace, lifting his arms to his shoulders, melting into him, open, yielded, still. He lifted his lips to give him a light kiss. "Marry me, my love. Take me up flying with you. Let me share your wings."

Without a thought, Mateo wrapped his arms around Nuri's back and waist as he had so many times before. But this time, it felt completely new, as if he held an angel asking for his wings to be restored. As he tightened his arms, he heard a soft chant coming from somewhere. He glanced at Zoya over Nuri's shoulder to see her smiling, fierce, triumphant, swaying back and forth, and lightly slapping her chest in rhythm to her song. He nodded to her in respect, and buried his face in Nuri's neck.

UP. They rose until they were even with the tops of the trees. *TURN.*

Nuri laughed in delight as they made a slow circle. "This is like dancing!"

DANCE. Mateo didn't think he was much of a dancer, but he agreed. He guided them through sweeping turns, rising and dropping as he'd often watched swallows do at dusk. Nuri began to hum, and Mateo tried to match their movements to his voice.

They both had felt it at the same time, the blending, sweet and complete. Their bond and its destiny. Mateo gasped. Nuri's song faltered for a moment. They gazed at each other in wonder, knowing they would always be one, no matter what happened.

"Close your eyes," Mateo whispered, as he closed his. *SPIN.* They spun so fast that Mateo could feel some of the flowers in his hair fly away from the force of their movement. He snuck a glance at Nuri and saw that his eyes were also open and focused on his. *SLOW. STOP.* Their kiss was not a promise. It was an acknowledgement.

DOWN. They descended like a feather—falling, certain, but in its own time and way. Mateo's feet landed first, and he tightened his arms around Nuri to make sure he didn't stumble. For a moment not measured, neither of them moved. Zoya's song had stopped. The night hung utterly still, full. Complete.

Nuri was radiant. Mateo felt like he glowed too. Everything was perfect.

Zoya was the first to break the silence. "This marriage wants marking," she said, picking up the bag at her feet. "Nothing too grand, but special." She stepped over to the shrine and set a small clay bottle on it, with three little matching cups on the slab. She broke the bottle's seal and emptied the contents into the cups. She handed one to Nuri and then one to Mateo before taking the third herself.

She raised her cup above her head, as high as she could reach. "By the grace of the seasons and the wisdom of all living things, I bless this union. May beauty be served through it always, so long as these two shall live!"

The newly married lovers raised their cups aloft in answer. Nuri replied, "May beauty be served through this union so long as we two shall live."

"So be it," Mateo answered. An explosion of magic fire poured from his chest, wrapping itself around Nuri, Zoya, the shrine, and even enveloping the trees at the edge of the clearing.

"Ah," said Zoya. "The promise is sealed, and none can break it. This is good." She lowered her cup to take a sip. She smacked her lips. "Delicious." She nodded. "Like your love for each other."

Nuri and Mateo extended arms so each could drink from the other's cup.

"Mmmm," moaned Nuri.

The liquid smelled of bitter herbs and sweet fruit and wood smoke. As Mateo sipped, it filled his mouth in an intense burst of all the flavors the aroma had promised. He managed not to cough. "I've never—"

"No, I'm certain you've never," Zoya said with a happy little cackle. "And we may never again. This is an old gift from very far away. Don't waste a drop!"

As Zoya put the empty bottle and cups back in the bag, the men gathered up their clothes and sandals. "Let's not put these on," Nuri murmured. "I promise you that would prove wasted effort as soon as we get to our room."

Chapter Twenty-Seven

The evening of the new moon came too quickly for Mateo. Each day approaching that moment had been steeped in a poignant tenderness, an unspoken awareness of Zoya's looming departure. It sat with them at every meal and softened every conversation. Together, the three had walked the circuit of the farm every evening, absorbing what Zoya had done on her own for so long—watching, listening for any disturbance, calling for care and balance if they found it.

The new moon's twilight came. Zoya prepared a meal for Nuri and Mateo, and sat with them as they ate. She occasionally sipped from a mug of dark broth that smelled like wet earth as they spoke in hushed tones. Finally, she put down her mug and stood.

"It's time," she said with a little smile. Both men made to stand, too, but she raised a hand to stop them. "Stay here. Take care of each other, and take care of the farm. Be well, and be safe." As soon as she stepped outside, Midnight landed on her shoulder with a squawk. Together, they disappeared into the night.

Mateo sat with Nuri at the table for a while, neither one speaking. There was nothing to say in the enormity of her departure. How could he feel so adrift in a house so familiar? It was as if Zoya had gathered up all her presence into a magical bundle and taken it with her, leaving the house hollowed out. Maybe she had.

Whatever the farm needed was up to him and Nuri now. He reached for Nuri's hand and squeezed gently. Nuri blew out the dinner candle, and still they sat together in the quiet dark.

After a while, Midnight came back and landed on the open sill, making growly chirrup sounds Mateo hadn't heard before, and then flew off. Something in Mateo settled. Part of Zoya was still here. They would manage somehow.

"Let's go to bed." Nuri stood up. "Tomorrow is a new day, and we need to get ready for market the day after."

As soon as Mateo opened his eyes, even before he reached over to see if Nuri was still there, his first thought was that Zoya was gone. Today, they would go to the market at Santa Inés as usual. They would trade as best they could for what they needed and sell what they could. They might buy a simple lunch for a coin or two from the purse Zoya had left them. But Zoya was gone. There would be no watchful, knowing presence beside their cart today, no one to consult if he had a question. Something in his belly told him he'd been abandoned, and he scolded himself for self-pity. He'd not been abandoned. His beloved snored softly beside him.

So yes, they would go together to market. Midnight would watch over the farm. They would come home to the countless voices and currents of life here. Together, they would tend to the animals, prepare dinner, eat and talk, then walk their circuit of care around the property—listening, communing.

Even though the sun was shining in a clear sky, Mateo could feel the cloud of despair and fear pressing down on the whole village as they approached—as if it hid from some looming danger, barely breathing. The gloom thickened as they entered the square, and it remained unbroken even though Nuri hummed a cheerful tune while setting up the chickens, eggs, and the few rabbits they had on offer.

Mateo nudged Nuri with an elbow. "Even though we don't really need them, I wonder if that woman our magic touched last week might be interested in bartering some vegetables for eggs. Or something else we have. Beatriz? I think that was her name. It would give me a chance to talk to her and find out how she is faring."

"Good idea. I'm going to make some music in a little while, see if I can encourage a few smiles."

"Something rousing, then?"

"No, certainly not at first. Too jarring. To banish this kind of darkness, you have to start quietly and build up."

As soon as he could get away, Mateo kissed Nuri on the cheek and left him to take care of their cart.

"Good morning to you, Beatriz," Mateo said as he approached. She straightened as her eyes darted to him and then took stock of the rest of the square, wary but determined.

"Good morning. We haven't met, but you know my name."

"My name is Mateo, and the man over there strumming his guitar is my hand-fasted partner. Nuri. We were here last week."

"Ah. Yes. Then you would know my name, wouldn't you?"

"I'd have come over after the incident, but it seemed you were being taken care of by friends. I didn't want to interfere then, but I do want to be a friend. I'm certain you are not a witch."

Beatriz nodded curtly, acknowledging his goodwill without giving anything away. "I do have good friends, and I'm grateful for them."

Mateo felt the fire in his chest stir, connecting again with her protection. "You have more good friends than you know. Has the issue been resolved, or are you still being harassed?"

She gave Mateo a cool gaze. "Why are you talking to me?"

"Perhaps you would like to trade some of your vegetables for our wares? We have eggs and chickens today as well as a few rabbits."

"Are the rabbits too old to breed?"

"We have three does and a buck, all in their prime. They've already sired or borne healthy litters and are in good health themselves."

"Let me take a look at them. I'll take all four if I like what I see. Without any sheep, I'll need other meat animals to get through the winter." She swept a hand at her barrow, her demeanor still cool. "Does anything here interest you?"

"Your tomatoes and aubergines catch my eye. We didn't have much luck with those this year. We could easily take all you've brought today. And those strings of hot peppers, too." He looked over at Nuri, who was now singing a rollicking ballad, and two or three folks had gathered around to listen. "Come over to look at the rabbits when you can, and we can talk more."

Beatriz nodded, then startled and looked over Mateo's shoulder as a hush fell over the square. Father Hidalgo entered, this time alone, walking with a solemn stride among the stalls and barrows. By the time he'd made his way to where Nuri stood, the little crowd of listeners had melted away. Nuri stopped playing. Mateo watched as the priest spoke for a moment. Nuri nodded, then lifted the guitar strap over his head and gently laid the instrument in the bed of the cart.

Mateo waited until Father Hidalgo had moved away from their cart and finally out of the square. When he'd disappeared, it seemed everyone still present could breathe again. "Come over to us at your convenience," Mateo said as he backed away from Beatriz. "We'll hold the rabbits for you until then."

When he got to their cart, he was shocked to see Nuri trembling, his body radiating fury while his face remained an impassive mask. "What did that priest say to you, my love? He must have said something terrible."

"He said," Nuri murmured, enunciating each word with furious care, "that smug, pretentious bastard said this was a time for prayer and repentance, not music that made people forget their troubles and want to dance." He took a deep breath and blew it out slowly. "Darkness posing as piety. Cruelty dished out in the name of the sacred. I know who I'd burn at the stake for being wicked! Music and dancing are sacred—how dare he?"

Mateo glanced around instinctively, making sure no one had overheard. "He wrongs your music, your heart's magic. Without wishing him harm, what would you have my magic do to him?"

Nuri looked away for a moment. "I don't wish him harm. He struck a tender place in me, is all," he said, his voice hurt and angry. "He repeats what I've heard most of my life—scorn for what I hold most sacred. My parents were the first to say I was wasting my life making music. They didn't understand how holy music was to me. I suppose it's one reason why I've never settled down until now. There always seems to be someone who insists music is dangerous, or worse yet, unimportant. It's happened often enough, but it hurts every time as much as the first. It's worst when it happens in the name of piety. Then I can barely manage my anger."

"But Zoya was different."

"She's always respected my music. It's why I've kept coming back."

Mateo put his arm around Nuri's shoulders. "So what do you wish for Father Hidalgo? Perhaps we can give him a gift."

"I wish that his heart might open to music, like a flower blooms in summer."

Mateo called to the fire banked in his chest. *Might this be so?*

Never against his choice. Offer the choice to awaken.

Mateo stroked Nuri's cheek and smiled. "I'm told he must have a choice, since he's not here to choose now."

"Of course. I want him to have a choice, too."

"At its time of choosing, and in its way, this magic, this gift, will offer him a choice—his heart can open to music like a flower in summer, or it can remain closed." Like a drumbeat, a pulse of fire plunged down through Mateo's feet, through the cobblestones, and deep into the earth.

Nuri turned back to their cart, brusquely swiping his hand over a wet cheek. "Good. May he choose well."

Sometime later, Beatriz came over to them, accompanied by one of the farmers who had protected her the previous week. They both examined the rabbits, which were all they had left by then. Nuri was his cheerful self again, humming song after song with a mutinous set to his jaw. The farmer approved the rabbits and watched as Beatriz helped Mateo load the traded vegetables into their cart. They said their farewells, although Mateo could tell Beatriz was still being cautious with them. He respected her the more for it, and told her so.

Nuri let Mateo lead Bray while he sang bawdy tavern songs in full voice all the way home.

Chapter Twenty-Eight

"It's a full moon tonight," said Nuri as he toyed with a slow melody on his guitar. "Two weeks until Zoya returns. Or thereabouts."

"Mmmm." Mateo opened his eyes and smiled at Nuri. "The time has gone faster than I expected."

"You were far away thinking about something else, weren't you?" Nuri asked. "What were you thinking?"

"Now that I can fly," said Mateo, stretched out on their pallet, hands clasped behind his head, "I think I'd like to travel a little. After Zoya comes back. I've never seen much of the world. This farm is the farthest from home I've been my whole life."

Nuri stopped strumming. "Do you miss it?"

"My hometown?" Mateo gazed into the candle, trying to decide. "No. A little, maybe." He pondered while Nuri played. "I suppose I miss a handful of the brothers at the monastery the most. Not the town itself or even my life in the monastery. But there's no reason to go back. In fact, they wouldn't want me back now even if I wanted to return, since I won't bring them Friar Calmas against the general's will and can't return the Mantle." He rubbed his chest. "I owe Father Xavier nothing. He expected Tun to kill me."

He caught Nuri's eye and smiled, helpless with affection. "Besides, I found you. I would never give you up for anything—everything—I had back there."

"So you want to see the world," Nuri said over a playful run through several chords. "Where would you go?"

"I have no idea. Maybe just as far as Santa Teresa to start. Not until after lambing, though."

"That's not too far from here."

"I've never seen the ocean."

"You probably should, at least once. It's big. And humbling, in a way." Nuri plucked a winding phrase in a minor key. "How would you make your way? People certainly won't pay to see you fly. They'd just as soon burn you at the stake for that."

"I could travel as a healer, perhaps. Using my gift to help them."

Nuri laughed and shook his head. "That's every bit as bad as traveling as a bard. Feast or famine. And more dangerous, too. I have some coin from my busking. You're welcome to that."

"Between us, I'm sure we could manage."

Nuri damped the strings, and the silence startled Mateo. "I don't want to travel anymore," he said softly. "I've lived most of my life going from place to place to find people who wanted to listen to my music. Now I want to put down roots, like a tree. Let the world find me for a change."

"I can understand that."

Nuri sighed. "Most of all, I want to put down roots with you. And if that's not possible, then at least for you. Travel if you must, but I want you to come home to me, over and over, for as long as you need to travel."

He laughed and looked up at the ceiling, his eyes sparkling with imagination. "I want to be that tall, gnarled old tree you see rising from the dusty road before you see our house. The tree that, at journey's end, spreads its branches out to you in welcome, reminding you of all the gifts that come with being home again. Then when you are finally done traveling, you can come home to me one more time, and stay."

Mateo rolled off the pallet to grasp Nuri's face in both hands, kissing him softly. "Yes. You will always be my home tree, no matter what. I promise." He felt his chest fill and shift into a deep calm. "I love you, my home tree."

Nuri hung up his instrument and Mateo snuffed the candle. They undressed and gently made love by the light of the moon shining in through their window.

Mateo woke when Nuri's arm struck him sharply in the head. "What's wrong?" The angle of moonlight slanting through their room was nearly the same as when he'd closed his eyes.

"Can't sleep like this," Nuri mumbled, scratching at his chest. "I itch all over. I have to find the right place. Not here."

"What do you mean?" Mateo shivered, fever-hot. His chest throbbed and burned. The relic felt like a hot stone.

"I don't know. I just know... something." He scrubbed at his face. "This isn't the right place. Outside."

As soon as they entered the yard, Nuri started waving his arms, awkward and erratic, pacing back and forth with growing urgency. "Not here. Not here," he kept muttering.

Frantic to help, Mateo reached out to touch Nuri's shoulder. His skin was fever-hot and as rough as an old fence post. In the moonlight, he could see that dark, uneven lines had spread all over his body. He could barely breathe. "Come to the well," he said, fear making his throat thick. "Let me work a healing at the altar for you if I can."

Mateo hurried to the well, with Nuri shuffling after him, barely lifting his feet from the ground as he moved. He lowered the bucket to fill it so he could bathe Nuri's skin. To his horror, it had become strangely hard as well as rough. He had to heal Nuri. But how? His mind spun, his chest was on fire.

"Ooh. This is better, love," Nuri crooned. "Much better. Close now." He started stumbling around, his bare feet scraping in the dirt. He bumped into the altar and stopped, arms spread wide, lifted to the moon. His face lit with a glorious smile.

"Ah. This is the right place," he said in a slow, cracking voice. "So good. Your home tree, my love. Here al-ll-ways. For-you."

Nuri's feet disappeared into the ground. His body shifted, thickened. Craggy bark came up over his skin as his arms stretched up and multiplied. Twigs sprang out, then leaves. Limbs creaked and popped as they lengthened.

Then—nothing but a tall ash tree that hadn't been there before, and a whispering stillness borne on a soft breeze.

The pain in Mateo's chest was gone. He knelt at the base of the new tree, the tree that somehow was Nuri, and pressed his forehead against the rough trunk, sobbing. "Nuri, come back. Please come back."

What had he done? "Nuri!" He was shouting, and didn't care.

It's alright, Mateo. This is wonderful, in fact. Exactly what I said I wanted. I'm an ash tree! Beautiful.

"Nuri?" Mateo stretched his arms around the thick trunk as far as he could reach. "Did you just say something to me? Talk to me. Tell me what happened, and how I can get you back."

I said I wanted to be your home tree, and now I am. This isn't what I expected, but it's splendid. Not at all what I would have thought. Being a tree is... so beautiful.

"No! I need you back as a man, Nuri! Nuri!"

You'll have to give me some time to figure things out. There's music here. A song... I'm becoming... slower now. The other trees are talking to me, but I can't talk to them and you and the same time. Go back to bed. We can talk when the sun comes.

"Bed?" Mateo laughed and swiped away crazy tears with the heel of his hand. "You think I can go back to bed and sleep after this?"

Maybe not. But rest. This is good, love. So good. Nothing wrong.

Chapter Twenty-Nine

"Nuri!" Mateo shouted, but nothing happened. There was no answer. Nothing but a sigh of night air rustling the leaves. He sat staring at the tree trunk. The tree that was Nuri. What had they done? What had *HE* done? This was his magic's doing. One moment, everything was more wonderful than he'd ever dared hope, and now it was all gone. How could he lose everything between one hour and another?

Nuri had made him so happy, filled his days with laughter and whimsy and music. With beauty. Nuri had understood his magic better than he did, could lift him out of himself with a smile or a kiss. He walked with him in the evenings to listen to the land. They had bonded!

In his heart, where all that exuberant life and gentleness had played, was now nothing. No, worse than nothing: a heavy absence. The silent ache of Nuri's not-hereness.

"Nu-u-u-ri-i-i-i!" Mateo cried out, unable to stop desperate tears, unable to keep his voice from rising into long a wail. His heart wanted to burst open, to reach into the tree to find his Nuri. "Come back! Say something. At least let me know you're there..."

There was no answer. Nuri had said he needed to talk to other trees. That was no comfort at all. In fact, it was worse. He was cut off from whatever Nuri was now—outside the sweet bond of belonging they had created. He'd been cut off. Abandoned. Abandoned. Mateo lurched forward, stretching his arms around the trunk, his fingers scrabbling at the bark as if to peel it back to find Nuri inside. But the bark was Nuri, too.

He pressed his forehead against the rough bark. As if something had taken possession of his body, he began to beat his forehead against the trunk. "Nuri. Come. Back. Come. Back." He could tell his forehead was bleeding. He could taste blood dripping onto his lips, stinging his eyes. He didn't care. He deserved the pain. He wanted to drive his blood into the tree, to reconnect, to be together again.

"Midnight!" Mateo shouted into the darkness. An owl hooted. "Midnight!" he shouted again. But Midnight didn't come, didn't even answer. He was no doubt safe and comfortable in his familiar roost.

Mateo stopped beating his head against the tree. Blood trickled down his face. He swiped his cheek. Good thing he wasn't wearing clothes. No, he didn't care about that. His heart was a stone.

He struck the knotted scar on his chest. "Damn you! You tricked me!" he howled. "You betrayed me! I called you a gift, but you're really a curse."

Inside his chest, the relic sat silent. Without warmth, without fire, without acknowledgment. "You promised to be the path to my happiness," he said between desolate sobs. "And I had it. Here. With him. Now you've ripped it out of my heart, my hands in but a moment. This is cruel happiness you've given me." The relic was as silent as the trunk of a tree.

By the time the sky began to pale, Mateo had run out of tears, out of rage, out of despair. All he had left was the pain of being empty. He was naked and cold. He didn't care. He got up to put on some clothes.

Zoya was gone. Nuri was gone. He'd promised to care for the farm. He would keep his promise. It would soon be time to feed the animals.

As soon as he entered their room, he saw Nuri's guitar hanging by its strap from a peg on the wall. Nuri's not-hereness hit him in the chest like a fist. He couldn't breathe. Their rumpled bedding, the guitar, the candle stub they'd snuffed out last night, their last night together—everything they'd shared only hours ago shouted at him with haunting silence. Nuri's terrible not-hereness. His throat ached from crying.

He looked out the window. The sun had risen. The farm wouldn't take care of itself. Mateo pulled on some clothes and headed out to work. Midnight was waiting for him on the roof of the nearest rabbit hutch and followed him around all day. Mateo was grateful—sometimes the inscrutable bird distracted him from the gnawing hollowness inside him.

When his chores were done, Mateo thanked Midnight and went in to find something to eat. As he put some food on the table, he caught himself setting two places out of habit. Putting the second plate and utensils back felt like a burial. He didn't light a candle. As he ate, the quiet of the house was unbearable. He kept his eyes on his plate and concentrated on chewing. Not looking at anything else seemed to keep some of the pain away.

After he'd cleaned up in the kitchen, Mateo walked the evening circuit alone. He tried to listen to the land as he and Nuri had done together since Zoya's departure, but his senses were dull, drugged by Nuri's absence. He could easily have missed something that would have been obvious on any other night, so he walked the circuit again, asking the relic to help him if only for the farm's sake. He was surprised to feel the warm pulse of agreement in his chest. His treacherous gift. This time, Midnight appeared unbidden and accompanied him, flapping silently from perch to perch as Mateo walked through the darkness.

When he'd finished, neither Midnight nor the relic had shown concern in spite of Nuri being gone. With a bitter sigh, Mateo accepted that he'd probably done this little job well enough.

He paused at the door to his room. He wished he could talk to Zoya, weep, and confess. He couldn't bear to be alone in their bed tonight. As exhausted as he was, he'd never sleep. He took his blanket to sleep next to Nuri.

He found a space between the roots and arranged his blanket. "Nuri? Won't you talk to me? Please say something, I beg you."

Mateo leaned against Nuri's trunk, waiting. There was no answer, but he refused to believe there never would be. Nuri would speak when he was ready. Mateo settled into his bed. As soon as he looked up at the waning moon peeking through the canopy, he felt the burn of desolate tears. He let them come. They didn't stop for a long time.

In the morning, he called to Nuri again, but there still was no answer. Midnight showed up as Mateo was shaking out his bedding, and followed him around as Mateo drifted half alive through the day's chores. He even sat on the sill and watched him eat. When Mateo went outside for his evening walk around the farm, Midnight landed on his shoulder and pushed his beak against Mateo's ear, making clicks and little growly chuckling noises. Mateo nearly wept at the comfort. Together, they made their circuit before Midnight took off into the darkness.

Mateo returned to the foot of Nuri's tree to make his bed. He put his hand against the trunk, aching for a sign. He felt... something, a presence, even though Nuri hadn't spoken yet. The presence surrounded him from above and below, as if all the trees crowded around him, breathing their companionship down on him, holding him gently in their silent strength. A pulse of warmth in his chest answered them. The trees whispered. He wept again, but sleep came more gently.

When Mateo opened his eyes, something sweet had opened in his heart. Something small and calm. He appreciated it for a moment, welcoming it. Perhaps a gift from the trees that had held him in sleep.

The day passed in a wordless procession of daily chores—feeding, mucking out, hauling water and hay, and repairs. Eating felt like a chore, too. Midnight would occasionally squawk at him or hop onto his shoulder for a moment, but other than that, Mateo trudged from chore to chore, aching but daring to hope to talk with Nuri again, even for just a moment.

After he ate, he sat against Nuri's tree while the sun set, not thinking. Just glad to sit, staring.

It was time to walk the farm. He stood and brushed off his trousers.

The farm is fine today. You don't need to check any longer.

"Nuri?" Mateo whirled around to kneel and placed his head against the trunk, stroking the bark with his fingers. His sobs got in the way of words. He touched his chest, begging for help to communicate. The relic warmed, and then like a bolt sliding home into its catch, his heart entered Nuri's. They were together again. He was home.

"Nuri, my love. Thank you..." He had nothing else to say for a while, happy to weep and feel their connection again. "Thank you."

I've been hard at work. I had so much to learn before I could reach for you.

"Doesn't matter," Mateo sobbed. "You're here now. We... I can feel you again."

So. I can tell you if the farm is in trouble. Any time.

"I believe you, but how?"

It's part of the song. The ground is thick with messenger threads. They tell us so much.

"The song?"

Yes, the song! Oh, Mateo! It's everything! Music and belonging beyond anything I could have imagined or hoped for, this vast life of the rooted. I've learned so much, and I have so much yet to learn from my elders. To sing the great cycles of my tribe. We stand between, uniting.

"I don't understand."

At first, I didn't either. It was too wide for my humanness.

"Nuri, please come back to me! I know that if you say you want to and I agree, my magic will restore you to be a man again."

There was a long silence. Mateo began to fear he'd driven Nuri away. "Nuri?"

I'm here. I'm not going anywhere.

A shiver of amusement Mateo didn't recognize danced around him and faded.

I didn't feel you laugh. I meant to make you laugh. All of us around you laughed.

"This isn't funny, Nuri! I want you to come back."

I already told you: I'm not going anywhere. I am here with you right now. You could join me as a tree, you know. We could make that agreement with your magic, too.

"No—I don't understand this!"

Have you asked your gift for understanding?

"No! It betrayed me—and you!" Mateo knew he was shouting. Birds took off from nearby branches, but he was too angry to care.

Did it? My love, don't be so quick to judge. You don't like what happened, but you haven't asked me if I do.

Mateo hesitated. "I can't." His voice cracked to a whisper. "I'm afraid you'll say yes."

Oh, my love. Well, ask me when you are ready to hear. Our love remains, you know. As strong and beautiful as ever.

"I love Nuri, the man!"

Have you not loved trees from boyhood? You told me you dreamed of speaking with trees.

Stunned, Mateo struggled to breathe. Had his magic manifested his boyhood fantasies? "I... yes, but not like this. Never like this. Never."

Why not? Oh. My roots. I'm being called to sing with the elders. We'll talk again. Ask your magic to understand, my love. I want you to call it your gift. That's what it is. Nothing is wrong.

Mateo stared at the tree trunk, feeling more lost than he ever had. Without realizing what was happening, his hands slowly traveled to the scar on his chest. It took him a while to find the courage to form the words that felt like defeat. "Please help me understand." He didn't feel an answer, but then he knew that sometimes he didn't. At least he had asked.

He made his bed under the tree, stared into the night, prayed to his magic and to Nuri's trees for understanding, and slept.

Chapter Thirty

When Mateo woke, the first thing he noticed was the chorus of voices. To his relief, he could hear again. As he sat up, he brushed at a tickle at his throat. A twig with a single leaf at the end of each branch fell into his hand. He looked up. It was a message from Nuri. Nuri had given him a symbol of being together. Two leaves joined by a single source. His first thought was to wear it all day, but he decided it was too fragile, too sacred for that. He went to their room and carefully threaded it back and forth through the strings of Nuri's guitar, just over the sound hole. He stepped back to see how they looked together, weeping and smiling at the same time. They were exquisite together. Painfully exquisite.

The workday flowed by in a steady stream, made lighter by the knowledge that he was connected to Nuri again. Soon, he would be able to talk with him again. When it came time to clean his shovel and put it away, he felt the warmth of satisfaction instead of the ache of emptiness.

He washed, ate, and hurried to Nuri's tree, calling to him before he could settle between the roots. "Nuri—can we talk?"

Hello, love—I was hoping we could. The farm is happy. The new moon approaches, and Zoya will be returning. I'm glad you'll have another person around in a few days.

"You can feel the phases of the moon?"

Of course. That's part of the song. I can see it, too, at the moment. I've already begun to lose my leaves, though. My eyes.

Mateo was horrified. He stared up into the canopy. It was turning color. "You'll go blind, come winter?"

Yes, it's part of our cycle. But we can always hear and speak. Through our roots and the messenger threads. We never leave the song, although it's quieter for us around the solstice. Then the quickening comes. But the moon is always part of the song, and we always sing together. I don't think you can imagine the beauty. I couldn't. It's what my human singing always reached for, how I wanted my music to feel when it came through—all the connections, singing together. That's my work now.

This sounded strange, but Nuri sounded so content. It was a while before Mateo could bear to speak.

"You gave me a twig with two leaves. Thank you. I wove it into the strings of your guitar. You gave up two of your eyes for that."

Yes, but I have plenty more for the time being. I'll grow new ones in the quickening. You should learn to play that guitar, if you're not going to join me as a tree.

Mateo could barely form the words against the weight of his despair. "I don't think I could bear to even take it down from the wall."

Nuri said nothing.

"Did you know you're an ash tree?"

We have a different name, but yes, I know. I love being one. It suits me.

"If I were a tree, what kind do you think I'd be?"

The shiver of tree laughter again danced in the air all around him. *You would be a sturdy old oak, I think. At least that's the name you know.*

Mateo tried to imagine himself as an oak. "I don't think I'm ready for that. At all."

Take your time. I know you're not ready to make that choice. I said I wasn't going anywhere. I'm rooted now. I love being rooted.

To his surprise, Mateo didn't want to argue or beg him to change his mind and be human again. "You said the song was your work now. What do you mean?"

Hmm. I'm still learning, but I can share what little I've learned. There are many parts to the song. Two are the voices of the rooted and the unrooted. The world needs both to thrive. We hold stories. So many. We trees sing of the rooted, obviously, and we provide a... a living place... and food for many of the unrooted. From the tiniest mites to birds. And people, if they pay attention.

"You mean for eating fruit or building houses?"

Not really. It's about the song. Poets write about the song all the time. Maybe they're the only ones who can hear. Think of the flock of migrating herons coming every year to nest in trees near the river, filling the air with their mating calls. The ground below them turns white with guano. The rooted and the unrooted giving to each other. Sharing and belonging.

Ordinary human affairs aren't as significant to us as humans might think. Humans are not at all as important as the song we sing. We are too busy to pay much attention to people at all.

"Even if they cut down trees to build cities?"

"That's the least important part of the song, I think. But I'm still learning. I don't want to talk about that tonight. It's going to rain in a while, and you should sleep inside tonight. Are you willing to do that?"

Mateo laughed—a sharp bark of love, nostalgia, and pain. "You still badger me to take care of myself." He took a deep breath and let it out, trying to banish the pain. He'd hang on to the nostalgia and the love. "For you, my beloved ash tree, I will."

Mateo stirred on his way to wakefulness, and reached for Nuri. He wasn't there. Of course he wasn't there. He was a tree. There was no point in grieving. Nuri would never want to become a man again. Mateo had heard that hard truth in what Nuri had said last night. The animals needed feeding. The morning dragged on.

When the new lamb butted the water bucket just as Mateo was about to fill the trough, the water splashed uselessly onto the ground. He had to hold himself back from kicking the animal. If this was his path to happiness, he wanted a better one. His resentment grew as he trudged back to the well to refill the buckets until he was trembling with rage. He refused to ask to fly, since this treachery was the relic's doing from the very start. For the first time in years, he wanted to hit something, to make something else suffer his pain, too.

Remember the lightning-struck tree.

Mateo dropped the empty buckets. "What? Now you decide to speak?"

Remember crossing the desert. The lightning-struck tree was happy in spite of what had happened to it. Living. Growing. Glorious.

Mateo snorted, dismissing the comparison. "I'm a man, not a lightning-struck tree stuck in the desert."

No difference, except you believe you have the right to have an opinion on what happens to you and that your opinion should matter. It doesn't. What happens to you is seldom your choice. What you choose to do in response is all that matters. You almost kicked the lamb. You chose not to. That matters.

"I was kind to animals before I first heard you. I'll be good to them even if you remain silent forever."

Do you remember what I told you about the beginning of happiness? Your happiness begins when you love the world as it is.

"How can I? Because of you, I've lost my Nuri, my heart, my wisdom, my hope of happiness!"

You can still love the world as it is. Your approval of everything happening in it is not required. Your disapproval will change nothing. Love and approval are completely different things. Let them be separate.

Mateo lowered the well's draw bucket and cranked it up. He filled one bucket, then the other, and started back toward the pens. He could feel some kind of familiar presence gently pressing against him, but he couldn't name it. It felt like remembering something important.

Remember when you could feel all of life all around you. It was beautiful and complete. A river of life flowing through all things.

"I remember. It was wonderful. But Zoya said I'd go mad if I stayed like that."

That flowing river is what you must learn to love, if you are to be happy.

"Is that really possible?"

It is the only way. Your happiness, your belonging, begins when you love the world just as it is. Can you love the world just as it is—not approve or disapprove, because that's not your business. But can you love it, whether you approve or not?

"No, I can't. I'm too angry. I hate that Nuri is a tree. I hate that he doesn't want to be a human again. I hate that General Tun and Father Xavier live in comfort while they continue to abuse the people around them without being called to account."

Then you have work to do.

Mateo poured the buckets into the sheep trough, careful to keep them clear of the crowding lambs. There was so much wrong in the world. "Does that mean evil men can escape the consequences of their deeds?"

The relic did not answer.

That evening, after he was settled against Nuri's trunk and Nuri had promised him that all was right with the farm, Mateo told him of his exchange with the relic.

Good, Nuri said after a long silence. *I'm glad to hear this. It harmonizes with the song.*

"But everywhere there is so much that is wrong."

Without doubt. But to rage at what you cannot change is wasted life.

"That's cowardice!"

Not at all. It's the first principle of the rooted: Respect where you are. It works for the unrooted, too, but not quite the same.

"What does that mean?"

You can't love what is a thousand miles away. That's just imagination. Knowing where you are shows you what you are called to love. Loving the world where you are is the key, the beginning of happiness your magic spoke of.

"What about loving a person a thousand miles away?"

Ah, now you're just trying to wriggle away from what I'm telling you. If you truly love someone, then you are connected to them as if they stood beside you. I sing with trees far away—many, many miles. The messenger threads connect us as if we stood together in the same grove.

You sing to a rabbit in your arms, not to a hundred rabbits in some other country. That is how loving the world works.

"So elsewhere, greed and cruelty go unpunished."

As far as you are concerned, maybe. Maybe not if it is in front of you. Think of how your magic works. It can't forge a binding contract with all the greedy or cruel people in the world. It could never happen. With your magic, you've always formed an agreement with one person at a time—someone right in front of you. Even in the square that day, you protected all who intended no harm—but your agreement was with me as I stood beside you. Know where you are. Begin with where you are when you show your love for the world.

Forget injustice that isn't relevant, my love. The relic's gift is not just for righting wrongs. It is also for healing, protection, all manner of miraculous beauty. That's how your gift works. Use it that way. That's how you love the world. By the way, Zoya will return tomorrow or the next day. Very soon.

Somehow, Mateo knew Nuri was right, even though accepting what he'd said felt like defeat. He couldn't use magic based on his personal opinion or preference. Was that why the relic sometimes hadn't answered him? It must have been.

What would it mean to accept that his approval or disapproval had nothing to do with loving the world? The idea was terrifying.

CHAPTER THIRTY-ONE

Something nudged Mateo's leg. "You shouldn't be sleeping out here."

"Zoya!" Mateo scrambled to his feet, making Midnight leap noisily from her shoulder as he embraced her. "Welcome home—it's so good to have you..." he stopped, unable to tell her that he had turned her nephew into a tree.

He squared his shoulders and looked her in the eye. He pointed back to the tree. "Nuri," he said, his voice cracking. "Nuri..."

"I know." Zoya smoothed his cheek gently. "I know. As soon as I set foot on the land, I knew. He's happy, yet we both miss him terribly."

Her tenderness was more than he could bear. He coughed and cried, clutched her hand in both of his, wracked with sobs. "I'm so sorry. We... I... I didn't mean to—"

"Shh. Hush, my boy. How could you? I know you didn't." She gave him a watery smile. "All in good time. Come inside."

Mateo watched Zoya make tea. "You're not limping anymore. I'm glad."

"Renewal did that. I'm strong again." She put the pot on the table and sank into her chair. "It's good to be home, though."

She pulled out her stick and began gently rubbing it with her thumb. "You've cared so well for the farm. Well done. Thank you."

With her other hand, she reached out to cradle Mateo's hand curling around his cup. "Now tell me what happened. Take your time."

When he was finished, Mateo wiped his tear-streaked face with his sleeve. "So that's where things stand. Nuri doesn't want to come back to being human. I know that's his choice, but I don't like it."

He sat back in the chair with a groan. "I can't like it. I love Nuri too much. I want him back. This isn't right."

"So you want to make the world fit what you want? That will never happen."

"I've been told that over and over. By Nuri, and this thing." He slapped the scar on his chest. "I still want to make *something* right. I have the power to do that, at least."

"What would you do? Punish bad people?"

"If necessary. And protect good ones."

"There's no end to that. That's just another way of trying to shape the world into what you want it to be."

Mateo thought about that. He felt the truth of it but didn't want to understand. "Then what?"

Zoya was quiet a long time. "I've never borne a child," she finally said. "I always knew that wasn't my path. But I've watched dozens of mothers care for their children. The good ones never withheld their love when their child did something they didn't approve of. The bad ones dangled their love on a string in front of their children like bait on a fishhook. Love is not love if it can be withheld as a punishment or given as a reward."

"But even a good mother has to address wrong behavior sometimes, doesn't she?"

"Of course she does. But never without love first. And during. And always." Zoya smiled at Mateo. "Correct your children—wisely—if you must, but your magic is simply asking you to be a good mother, which involves more than just correction. I know you can do that."

"I think I see." Something heavy and dark pushed up from his memory, slowly showing him why he ached to belong somewhere. "I think my mother was a good mother, but secretly. My father used his approval like that, as a kind of key. Even to belonging in the family. I never knew when he might lock me out. I think that's why I finally left for the monastery."

"You do belong here, though. You know that, don't you?"

Mateo studied Zoya's face, feeling her love, her acceptance, even forgiveness, filling in an old hollow place. "Yes, I know I belong here. In spite of... Thank you."

Zoya gave a brusque nod and pushed away from the table. "Good. Let's get to work. This evening, we'll talk with Nuri together."

Chapter Thirty-Two

Zoya seldom joined him after their first evening together with Nuri, saying Nuri had more to teach him if he was willing to learn.

As the days continued to shorten and make their pilgrimage toward the winter solstice, Mateo sat with Nuri every day, sometimes talking, sometimes communing in silence. Nuri lost his leaves as they dried and fell and could no longer see. It was part of the song's rhythm, he insisted whenever Mateo fretted about it. Now was his time to listen more deeply to the roots and the messenger threads, which brought news and conversations from fields and forests as far away as the river and Santa Inés. Sometimes even farther.

As he had even when human, Nuri enthusiastically shared his stories and songs. Now, instead of the ones learned in his travels, they were ones he'd learned from his tree family. The stories were slower, gentler, deeper. More inspiring.

Even though Mateo was certain he didn't completely understand, he could feel in Nuri's stories the same beauty of interdependence he'd felt in Zoya's garden so many moons ago, when the relic had first become part of his body. But now the stories had more kindness, and they gave charming, tiny, and transient details as well as the glory of a transcendent flow. Mateo always had stories from his day, too, although some of them didn't seem to interest Nuri much beyond the fact that they were Mateo's.

"I harvested two rabbits this morning," Mateo said one afternoon as he leaned against Nuri's trunk. "For the first time, I wondered about whether or not that was a good thing to do. I didn't get an answer from my chest. What do you think?"

"I think it's an interesting question for you to ask," Nuri said. *"I also think humans make far too much of life and death, especially their own—as if their life and death were more important than any other, as if both life and death weren't always essential parts of the song."*

"What's more important than life and death?"

"The song is more important. And sunlight. Water. Wind. Soil. Seasons. Life and death are merely seasons."

"And the rabbits?"

Did you treat them with respect and care while they lived?

"Yes."

Did you treat them with respect and care when you killed them?

"Yes."

Will their bodies go to waste?

"No."

Will you stretch their pelts to dry before taking them to market?

"They are already mounted on the drying boards."

Then they continue, part of the song through you. Sing their lives and deaths without shame.

Mateo pondered this. It wasn't only about rabbits. It was about him, too. About Nuri and Zoya. About everything in that unfolding glory that nearly drove him mad when he first touched it. He didn't pretend to understand, but maybe he didn't need to. His chest filled with a call to join the unfolding. The relic—his double-edged gift—wanted him to be part of it. He wanted that, too. To join the unfolding. To belong in it.

Zoya set the steaming pot of rabbit stew on the table and set aside the lid. The scent of rosemary, garlic, and sage wafted out, calling Mateo to take a deeper breath. "Mine never smells this good, Zoya. What do you put in it that I don't?"

"Witchcraft, tried and true," Zoya said with a chuckle as she sat. She ladled some into her bowl. She handed the ladle to Mateo and tore a chunk of bread from the loaf.

"Speaking of witchcraft, I've invited my apprentices, Magdalena and Paloma, to come to the farm and live with us."

"I've seen them around often enough, but I can't say I know them. Nuri—" Mateo swallowed against his grief. He reminded himself this wasn't about him. "Nuri talked to them more than I did. They're twins, right?"

Zoya gave a curt nod. "They're getting pressured to marry, but neither of them is interested in marriage at this point. We'll need to refresh the farm's protections next time they're here so they're properly included."

"Of course. I assumed they already were."

"I want to make it more specific now that they'll be here all the time. They're at the age when parents expect them to leave their family home. Customarily, of course, into a husband's house. But even if they don't marry, they'd be expected to leave. I want to make sure they're safe here—no angry brothers, pushy suitors, or bossy priests."

"They seem happy learning your craft."

Zoya nodded. "They'll help with the farm, too. They already know how to spin and weave. They'll be a big help, especially if you're not here."

Mateo dropped his spoon. "Are you asking me to leave, Zoya?"

"Not at all. But what I see of your path is not clear. Some big choices ahead. I don't think your path is clear even to you."

"What's clear to me is that I can't leave this place. I have to live here. You are my family, you and Nuri. Even now, he's my other half."

A terrible chill ran through him. "Do you need me to leave because the girls are coming? I'd welcome them as my family, too. If they wanted me here. They were always more comfortable with Nuri than me. Do they know about what I did to Nuri? They might hate me for that…"

"Stop this nonsense, Mateo." Zoya covered his hand with hers, squeezing hard. "I'm not sending you away. What I said is that your path isn't clear to me and that I don't think it's clear to you, either. Is it?"

"No," he confessed, feeling lost. "It's not. I feel like I'm trying to learn how to be in the world. Maybe even to be happy again. You said my magic was asking me to be a good mother to the world." He scratched his chest. "With this. With you. With Nuri. I don't see what any of that means yet."

"You've grown so much. But there's much more to come. Of course I see unfinished business for you. I don't know what that might be. Not my business, really. Time will tell."

Mateo sighed, giving in, accepting. "I hope it's not a lot of time. I'd really like more clarity soon." To his surprise, the relic heated in his chest.

She patted his hand and pointed to the door beyond the stove. "They'll stay in that room. I'll need your help in getting it ready."

"Of course. When are they coming?"

"As soon as they leave their old home. The sooner, the better." She stared hard at him, not letting him look away. "Trust me. And your magic. Trust the girls and their intentions."

Mateo nodded slowly, feeling his foolish fear subside. "I do trust you." He paused, letting it go. "I may not be so clear on my path, but whatever happens, I'm very clear on where I belong. That's here."

Zoya rose from the table. "Good. That's as it should be, then. Our paths are already so deeply knit together that they will never separate no matter what happens."

Chapter Thirty-Three

One market day after the solstice, Paloma and Magda—as she insisted on being called—joined Zoya and Mateo by their cart in the square. Each carried a modest bundle wrapped in a scarf, holding each other's hand in a fierce grip. It looked to Mateo like they'd both been crying. Zoya gave them each a hug.

This must be the day they would come to the farm. Mateo smiled at them, hoping they could feel his empathy and welcome. Words seemed too coarse for the tender moment. Zoya seemed to agree. She silently took their bundles and tucked them under the seat of the cart.

The moment they had nothing left to sell, they harnessed Bray and were on their way to the farm. Their silence continued on the road, as it still seemed there was nothing to say. Zoya sat in the cart and held Bray's reins. The girls, still clinging to each other, walked on one side of the cart with Mateo on the other.

A heavy sadness hung around them on the road, yet the girls walked with resolve and perhaps even defiance. Mateo directed his attention to his chest and asked if there was anything he could do to bring comfort to the group, and he felt a rush of hope rise up in him and flow outward. Zoya sat up, immediately alert, then caught Mateo's eye and nodded. After a while, Paloma started humming a little tune that Mateo didn't recognize. Magda eventually joined her, though her voice occasionally cracked as she sang. By the time they turned from the road and Midnight greeted them from the nearest tree, they both were singing in full voice.

Dinner conversation that night was still quiet but no longer cloaked in the muted tones of mourning. The girls spoke of their final moments with their family, most painfully with their angry older brother. He'd essentially disowned them, claiming they brought shame to their family by rejecting the suitors he'd arranged. Zoya spoke of Nuri and of how, even though it seemed that transforming him into a tree had been a mistake, he was deeply happy. Life was full of change.

Mateo cleared his throat and gave voice to what he'd been thinking since he'd asked his magic for help. "Paloma, I think you love music as Nuri did. Is that so?"

Paloma blushed. "I do, although I doubt I'll ever be as good as he was. He encouraged me almost every time I came to the farm. Why do you ask? No matter how good I became, I'd never be allowed to perform in the square on market day like he did. People say only women of bad character would do that."

Mateo put his hand to his throat as if to dislodge the words that stuck there. "He left... his guitar is still hanging on the wall in our room. My room. I know he'd be pleased for you to have it." He scrubbed at the corner of his eye. "I think it wants to be played, not collect dust."

"Oh!" Paloma's eyes sparkled in the candlelight and overflowed. "That would... I've never had... thank you. His guitar. Oh."

Magda gave him a curious smile. "That's very generous. But don't you want to keep it?"

"Part of me wants to keep it hanging on my wall forever. But it can't make music there. Nuri would hate that. I'll never learn to play it. I know that much. So I'd like it to be used and enjoyed. Played by a family member who loves music like he did. Does."

The pain of missing Nuri crashed upon him in a suffocating wave. What he would give to hear him play that guitar again! He didn't bother to wipe away his tears, a little surprised he had so many. He thought he'd cried them out already.

The next morning, the four of them walked the farm while Zoya pointed out repairs and projects for the future as well as what work had recently been done.

"The whole farm feels like magic!" Paloma exclaimed as they returned to the house. "We've come here so often over the last year, but we always just went to—" She looked to Zoya, who nodded.

"He knows about the spring," she said. "And he has his own magic. Very different, but compatible. We are fortunate to have found each other, all four of us."

"We can contribute with our common skills even if we can't work much magic yet," Magda said enthusiastically. "Instead of trading raw rabbit hides and unwashed wool at the market, we can make them more valuable. I know how to tan the hides with willow and oak bark. If you have a draw knife, I can use to peel branches. And if we spin the wool into skeins ourselves, we can dye them different colors with onion skins or all sorts of other plants."

"Those are good ideas," Zoya said carefully. "Let's see how we can fit those efforts into the rest of our work. Your studies and daily tasks come first and might take more time than you imagine." She patted Magda's arm. "Still, it would be lovely to spin yarn again. Mateo just moved my wheel and swift out of your room. We can find a place for it again if we need to. Let's see how our work unfolds."

Calmas.

"What?" Mateo was so surprised at the relic's voice that he spoke out loud. Zoya raised an eyebrow at him.

Brother Calmas. Your work unfolds. Your next work is with him. Tonight.

He tilted his head toward Zoya in resignation. "We have to talk," he murmured.

Paloma glanced between Zoya and Mateo and put her hand on Magda's arm. "Why don't we prepare lunch while you talk?" she said. "About an hour?"

"That's very thoughtful of you," Zoya said, drawing Mateo away from the door and back onto the garden path.

When they were alone, Mateo said, "Let's go to Nuri's tree. If he's listening, I want him to hear."

"You received instructions," Zoya said, her voice flat and cautious.

"Yes. The relic says I have to visit Brother Calmas tonight."

Zoya halted mid-step. "That's not your business to finish any longer. Best not to stir trouble with General Tun."

"The relic says otherwise. I have a feeling it's because I didn't have the chance to ask him directly whether he wanted to stay at the fortress or return to the monastery. I have only Tun's word as to why he's there. What if Tun is holding Brother Calmas hostage?"

"Why does that matter?"

"I need to know. You told me my magic was asking me to be a good mother. I've been thinking about that. I can't do that if I turn my back on my guidance. I have to hear his choice for myself."

"Even at the risk of bringing Tun's anger down upon us and the farm?"

"We've already established protections for the farm and all who live here. They will hold regardless of what might happen to me. If you wish, we can strengthen them again."

Zoya stopped on the path, took out her stick, and whispered something to it. "You go on to Nuri. I need to be in my sanctuary for a while." She strode off toward the spring.

Mateo settled against Nuri's trunk. "Are you there, Nuri? Can we talk?"

Yes. The ground has been humming with all the changes. The young women. That feels good and important. And something has unsettled you. We can all feel it.

After Mateo recounted what had happened, Nuri made a slow humming sound, then fell silent. Mateo waited.

This is important for you, I feel. But apart from seeing its role your own destiny, I have nothing to offer. You have to go; you are connected to this man. The farm is safe, but you travel into danger. I can't follow what you do. There are no trees inside the fortress.

Mateo leaned back against Nuri's trunk. He wanted to sleep, but the angle of the sun told him that lunch would soon be served. He was a little surprised by how at peace he felt. Maybe that was Nuri's wise serenity. He didn't know what would happen, but all was as it should be. He stood and made his way to the house.

Zoya came in just as Mateo was helping the girls clean up. "Come sit," she said to them. "This affects all of us."

When they were settled, Zoya took out her stick again and ran her thumb over its twists and curves. "Mateo is going on a journey tonight. He might be back tomorrow, or never. I can't see. I advised him he needn't do this, but I was wrong. I let my preference cloud my vision. This is unavoidable." She reached out with her free hand and patted Mateo's. "Go with our blessing and deep affection."

"Do you want to check the farm's warding together?"

"I already did," Zoya said, her voice tight. "Our protection is strong and clear. The farm is safe, and we'll be fine. It is you who will not be safe. But you must travel the path your magic has given you."

Mateo wanted to thank her for her affection and her blessing, but to say it aloud would be almost as final as saying goodbye. He smiled instead. "I must. Perhaps especially when the path feels this dangerous."

After darkness fell, Mateo went outside, ready to fly to the fortress. He rubbed his chest, reaching in to the relic. "I can fly under cover of night, but you will have to direct me to where Brother Calmas is."

You will be at his window shortly.

With that, Mateo focused on flight, lifted into the air, and shot into the night toward General Tun's fortress. In less time than it took to carry a bucket of water to the animals, he landed among the trees facing the tower he'd been thrown from months ago. This was more dangerous than anything he'd ever done. His whole body hummed with excitement.

"This is where you gave me my new life," he said to the relic. "Now what about Calmas?"

Follow the pull.

As he had that first morning standing in the middle of the road asking which direction he should take, Mateo swept his attention across the wall of the fortress until he felt the tug. He lifted into the air and circled away from the main road to follow it. The pull led him to a high open window. He peered in. The room was small and nearly bare. A man slept on a bed in the corner with a crude wooden stand next to it. A table and chair stood next to the window. It was as simple as a monk's cell but larger. He floated through and landed on the rough plank floor, which creaked as he settled.

The man in the bed stirred and sat up. "Who's there?" he asked, squinting into the gloom.

"A friend, Brother Calmas." Mateo was surprised the man sounded more curious than afraid. "No reason to fear. I mean no harm. I have a story behind my visit, and a choice for you once you've heard it."

Mateo watched Calmas fumble at the stand beside his bed to find his tinderbox and light a candle. Strange. The waning moon had risen. Surely he wouldn't need to light a candle in order to see someone standing by the window. As the wick caught, its light revealed a man whose tired face seemed many years older than his body — empty, but unafraid.

"You know my name, but I don't recognize your voice." He draped a long cord over his shoulder as he leaned back against the wall behind him. "I don't know how you slipped past the sentries, but if you mean to harm me I will sound the alarm before you can try."

"I swear I come in peace," Mateo said, his voice as gentle as when he talked to his hens. "We've never met, although we once called the same monastery home. Earlier this year I traveled across the desert from San Fortunatus. That's the beginning of the story I want to share, which will end with the choice I offer you."

"San Fortunatus. That's a name I haven't heard for a long time." He shifted his weight against the wall, but left the alarm cord on his shoulder. "Tell me your story, then."

Mateo pulled the chair away from the table and sat, facing Calmas. "This spring, the Prior, with the authority of the Abbot, threatened to expel me from the monastery unless I delivered a sacred relic to General Tun. This relic, the Mantle of St. Sarvras, was supposed to win your return to the monastery to continue your work there. I nearly died in the desert. It was very difficult. But I managed to make my way to San Pedro. The parish priest informed me that the relic entrusted to my care had been discredited many years ago and that its status was widely known. I insisted on completing my mission. Father Bartolo kindly allowed me to recover before continuing on to Santa Inés and this fortress.

"To my bewilderment, the general informed me that it was Father Xavier who paid him to keep you here. I insisted on offering him the gift, regardless of his pact with the Prior. He wouldn't listen, and instead ordered me thrown from the rampart. By a miracle, I survived, but Magnus—the monk who survived the desert to deliver a discredited relic to a general who didn't want it—disappeared as if he had indeed died.

"I have since built a new life. I've taken a new name: Mateo. But something in me will not rest until I know what you want. The general's word is not enough for me to let go of my obligation to your situation. So I am here tonight, asking if you wish to return to the monastery or to stay here. I don't really care what you choose. In order to put my part in this to rest, I need to hear what you want, not what someone else wants."

Calmas was silent for a while. "That is a remarkable story, Mateo. Powerful." His shoulders slumped, and he stared at his hands folded on his lap. "I have no reason or wish to go back to San Fortunatus. My life here is good enough. I have a good place to work. Good light. The general visits every now and then. He appreciates my work. He's given me an assistant to mix my pigments, simple comforts. I love my work. This is enough for me."

"If General Tun respects your work, why would Father Xavier have to pay him a stipend to keep you here?"

"That's a bargain I'm not privy to," he said softly, "but I can guess."

Mateo could feel Calmas struggle to give voice to something difficult, and he silently waited, sending him what comfort he could.

"Father Xavier was... fond of me when I was younger. Until his affection shifted to another. I suspect that has something to do with his arrangement with the general, who is clever enough to strike a profitable bargain, gaining an artisan as well as the money to keep him."

He looked up at Mateo, looking resigned and sad. "My eyesight has begun to fail. The general has promised to continue to care for me when I can't work anymore. When I'm blind. I fear I'll need that care sooner than I'd like, but I want to finish a few more pages, if not the manuscript. I can't afford any disruption of my work, even if the monastery truly wanted me to return."

"I understand, and I respect your choice," Mateo said, fighting his anger. Here was another man abused by Father Xavier and thrown away. Another who deserved some kind of accounting from the Prior. Mateo would take care of that soon. But that wasn't what was most important right now, facing this tired man. He wanted to heal Calmas. He reached inward. *Is this possible?*

A pulse of power warmed his chest. "What if I could restore your eyesight? Would you want that?"

Calmas snorted. "Of course I would want that. But it's not possible."

"You don't have to believe it's possible. I can believe enough for both of us. All you have to say is, 'You can restore my eyesight.'"

Calmas brushed a tear from the corner of one eye. "Either you are a very cruel man, or you can work magic. I can't tell which."

"If I am a cruel man and I'm lying, you lose nothing if you try. You can summon a guard and they can take me away to be punished. If I have some kind of gift and can restore your eyesight, you get to see the world again and do the work you love longer than you thought you could."

"Very well." Calmas sat up straight and proclaimed in a loud voice, "You can restore my eyesight."

"Yes," Mateo murmured. "I can restore your eyesight, true and clear." For an instant, the relic's fire opened, blossomed up and out from his chest, then faded.

Calmas shuddered and then shrieked in surprise, in joy. "I can see! I can see again! God bless you!" He leapt from the bed and embraced Mateo, laughing and weeping.

Mateo returned the embrace, wordlessly grateful. Happy. Here in the shadow of so much deceit and cruelty from Father Xavier and the general, he'd brought some good. Blessing.

Someone pounded on the door, then threw it open. Two armed guards strode inside, followed by a page bearing a torch.

Go with them without resisting. Our work here is not yet finished.

"Say nothing of your healing, Calmas," Mateo whispered into his ear. "Protect yourself. Let them take me." He filled with a certainty that could belong only to the relic. "Even if they try, they will not harm me."

Calmas stepped back, fearful, but nodded in agreement.

"Who are you," one soldier said, stepping forward with his sword drawn and pointing to Mateo, "and what are you doing here?"

Mateo shrugged. "I came in through the window to visit my friend, Calmas."

The soldier turned to Calmas. "You should have sounded the alarm."

"I was confused.. I awoke and he was here. I didn't know what to do."

The soldier grabbed Mateo's hands and swiftly tied them together behind his back. "His Excellency doesn't take kindly to visitors coming here without his permission. I doubt you'll live out the night." He marched Mateo to the door, where the other guard and the page waited.

Mateo didn't resist. Finally, he and the relic would bring justice.

Chapter Thirty-Four

Led by the page carrying the torch, Mateo walked between the two soldiers. They went down a long hallway and narrow stairs, coming to a landing where the stairs widened and became ornate. At the bottom, the first soldier pulled a cord next to a heavy door. The scrape and thud of a bar being lifted sounded from the other side. After a moment, the door was opened, and Mateo was marched inside.

Mateo recognized the reception hall. He'd entered from the other end this time. Soldiers still lined the wall. General Tun still sat on his throne, clad in the same garish ornaments as before. In front of him, it appeared that two soldiers were wrestling in some combination of practice and entertainment. The general raised his hand, and the wrestling stopped.

"What have you there, Sergeant?"

The soldier saluted, bringing his fist to his chest. "On our patrol of the upper corridors, Your Excellency, I heard two voices coming from Brother Calmas's room, then shouting. We entered and found this man with him."

General Tun dismissed the wrestlers with a wave. "Bring him closer."

The two soldiers marched Mateo to the rail in front of the throne and knelt. This time, Mateo knew to kneel as well.

"So." The general's voice was ominously mild. "What are you doing in my home uninvited?"

"Your Excellency, I'm an old acquaintance of Brother Calmas. I had heard that he was ill, and was concerned for his welfare—"

"You insult me. Men have died for less. Do you imagine I would not provide for the welfare of someone under my very roof? Or anywhere else in my domain? The welfare of all my subjects—all of them—is my first concern, always."

The relic's fire rose and flowered out through Mateo's body, waiting. Mateo understood. This opportunity was perfect. "Yes, Excellency. Your first concern is always for the welfare of your subjects. I meant no insult, Excellency. Everyone knows this."

Like a bolt of lightning, the relic's fire shot into the general, who sat up straighter, looking surprised and uncertain. Mateo watched the general's face gradually soften, until a beatific glow shone from his eyes.

"You are wise beyond your years, young man," he said gently. "I admire that. I promise you, Friar Calmas will be cared for well. His work, dedicated to the glory of God, will last long after he is gone. And me. Go in peace, my son, with my blessing."

"Thank you, Your Excellency." At the edge of his vision, Mateo saw the surprise and confusion on the faces of the soldiers beside him. He stood, waiting for them to move.

General Tun cleared his throat and focused on the soldiers. "What are you waiting for?" he said, with the impatient edge of command in his voice. "With my blessing, this man is to be released immediately."

"Yes, Excellency," the soldiers said. One moved to untie Mateo's hands, fumbling at the cord in his haste.

"No! Wait, Your Excellency!" Another guard stepped forward. "This man practices witchcraft among us!"

Mateo took a deep breath. Anselmo. Surely he wouldn't choose a lifetime of suffering by reporting what had happened at Zoya's farm. Would he? Did the man hate him that much?

The general scowled and pointed at Anselmo. "Hold this man!" Instantly, there was a soldier on either side of him and one behind.

"Tell me. How do you come by this deadly knowledge of his witchcraft?"

Anselmo glowered at Mateo. "He repeats things. He bewitched my cousin into telling everyone the truth of his misdeeds. He was murdered because of it."

Tun threw back his head in a belly laugh. "And what witchery would cause someone to tell the truth, I ask?" He leaned forward, his face flushed and angry. "Should you not be rejoicing in truth like every virtuous man?"

Anselmo paled as he realized that he'd made a mistake. "His life for my cousin's!" he shouted, drawing a dagger and lunging toward Mateo.

"Kill that swine!" Tun commanded.

The guards at Anselmo's side grabbed his arms. In the same instant, the one behind him drew his sword and struck, driving it through Anselmo's torso from the back. He gagged only once and crumpled to the floor with a groan, blood spreading around him in a puddle. Filling with pity, Mateo watched the light leave his eyes.

The soldiers bent to gather up the body and carry it away.

The general turned again to Mateo. "Do you practice witchcraft, young man?"

"No, your Excellency, I do not. I labor on a farm."

"Then go with my blessing," he cast a quelling look around the hall. He was making a declaration. "And my protection."

Mateo was briskly escorted down the stairs of the keep, across the fortress bailey, and shoved out the wicket gate. He didn't dare move until he heard the inside bar slide back across it.

He walked along the road until he found a secluded spot among the trees. What would happen now, with the general's new dedication to the welfare of his people? Some would no doubt celebrate it, but others would think their power and wealth might be at risk. Turmoil was coming. But that was not his problem. He'd brought something good. A worm of misgiving said something wasn't right, but he ignored it. He lifted and flew home to Nuri, to Zoya.

The next evening after supper, Mateo settled his back against Nuri's trunk and recounted his adventure at Tun's fortress. "So that's what happened," he said when he'd finished. "And I don't really know what to make of it. Restoring Brother Calmas's eyesight felt right. I felt something beautiful in it. But when dealing with General Tun, I didn't feel the same beauty, even though it seemed like I was helping more people. It wasn't what I thought it would feel like. At all."

What did you expect?

Mateo sat silent for a while, embarrassed by a sudden discovery. "I expected to feel bigger somehow. Triumphant. Righteous. But I didn't. I felt... empty."

Maybe the difference is in following the song. The song has to be at least as important to humans as their other plans if they are to hear it. Probably more. You felt beauty in the healing. That tells me it was part of the song. It takes people time to know how to listen.

"Can you teach me?"

It's better, I think, that at this point you ask your magic to teach you how to listen. So much depends on choices you haven't yet made. Singing with us trees may be too difficult at first. Or perhaps it's not your part of the song to sing.

"Wherever my choices may lead in the future," Mateo said, feeling the solid weight of what he was saying, "I know I need to visit San Fortunatus and confront Father Xavier."

Even after you found no satisfaction in facing General Tun?

"I never intended to face the general. That was all the relic's doing."

Hmm. Perhaps.

"Brother Calmas wants to stay at the fortress. That's his choice. But he's the first man I've met who was used by Father Xavier as I was. That means something to me. My return to the monastery is not just for me."

Chapter Thirty-Five

"Don't let the water get too hot," Zoya called over to Magda. "Just warm enough to get your attention if you touch it." She walked over to the stove and stuck her finger in the pot. "Too hot. That will make the wool want to stick together. Take it off the stove and let it sit for a while. You can put my cleansing compound in now, though. Just a dozen drops."

She returned to Mateo, who had come into the kitchen for something to eat. "Trading for wool last week was a good idea, but I don't think we should go into town again for a while. Maybe by then, the tumult you set in motion at the fortress will have played out more."

"So far, what little I've heard has been encouraging."

"Yes, but you haven't been talking to the people who stand to lose anything in the changes. The people who benefit from the way things already are do not welcome change so readily."

"That's certainly true, but those folks are no concern of mine." As Mateo opened the door to go back outside, Midnight landed on the sill, cawing loudly. Even Mateo knew he didn't bring good news. Zoya pushed past him and let the bird hop onto her shoulder, where he bobbed and clicked and called.

She looked back at Mateo. "The general has been murdered," she said, her face grim. "We definitely need to stay out of the chaos of town affairs for a while."

Mateo winced. "How long, do you think?"

"Whoever killed him no doubt leads a faction, and I expect some other faction will try to remove the new ruler soon. We should stay out of the way for at least two moons. Midnight can bring us news in the meantime."

"Good," Mateo said decisively. "This feels like the right time for me to go to San Fortunatus."

Zoya shook her head. "You've heard all my arguments against that already. You're still going?"

"I have to. Now that I can fly, I should be gone for no more than a week. The nights are long, so I can probably get there in two."

"I suppose this is the best timing we'll get while local authorities are caught up in this coup. I still wish you wouldn't go at all."

Mateo took a deep breath, wanting Zoya's approval. "I have to."

"I know you do. I feel that. Allow me my wishes. I still wish otherwise."

"I'll leave tonight, but let's check our net of protection first."

Zoya nodded, looking sad. "Good idea." She turned away. "I have a sturdy cloak here that belonged to Nuri. You can wear that."

A waterskin rested in an inner pocket along with some vegetables from the root cellar. It felt strangely familiar, as if he were again setting out from the monastery to deliver the relic to someone on the other side of the desert. Again he carried everything he needed.

He'd even pondered taking his old staff with him, with its crudely carved notches on it to keep track of the passing nights across the desert. He'd found it, but as soon as he picked it up, he knew he wouldn't need it. Instead, he'd cut it up for kindling, which seemed a better use for it now.

Mateo wrapped the cloak around him and spoke to the relic, asking for swift flight and protection from both cold and notice. Setting his intention on the chapel at the monastery, he lifted into the air and headed east. The cold air bit at him, so he asked for more of a shield. He followed the road to San Pedro, watching it speed by beneath him. There was the simple church on the square where Father Bartolo was undoubtedly hearing confession this evening. A moment later, he was flying above the desert.

For many miles, he followed the road, unconcerned that he might be seen. Then what must have been the glow of a campfire beside the road appeared ahead. He veered away, keeping the fire between himself and the rising moon, and he returned to flying above the road only when he was well past the camp.

When the horizon began to lighten, he decided to look for a place to rest. He noticed heavier vegetation in the midst of a stand of scrub trees, which looked promising. He descended and slowed to survey the area. To his surprise, he recognized the place once he'd landed—it was the tiny spring where he had first heard the voice of the relic, offering to be his path to happiness. He felt a poignant symmetry to being here again, headed this time in the other direction. He drank his fill from the spring, ate a carrot and a chunk of bread, watched the sun rise, covered himself with his cloak, and slept.

Mateo woke several times during the day, but when he rose as the sun set, he felt steady and refreshed. Ready. He ate and drank, feeling the weight of his coming confrontation. He reminded himself that, when facing Father Xavier, his intention had to be more about closing a chapter of his life than punishment masquerading as justice. He touched the relic, asking for wisdom to do this right. Then he asked to fly to wherever the Prior might be and shot into the deepening twilight.

It wasn't long before he saw the monastery sitting on its hill above the village. Mateo filled with an odd mixture of sadness and revulsion—sadness for some of the men and revulsion for the ugliness which had been shrouded in the vestments of piety for too long. He bypassed the town and the road to the monastery gate, and instead landed near the chapel. The pull in his chest told him that was where Father Xavier was.

Mateo pushed back the hood of his cloak, pulled open the door, and walked into the narthex. The chapel's lofty peace, the smell of the candles, and the profound quiet were all so familiar yet utterly foreign. For a heartbeat, he again wanted the certainty it offered. No, he didn't. The price was far too high.

He slowly walked up the aisle of the nave toward the altar, where Father Xavier was preparing for Mass. A handful of brothers were already kneeling in the stalls, but not one looked up as Mateo passed.

Father Xavier didn't look up until Mateo stood at the first step below the altar. "Who are—" he began, before he recognized him. The Prior startled, fear passing across his face in a parade of questions.

He schooled his features into untroubled authority. "Magnus. This is something of a surprise. If you've succeeded in your assignment and have brought back Brother Calmas, you can petition for reinstatement in the morning."

"My name is no longer Magnus, and I have no desire to petition for reinstatement. Brother Calmas wishes to remain at the general's fortress."

Father Xavier sniffed dismissively as his shoulders relaxed. "Then you shouldn't be here at all. This Mass is for the brethren only. Laity must worship in the village."

"Among other reasons, I came to inform you that your longtime ally in wickedness, General Tun, is dead by an assassin's hand."

Father Xavier froze, then he carefully placed the chalice where it belonged. "And so now you think to kill me in this holy sanctuary?"

"No. I did not kill the general, and I will not kill you, even though—" Mateo saw the door to the sacristy open. The Lord Abbot was dressed in vestments for the Mass. Tonight's Mass must be a special occasion. How appropriate.

"What's this about General Tun?" the Lord Abbot blustered, his face a perilous shade of red.

"Father Abbot, it's good of you to join us. You may not know the extent of your Prior's long history of deceit and iniquity, but I think you saw enough of it and carefully looked away. I am here to denounce you both in this place you call sacred."

"This is not the place," the Lord Abbot huffed.

"On the contrary, it is the perfect place," Mateo said, his voice rising. "Father Xavier tired of having me in his bed, just as he'd tired of a long list of young men before me. Including Brother Calmas. Surely you noticed how so many novices suddenly disappeared before they could take their solemn vows, didn't you? It doesn't matter now. That shameful parade stops with me."

"You sully this place of worship with your slander!" The Lord Abbot shouted. "I will not allow it!"

Mateo didn't need to call to the relic for strength to see this through. Its fire rose around him like another cloak. "You have no choice but to listen," he thundered. "Over many years you have abused or allowed the abuse of the men you claim to lead," he shouted. He smiled as he heard his voice reverberate down from the vaulted ceiling. Both the Lord Abbot and Father Xavier looked stunned.

"On the strength of your Prior's lies, you sent me into the desert to die." He waited for his echoing voice to decay. "And if I survived the desert, you thought General Tun would do your dirty work for you when I offered him an object for his chapel that he already knew was fraudulent. You *knew*. Everyone knew!"

Mateo climbed the steps to face the abbot and Father Xavier. "I survived both the desert and the general, and I return to denounce you. Your corruption ceases tonight," he said, waving at the giant crucifix above them, "before all you claim to hold sacred."

The abbot scurried back into the sacristy as quickly as his obese body could manage, leaving the door ajar. Father Xavier, however, stayed where he was, his face now a schooled mask of outrage. "Do you think anyone will believe you over my word?" he sneered. He gestured at the sacristy door. "Our combined word?" His face turned smug with disdain. "You are nobody, while I am a respected pillar of this church with many years of dedicated service."

Mateo nodded, feeling the contract take shape. "Yes, Father Xavier. You are a pillar of this church." The relic's fire sprang out, cold and hard as stone. "You will serve the church for many more years."

The Prior's face changed from outrage to confusion in a heartbeat, and then to terror. "What have you done?" he coughed. "You... gh-hhh."

Father Xavier slowly stretched heavenward in a graceful column. The vaults of the ceiling rearranged themselves to meet the crown of his head. His face, frozen in terror and large enough to be recognized from below, now peered out from the extravagant marble acanthus leaves of the pillar's capital.

The abbot had returned in time to watch in horror. He stared first at the new column in his chapel and then at Mateo. He reached over to the altar and grabbed the chalice. "Here," he said, his voice wobbling as violently as his hands. "I went to fetch gold, to pay you to go away. Take this chalice, too. Never return!" He thrust a small bag and the cup into Mateo's hands.

"The wrath of God upon you! You've desecrated this holy..." The abbot's face turned a ghastly purple, then he clutched at his head and cried out a wail of pain. His eyes rolled backward, and he fell to the floor with a heavy thud. A trickle of saliva leaked from his open mouth. His eyes twitched and stopped.

Mateo watched the abbot die. He shrugged. He hadn't expected that, but his death felt more appropriate than Anselmo's.

He put the cup and the bag in his inner pocket along with his remaining carrots and the rest of his bread. He turned and descended the steps into the nave. Only then did he remember there were other monks present. Now they knelt together in a cluster in the aisle, heads bowed, murmuring prayers and crossing themselves again and again. As when he entered, not one of them looked up as he passed.

Standing outside on the steps of the church, Mateo looked around, letting his deep breaths flow in and out. A joyless finality settled on him. His heart was empty, blank. He was finished here.

The moon would rise soon. The silhouettes of the orchard trees were just visible. Such a beautiful place, so carefully tended. Care poisoned with ugliness. He would never see it again. To his surprise, he raised a prayer—he hadn't expected to pray—that others might still find beauty here when the echoes from this night's events had faded. He pulled his cloak around him, lifted its hood, and rose into the air. He was eager to get home.

Mateo watched the desert roll by beneath him, thinking still of the beauty of the land of the monastery. He'd loved it when he lived there, especially the peaceful fields and orchards. That peaceful beauty had struck him again, in powerful contrast to the human ugliness he'd confronted there.

Was he obliged to challenge the machinations of men while the earth beneath their feet lay open and generous, already singing its song of beauty for all to share? No. Would anyone listen? Surely a few. Maybe more could.

Reaching to the relic, he asked to be guided to a place without a spring but where one waited to be found, and where he could rest when morning came. He felt the answering tug, and he shifted his direction slightly, smiling into the night, feeling clean again.

As morning approached, a pulse from the relic told him he was near. He flew higher to get a broader view beyond the road and saw a cluster of giant rocks pushing out of the sandy soil. Another pulse. That was the place.

Once he was on the ground, the rocks proved larger than they appeared from the air. He would have shade all day if he needed it.

He looked around for signs of where the spring might be. His gaze fell again to the base of the outcropping.

Dig.

Mateo picked up a dead branch lying near some brush. It wasn't an ideal digging tool, but maybe the water wasn't too far down. He started to scrape and dig, scooping out the loosened dirt with his hands. The stick worked well to loosen dirt and stones, better than he expected, but his hands proved to be inefficient as a scoop. He paused to shed his cloak, which made a clunk as he dropped it on the ground. The chalice. He laughed as he drew it out. Who would imagine a bejeweled gold chalice from a church altar would one day be used to excavate a hole in the desert?

Hours went by. Mateo was now standing waist-deep in his hole. Two of the gems on the chalice had come out of their setting, and the lip had begun to show significant wear. He stopped to wipe his face. How much farther would he have to dig?

Call the waters to the surface.

He shook his head with a smile. He should have thought of asking. He climbed out, squatted next to the hole, and gathered himself. "Spring water, come to the surface. Bring your life to this land, if you choose."

A bit of soil at the bottom of his pit darkened. The dark patch spread, and then a muddy burst of water drove out rock and soil, splattering Mateo and the ground around him. The flow decreased after that, but the hole filled and eventually overflowed, only to disappear into the earth again a little distance away. Mateo knew it wouldn't be long before grasses or other small plants started growing, preparing the ground for whatever might grow next.

He leaned back against a smooth place in the rocks. The water in the hole slowly clarified, trickling out into the sandy soil. This felt... good. A gift without guile, without expectation of a deal struck behind closed doors.

The relic warmed in his chest. "This is part of the song, isn't it?" He asked. He didn't even need the pulse of confirmation that came. He knew.

"Nuri always could hear the song, couldn't he? Probably from childhood."

Yes. To some degree, all who create beauty do. Music. Art. Those who have reverence for living things can hear it. If they choose to listen.

He startled at a sudden thought. "That's why you offered to be my path to happiness. You offered me a chance to learn how to listen."

Yes.

"Did you know this was where my path would lead? Right now?"

The song does not have parts set down in ink. There are so many choices, so many paths. All can be part of the song, as the song fulfills itself in the unfolding. You merely have to listen. Attune to it. Choose to discover. Choose with courage and then let go. That is happiness.

"Please help me attune to the song." The relic's warmth bloomed in his chest so strongly that it made Mateo gasp in a long breath. Everything in his vision shimmered.

When Mateo startled awake, the sun was close to setting. He hadn't remembered falling asleep. In his dream, he'd been reaching toward a question for the relic, something about letting go. He couldn't remember.

He checked the spring, which flowed steady and clear. It felt like part of the land now. It would last. His heart and eyes overflowed as he filled with gratitude. He ate his remaining carrot, filled his waterskin, and put the damaged chalice back in the cloak's pocket.

What would he do with a cup like that? He had no use for it, and Zoya might not even want it on the farm at all. Perhaps Father Bartolo in San Pedro? He might be able to break it down and use the wealth from it. He would offer.

As dusk fell, Mateo flew alongside the road, following it up to the crest of the hill he remembered so well. He landed and walked down into the town.

When he reached the square, he saw Bartolo closing the church doors. "Have you just finished hearing confession?" Mateo asked.

"Yes." The priest turned slowly, squinting in the darkness as if trying to place him. "Is your need urgent? If so, we can go back in."

"I didn't come to confess, Father Bartolo, but to thank you again for showing me kindness the day I stumbled into your church a few months ago. We discussed the Mantle of San Sarvras over a meal."

Father Bartolo's face lit in recognition. "Ah! Welcome again," he said. "I'm glad to see you're now in better health." He peered more closely at Mateo's clothes, and his face became more cautious. "From your dress, I take it you no longer follow the life of a monk."

"I do not. I've changed. Is there somewhere private where we can talk?"

"Certainly. Come to the manse. May I offer you a meal?"

"Thank you, but no. I ask only for a moment of your time."

Father Bartolo opened the door of the manse and ushered Mateo in, gesturing to chairs near a crackling fire. "I see Miranda has anticipated our arrival. Let us at least sit."

When they were settled, Father Bartolo fixed Mateo with a penetrating gaze. "I am truly glad to see you again. I prayed for your safety after you left. You were headed into the jaws of danger at General Tun's fortress." He crossed himself. "You seem to have fared better than the late general did."

"Thank you for your prayers. I have no doubt they helped."

"I hope you are not going to offer me the discredited relic."

"The relic is no longer mine to offer," Mateo said, reaching into the pocket of his cloak. "But I do have something else of unusual provenance." He pulled out the battered chalice and fished around for the loose gems.

Father Bartolo sucked in a sharp breath. "Is that—"

"In a moment of great distress, the Lord Abbot of San Fortunatus recently thrust this chalice into my hands," Mateo said. "Today, I used it to dig a small spring along the desert road, which I hope will comfort many travelers in the years to come."

He ran his thumb over the disfigured lip. "I'm afraid it suffered some damage in the process." He held it out to the priest. "I thought you might repurpose the materials to aid your parish. If you wish."

Father Bartolo reached out slowly. "You dug a spring in the desert with this chalice," he said, musing, turning it over in his gnarled hands. "Life more abundant."

"I'm not sure I understand."

"No matter. Just ruminating." He placed the chalice on a table beside his chair, firelight dancing across its scars and gaps. Mateo reached over and dropped the loose gems into it.

"Thank you," Father Bartolo said. "Perhaps it's time for the church to benefit the people in ways other than spiritual ones."

"Then I leave it in your good hands," Mateo said, getting up to leave.

"Will I see you again?" the priest asked.

"I doubt I will pass this way again, Father. But I'm confident the story of this cup will have a happier ending now than it might have had only days ago. I wish you peace." Mateo put one hand over his heart in salute, smiled, and showed himself out.

Chapter Thirty-Six

As Mateo neared the farm, he peered ahead into the darkness for Nuri's tree. His home tree. At first, he couldn't identify it among all the other naked branches, but he could feel him nearby. His heart reached to connect, and instantly, Nuri's song came up surging into him, welcoming him home. A welcome and an invitation to stay. Nuri, keeping his promise.

Through the window, he could see a candle still burning on the table. He'd go in and say hello before going to his room. He was home. Flying was exhilarating, Mateo thought, but he liked coming home better.

Flying belongs to the song of the unrooted. Perhaps your part of the song belongs to the rooted.

Mateo stopped at the doorway. That felt like it might be true. He needed to think about what that meant.

Midnight landed on the eaves of the house, chuckling quietly. Mateo waved at him and went inside. No one was there. Had Zoya left the candle burning for him? The room felt... different. Maybe it was the presence of the sisters. Or maybe he was different. Changing. Or maybe attuning. He blew out the candle and went to his room.

When he came to the kitchen the next morning, everyone was already busy, flowing around each other in a dance, as if there was some silent music in the air. Paloma put out eggs and bread and made tea for him. Magda was just heading out to the animals, bundled against the morning chill.

Zoya sat with him, gently rubbing her divining stick as he ate. They chatted about everyday things. The days were already noticeably longer. Magda wanted to start tanning the rabbit hides—did Mateo know where the draw knife was? A sharpening stone? Paloma knew how to make hard cheese, and as soon as the ewes began to produce, she would make some. He'd never seen Zoya so at ease, so optimistic. Something important had changed.

A thought surprised him—was he still needed here on the farm now that the sisters were here? He could still make himself useful, certainly, but the place had changed since their arrival. He'd felt it strongly last night when he'd arrived. It felt more whole. It was still his home, there was no doubt about that. Maybe what he felt was his own part changing. If so, he wasn't sure what that was yet.

"When you've eaten," Zoya said, "we should walk the farm together and say good morning."

Mateo nodded. "The place feels different to me. Happier, maybe. More alive."

Zoya smiled and patted his hand. "I'll wait for you by the well."

Mateo joined Zoya at the well without a word. He peered down into it—he'd never thought of it as a dark window into the earth before, but that's what it was. A sacred, dark window for the earth to look out. They walked their slow circuit of the farm just as they had before she'd left. As expected, he felt a kind of harmony winding its way through and around everything. So full of peace. That's not something he'd felt often, at least not before coming here. He'd learned peace here, especially with Nuri.

He reached into his pocket, pulled out the bag of gold coins, and handed them to Zoya. "The abbot thought this would buy my departure when I confronted Father Xavier. I thought it might serve the farm well if some emergency arose."

Zoya took the bag, nodded, and slipped it into a pocket. She stopped, looking at him quietly for a moment. "This experience was important for you, I think. You've changed."

"Yes. Couldn't say how, but I feel it, too."

They walked the trail toward the road, listening.

"Did you bring just retribution to him? This Father Xavier?"

"He used me for sex, then when he tired of me, he arranged for my death. He summoned his own version of justice."

"Through your magic?"

"Yes. Through my magic."

Zoya stopped again. "How did that make you feel? This is an important question."

"Sad and weary." Mateo took a deep breath and tried to put what he'd been thinking into words. "Before I left for the monastery, you said my magic was asking me to be a good mother. Love before consequences. And during, and after. Tender, uncompromising love. I don't love everyone. I can't. I never loved Father Xavier, and he never loved me.

"Living as a bringer of justice to wrongdoers..." The sight of Father Xavier's anguished face thrusting out of the marble leaves of his pillar came back to him, and he shuddered. "I don't have it in me. I wanted him punished. I think what most people mean when they say justice is really punishment. I'd much rather bring healing than justice. That feels as though it has a lot more to do with... what Nuri calls the song."

"The song," Zoya said.

"Yes. The song. When I got to the farm last night, Nuri welcomed me home. I felt him as if he was physically hugging me. He wrapped me in his laughter, his love. I could feel him singing his wisdom and his peace so clearly. And I felt something similar this morning here in the kitchen. It's all around. That means more to me than meting out righteous punishments ever could."

"Good," Zoya said firmly. "I'd hoped for that, but I knew you had to choose." They walked on.

Mateo felt lighter. He greeted each lamb, each rabbit with a caress. "Does Magda do most of the animal care?" he asked.

"All of it. She loves them, and it shows."

It did. Mateo saw and felt it. They were hers now, no longer his. That felt a little sad, but right, too.

As they turned from the pens toward the house, Zoya stopped again and put her hand on his arm. "Someone will eventually come looking for you, you know. From the monastery. Or the fortress. It could be a long time from now, but eventually, someone will come. They might not even have ill intent, but they could find out more about our lives than we want them to."

"I know it's not the full answer," he said gently, "but let's strengthen the protections against ill intent for this place and those who live here. It's a start, at least."

"What do you want to do?" Zoya studied him, patient and kind. "That perhaps is the most important thing to find out. You don't have to decide what to do right away. You hear more of the song now, especially the song in the land. I think you should take some time to meditate and listen, maybe sit with our Nuri for a while."

"I need to listen. I can't stay, and I can't leave." He looked around at what he loved and couldn't leave. Maybe he could have done things differently. But he hadn't. This was his reality. He ached with sorrow but breathed out a sigh, reaching for acceptance, reaching to love the world exactly as it was.

Chapter
Thirty-Seven

What did he want to do? That was the question. Wielding great power to do big things wasn't his answer. He'd mulled over the grand questions of justice as if they might provide the answer, and they hadn't. He instinctively knew that they had to be part of any answer, but not the source. So the question remained—what did he want to do?

First, he wanted to listen. He sat against Nuri's trunk but didn't call out to him. He needed to listen on his own for a while. The trees whispered all around him. They had a beautiful language. He'd always known that since boyhood.

If he could have what he wanted, he'd remain human. Even if becoming a tree proved as wonderful for him as it was for Nuri, it would mean death to his human self. He would have to give up flying as surely as the ant had shed his wings. He would never even go for a walk to the animal pens. What would he see when he had leaves?

So, yes. He'd prefer to stay human and live safely here on the farm with the others forever, but he knew belly-deep that wasn't possible. Failing that, he'd prefer to stay human and somehow still share the relic's magic with others. He didn't see how; he'd already set too much in motion.

He wasn't as wise as Zoya, who knew how to remain unnoticed, but that wouldn't be his way. He'd eventually do something unusual and trouble would ensue. Word would spread, and being burned at the stake would accomplish nothing.

People had a part in the song, too, but it seemed each one had to learn it for themselves. Trying to teach people as if they all had the same part sounded very much like another kind of catechism. That was one thing Mateo knew he did *not* want.

The relic's magic had shaped his journey since leaving the monastery. His trek across the desert, being liberated by Tun's failed execution, finding Zoya, and finding Nuri all came together here at the farm. Was that journey over? Mateo startled at the realization that his story, this journey, had been the relic's as much as his own.

"What do *you* want to do?" he asked the relic, rubbing his hand across his chest. The relic didn't answer.

Had it herded him to this moment of decision? Mateo could imagine it might have—he'd certainly been manipulated before. He decided he didn't care. It really didn't matter how he got here.

What mattered—the over-arching truth—was that he missed Nuri. Yes, as a human, which was selfish of him. He could still talk with him, but it was as if Nuri was hidden behind a wall he couldn't get through. It wasn't enough. He ached to hold Nuri in his arms again. To be joined in body again.

Nuri was his home tree. That was the crux of it, regardless of everything else. That was what Nuri had said he wanted to be, and that was what Mateo—in fond, stupid playfulness—had agreed to, before... before everything changed. Before he'd lost him.

Yet Nuri's non-human presence had soared up to him as he came home and greeted him joyously, just as he had promised he would. If Mateo became a tree, what might his non-human presence do?

He didn't think he was capable of loving the world exactly as it is without Nuri, who had already shown him what real happiness could be. He wanted to love the world as it is. He knew now that he always had.

The idea of becoming a tree frightened him, but if that was the only way to be with Nuri, keep the farm safe, and offer his magic to people that mattered, then maybe that was the path to what he wanted. Maybe he could love the world as it is by being a tree, too.

On the road to the fortress so long ago, he'd imagined that, instead of being hidden away in General Tun's chapel, the relic could somehow be made available to anyone. Available to anyone who sought its healing, assistance, or blessing. He and Nuri had even built an altar with that intention. He knew he wanted to be a bridge between the relic's magic and people who needed it, and he wanted to be happy while being that bridge.

The sun set. He was about to ask the relic for guidance when he discovered he didn't need to. He already knew.

Joining Nuri would give him everything he wanted to keep. He looked around, imagining not seeing the farm, not feeling as a human. Feeling and seeing some other way. Remaining human meant losing more than he was prepared to give up. Joining Nuri was more important to him than keeping his human self.

He'd let Zoya know he'd figured out what he wanted to do.

Chapter Thirty-Eight

Zoya looked up from the stove as he entered the kitchen. Mateo could see in her eyes that she already knew. She gave him a tiny smile, moved her pot from the heat, and pulled out her stick. "Let's sit at the table," she said.

When they were settled, she didn't wait for Mateo to start. "It feels like you've decided to join Nuri," she said.

Mateo nodded, his heart pounding. "It makes the most sense to me. You may see something I've missed." He raised a hand with his fingers spread. He looked at it, sad and a little afraid. He wouldn't have hands soon.

"No one who comes looking for me will find me, but I get to stay where I want to be. With all of you, in my home." He folded down a finger, appreciating its beauty. Saying goodbye.

"After I survived the desert but before I got to the fortress, I had a vision of the relic's magic made available to all instead of being put away in Tun's chapel. Nuri and I..." his throat tightened. "We can offer that magic together." He croaked out a laugh. "We even said our altar was the shrine of the trees." He folded down another finger.

"I think it's the right use of the magic. I don't want it used to become enmeshed in human schemes. Better to engage people who ask for personal help—for themselves or a loved one—one at a time. If I still have a say in these things once I'm a tree, my part of the contract will be that whatever help they receive will enable them to learn their part in the song humans are supposed to sing." He folded down another finger, thanking it, thanking his hand and his whole human body.

"And whether it's noble or selfish, I don't care—I get to be with Nuri again. To touch him and hold him. My human life without him would be incomplete no matter how many wonderful things happened to me. This way, I'll be with him, and we may be able to be a magic bridge between the world of trees and people with good hearts."

Zoya was silent for a while, and then she placed her hand over Mateo's. "It sounds exactly right to me. The girls and I will serve as stewards and protectors of the shrine of the twin trees. I promise you that."

She blinked away tears and smiled. "I would ask to come with you, but someone has to stay and teach the magic I know. That's not your path, Mateo, but it's mine. I'm as rooted to this place as our Nuri. And soon you."

She reached forward with her hands grasping Mateo's. "So let us seal our agreement," she said, her eyes glittering in the candlelight. "This farm will be a safe place for our magic, welcoming only those with kind intent, as long as the seasons turn."

"Yes," Mateo answered, feeling the familiar fire blossoming. "This farm will be a safe place for our magic, welcoming only those with kind intent, as long as the seasons turn." Mateo felt the magic spread down through the floor of the kitchen and out into the night, enveloping every stone and twig and living thing on the farm.

He blew out a breath. It was done. Would the magic feel like this once he was a tree? He'd find out. Part of him said he didn't want to find out, but he knew better.

"Will you go to him tonight?" Zoya asked softly.

"Yes. No point in waiting longer."

"May I come and witness?"

Mateo stood, offering Zoya his hand with a contented smile. "I'd like that. You are the steward of our magic farm." The relic agreed.

Midnight settled silently on Zoya's shoulder as they made their way to the shrine.

Mateo stood still for a moment, facing Nuri's tree, letting his fears settle into place next to his hopes. When he was ready, he took off his clothes and stepped as close as he could, wrapping his arms around Nuri's trunk, pressing his cheek against the bark.

"Nuri," he called out. "Let me come to you. Say the words, Nuri. Say that I can be your twin tree."

Like music rising from the ground, Nuri's voice came. It penetrated Mateo's bones and made the air shiver all around him.

You are my twin tree.

Mateo felt the magic leap from his chest, curl upward into the branches, and then plunge down, down, down into the earth. His eyes stopped seeing, but he didn't mind. It was natural, like closing his eyes while listening to Nuri sing.

He felt his toes drive into the soil, felt his body twist and stretch. He heard the hum of the messenger threads all around him, welcoming.

He grew more arms, each one reaching for the sky, leafless, utterly content not to see. And still he changed. His roots swelled, wrapping around Nuri's, touching, touching, touching him again. Oh, so wonderful, touching, rubbing, plunging, caressing, twisting together all the way down, down into the damp welcoming soil, where there was nothing but belonging and joy and contentment. His leg split to wrap around one of Nuri's roots. Nuri, Nuri, Nuri, my Nuri, my Nuri.

Nuri was changing, too, his roots spreading wide in welcome.

His senses changed. The messenger threads weren't like light above the ground, but somehow exactly like sunlight, vibrating with life.

His trunk grew against Nuri's, pressed against him, rubbed his delicious bark with his own, laughing silently, stretching up but plunging below and spreading, piercing, prying, winding, binding. He felt their roots twining into the most delicate threads to where there could only be vibrating space between them—where even the slightest contact would be a violation—space for their communion.

And then the song came flooding. The song was everywhere. Beneath him, above him, all around him. He tried to gasp at its beauty, but he had no lungs. He didn't need them anymore.

He gradually became aware of other trees, reaching to him from where they were, welcoming, waiting for his change to complete. He surrendered, overwhelmed.

Then the messenger threads sang to him in his new language... There was the altar, there the well. He kept reaching out, loving the way he found a softness in the ground, humming at the gnarled twists and humps growing out of him.

The relic was like a full moon in his trunk, right where it pressed against Nuri's. He felt Nuri growing around him, too, just as he had grown around Nuri. Rooted. He began to sing, clumsily to begin with. His voice was different from Nuri's, whose voice was clear and graceful and pliant and generous. His sounded heavier, slower, stronger. He liked them both. They sang together perfectly. They belonged together.

Epilogue

In many ways, the world around Santa Inés continued on very much as it always had. Farmers and artisans came to market on Saturdays. The river flowed, and seasons turned. Babies were born, people got married, and others died while men hungry for power maneuvered and lied, scheming to carve out an advantage for themselves. Some strongman ruled from the fortress until he was murdered and replaced by someone else.

But underneath the busyness and effort and danger of everyday life, word spread, quiet as a whisper, of the shrine of the two trees—where the graceful ash and the sturdy oak twisted together like lovers behind a simple stone altar.

Many came, and most were strengthened and grateful. There were those who fretted afterward and intended to denounce such witchcraft to the authorities. Somehow, their grasp of the details faded before they could report what they had done, until the memory of their visit evaporated altogether.

But those who harbored kindness and generosity and respect for community in their hearts also came and later recalled a feeling from childhood they'd forgotten, opening a door to wonder that most folk didn't care to trust.

Often those who received healing, or small relief from troubles they brought to the farm's rough stone altar, swore afterwards that they could hear music as their blessing descended—a melody played on strings or maybe someone singing. And although only a few could repeat even a note of the song itself, all remembered what the song felt like when it touched them.

Afterword

Thank you for choosing to read my book.
I hope you were moved and satisfied.

Word of mouth is powerful!

When a reader leaves a review on Amazon, Goodreads, or elsewhere to let others know they enjoyed the book and why, they are helping an author like me—more than you might imagine.

I hope you'll consider leaving a review for The Relic.
Thank you!

Wherever you found this book, I hope you'll take a look to see if any of my other stories might interest you.

I love to hear directly from readers, too:
I can be reached at stories@lloydmeeker.com or through my website.
I hope you'll consider subscribing to my sporadic, low-key newsletter.

Thank you for spending this time with my characters, and until we meet again, I wish you a good and fulfilling journey.

ABOUT THE AUTHOR

Having led what can only be described as an unorthodox life, Lloyd A. Meeker can honestly say he's grateful for all of it, and he's got stories to tell.

Born and raised in a religious intentional community in rural Colorado, he's been a minister, a light aircraft pilot, a community orchestra conductor, an office worker, a janitor, a drinker, and a software developer on his way to writing novels.

A four-time cancer survivor, he's practiced and taught subtle energy healing all his adult life. He's sung in church and rainbow choirs, and currently channels his passion for music into learning the mandolin.

He and his husband met in 2002, and live in Montpellier, France.

His titles include The Last Lady of Albessind, The Garden Witch, Traveling Light, Russ Morgan, PI, and Stone and Shell. His novel The Companion was a finalist in the 2015 Lambda Literary Awards.